Terri,
Enjoy Reading!
D C Clut

PENNIES FOR JOSEPH

A NOVEL

PENNIES FOR JOSEPH

A NOVEL

DONNA C. EBERT

PEN-IT PUBLISHING
CEDAR GROVE, NEW JERSEY

This book is a work of fiction. Names, characters, places, and events are products of the author's imagination or are used fictitiously. Any resemblance to actual events, locations, or persons, living or deceased, is purely coincidental. We assume no responsibility for errors, inaccuracies, omissions, or any inconsistency herein.

First printing 2008

ISBN 978-0-9801115-4-5
LCCN 2007942145

ATTENTION CORPORATIONS, UNIVERSITIES, COLLEGES, AND PROFESSIONAL ORGANIZATIONS: Quantity discounts are available on bulk purchases of this book for educational, gift purposes, or as premiums for increasing magazine subscriptions or renewals. Special books or book excerpts can also be created to fit specific needs. For information, please contact Pen-it Publishing, 878 Pompton Ave. Ste B2, Cedar Grove, NJ 07009; 888-845-4708.

ACKNOWLEDGEMENTS

Thanks to my family and strong circle of friends who cheered me on during the process of writing and publishing this novel.

Thanks to Janina Burns who read a very sketchy first draft and still convinced me I had something to work with. Thanks to Cie Lael and Frank DiGiaccomo for encouraging me to persevere. Thanks to Michael Guarducci, my patient English teacher.

Thanks to all my early readers who helped me define the characters by reading as many drafts as I did.

Finally, thanks to my husband, my biggest cheerleader.

CHAPTER ONE

"Rosie, I can run faster than you can," Joseph sings, tugging my pigtail.

"No, you can't." I skip ahead on the heels of last year's saddle shoes. Joseph catches up. His freckled nose crinkles—a hint that an idea is brewing.

"Let's race to Ciccone's Bakery. Loser gives winner all the chocolate candy from trick-or-treating today," he says.

"I don't feel like it," I say.

"You're just chicken."

I'm not in the mood to dillydally. All I want is to get home. My stomach is all wormy since I woke in the morning drenched from Joseph's weak bladder and noticed the deep empty sag in the mattress next to Mama.

My twin twirls the charcoal curls he inherited from Mama's Sicilian ancestors, hoping I'll cave into his dare. I shrug and offer him a pinky.

"To Ciccone's," I say.

We pinky shake and line the tips of our toes on the cracked cement.

"On your mark, get set, go."

Joseph leaps into a full sprint. His stride is twice as long as mine. Born eleven minutes before him, I weighed thirteen ounces more, but at eight years and eight months old, he is two inches taller than me and plenty faster.

My ears are tuned to the sound of Joseph's sneakers pounding the pavement a yard ahead of me. When I reach Ciccone's, Joseph is bent forward gasping, his hands pressed just above his knees, his curls damp and frizzing.

"Told you I'm faster," he says.

"Big deal," I say. "No one cares anyway."

"Loser, loser," he says.

"Sticks and stones may break my bones, but names will never hurt me," I sing, trailing behind him on the walk home.

Mama paces on the porch, wringing a dish towel. "Where've you been? Teresa got home an hour ago. I was worried sick."

"Joseph says he's going to take all my Halloween candy away from me," I say, skirting by her.

"I won it fair and square, 'cause I'm faster than her," he says, clutching a fist at his side.

"You're not taking nothing from her. Now get inside and put your costumes on before you both skip Halloween this year." Mama swats our butts as we scurry away.

I shove Joseph.

"Sore loser," he says.

Our house is damp and poorly lit by a single bulb dangling from the ceiling, all its wires exposed. The oven door is open, toasting the room. Our sister, Teresa, is busy setting the table. Her legs are long like Daddy's but lanky like Mama's, and black leotards bunch at her knees like loose skin. Strangers dramatize their shock when they learn Teresa is Mama's daughter, not her sister. Even to me they look more like twins than Joseph and I do, beginning with the black roots on top of their heads, down to their middle toes being longer than their big toes.

"You two are in big trouble," our sister warns, ladling steaming pastina into bowls.

"Shut up," Joseph says.

Mama's on our heels. "Get your costumes on. There's not much time before it gets dark out."

In front of the flaming oven I strip off my dungarees and sweatshirt and stretch on a black one-piece leotard. Sitting erect, I allow Teresa to apply black liquid liner to my eyes, which are my best feature because they're not just ordinary brown; they're brown with gold speckles.

Dabbing frosted pink lipstick on my cheeks and lips, Teresa sighs, "There, all done."

I glimpse the compact mirror. I don't look close to being as pretty as Teresa.

"You didn't put enough on," I say.

"That's plenty," Mama says, inspecting my face. "You're lucky to be wearing makeup at all."

Teresa's hair is blackish purple like an eggplant. It is center-parted and slicked with Dippity-do, straightening her natural waves.

"I want my hair to look like Teresa's," I say.

"You're hair is too thin and straggly," Mama says.

Relieved I don't have to wear a plastic mask with the elastic that pinches your scalp, I don't press on.

Joseph's Halloween costume is the same every year: a cape sloppily cut out of black crepe paper and a branch whittled into a magic wand sprinkled with iridescent glitter. Tapping the wand on a black felt hat he found in the vacant lot across from the school, he bows.

"I am Joseph the Great."

"Do a magic trick for us," I say.

"Show us the disappearing scarf one again," Teresa says.

"There's no time. Sit and eat," Mama interrupts and lights a cigarette over the blue flames flickering on the stove.

"Is Daddy coming trick-or-treating with us?" Joseph asks, slamming his wand on the table next to his bowl.

"He has to work tonight."

"But he promised to teach me a new trick," Joseph says.

"He'll have to show you another time." Mama gazes into the compact mirror, fussing with her hair. She has that worried look that makes me not want to eat, sleep, or stray from her side.

Blowing on the pastina that's too hot for my liking and eyeing Joseph, I brag to Mama about how my teacher said I'm smart enough to skip to the next grade.

Mama puts her hands on her hips. "Well, you can tell your teacher you're fine just where you are. With your brother."

"Who cares? Let her go to third grade. I have my own friends," Joseph says. Bits of pasta stick to his lips.

"You're just jealous 'cause you're not as smart as me," I say, but down deep I'm glad Mama says I have to stay with Joseph.

"Shut up, both of you," Mama says, rubbing her head like we're giving her a headache.

"I'm thirsty; I want milk." I get up to fetch some in the refrigerator.

"There's no milk—drink water," Mama says.

"I want more," Joseph says, tapping his empty bowl with his wand.

"There is no more." Smoke rolls off Mama's tongue.

"Here, Joseph, have mine." I slide my half-eaten meal across the table. "I'm saving room for candy."

"Eat your supper, Rosie," Mama says, swiping Joseph's empty bowl. But my stomach is still clenched like a giant fist is squeezing my guts. "I'm not hungry."

Joseph smirks and delves into my bowl.

Before we leave, Joseph proudly presents the three brown grocery bags he designed the night before. Our names are scrawled on one side with crayon, and on the opposite side a jack-o-lantern smiles at us.

After Mama switches the gas jets off and grabs a sweater off a nail, we file out the door giggling.

From our house in the First Ward, we walk quickly past the projects, which is where Mama says dope addicts live. Joseph whines the entire time. He wants to go trick-or-treating with his best friends, Peter Hogan and Gerry Meyers, but Mama says he's too young to go off on his own. She believes that on Halloween crazy people come out of the woodwork like cockroaches, and she intends to inspect the treats we collect for razors and poison.

We slow when we turn onto a tree-lined block, rowed with brownstones. On the steps, in ceramic pots, orange, gold, and cranberry mums are beginning to dry up. Cardboard skeletons and witches are pinned to front doors. Property owners are raking the last of the fallen leaves into heaps at the curb. They smile and nod as we walk by. Mama says this is where she'd like to live one day, and I say I would too.

Finally, we reach the Hills, where Mama refers to the maze of homes as mansions. It isn't the first time we've come to this section of town on Halloween. The people who live in the mansions spoil us with whole chocolate bars and quarters, rather than the Tootsie Rolls and pennies we'd be sure to get in the First Ward.

Teresa, Joseph, and I venture onto the sidewalks to join a flock of girls parading in laced satin Cinderella and Snow White costumes; diamond tiaras sparkle on their heads. There are ballerinas with silk ribbons in their hair and slippers on their feet. The popular costumes for the boys are Batman, Robin, and Superman; black capes flow down their backs like a river.

To me, the houses we approach resemble castles, lit up for everyone to see, unlike our home where the shades are always drawn and the lights turned off. Peering inside the castles, I glimpse wall-to-wall shag carpeting and imagine squishing my toes into the soft wool. There is wood burning in fireplaces; the mantles are cluttered with family portraits, and the dining room tables set with linens and china like the ones at Bamberger's Department Store. Wrought-iron banisters secure staircases as wide as the Municipal Building's steps.

Men who toss treats into our bags wear smiles as white as their shirts, and the women sashay to the doors in skirts and high-heeled pumps, their hair teased in beehives and their nails manicured.

"What are your names?" a woman asks, pressing three Hershey bars to her chest. Her red-painted fingernails look like drops of blood next to the dark brown wrapper.

"Teresa."

"Joseph."

"Rosie," I say.

"And what is your last name?"

"Scarpiella," Teresa says.

"Where do you live?"

"In the First Ward," Joseph says.

The woman tucks the chocolate bars behind her back, and I think she is going to play a trick before she gives us our treats—but then she grabs a fistful of hard candies from a glass bowl on a foyer table and tosses them at us.

"Run along now," she says, slamming the door.

Joseph bends to gather the loose mints. I tell him to keep mine.

Tailing us, Mama's eyes are fixed on the strangers greeting us. While Joseph is one house ahead of us, I overhear girls poking fun at his paper cape. I tug Teresa's elbow.

"What is it?"

"Nothing," I say, allowing the girls to pass. As they do, I step on the witch's dress. It tears.

The witch spins around. Her front teeth are blackened with chalk. Her natural nose is crooked and long like the wicked witch in *The Wizard of Oz.*

"Hey, you ripped my dress, you little jerk," the witch says, glowering at me.

"It was an accident," I say, smirking.

She inspects the torn hem, flips me her middle finger, and scuffles off with her ballerina friend.

"You did that on purpose," Teresa says.

"So."

Joseph fidgets at the corner. He dares to cross without Mama's permission. We reach him, and Mama glances up and down the street before nodding. Joseph darts across to join the boys he's befriended.

"Wait up," I say, chasing him.

"Wait for me, too," Teresa says.

Joseph is farther ahead. I prefer to skip the houses that separate us, but Teresa, who is unwilling to miss out on a single piece of candy, begs me to stay with her. When we're finally reunited with Joseph, Mama gives the signal that it's time to head home. I don't resist; my arms and legs ache. And I'm afraid of the dark.

"Why do we have to go home now?" Joseph whines, marching backward up the street.

"Because it's getting dark."

"But I'm a boy, and I'm not scared of nothing."

"Don't answer me back, Joseph, or I'll take every bit of that candy away from you."

It's bone chilling, and the wind swirls piles of neatly raked leaves. Crows are mingling on bare branches. Teresa and I take turns sharing the sweater Mama brought along. But when it is her turn, she notices I'm shivering and that my teeth are chattering. She removes the sweater and wraps it around me.

"You can wear it the rest of the way home."

Joseph amuses himself pouncing on heaps of leaves. As we get closer to the First Ward, we bump into school friends. Again, Joseph asks if he can stay out.

"You can stop at a few stores—that's it," Mama says.

"That's not fair," he says.

Carmine's Deli, on the corner of Hyde and 18th, is still open. Mama crouches with one knee on the sidewalk. She rummages through our bags, collecting loose change. We follow her into the store, singing trick-or-treat. At the counter, Mama asks for a pack of Pall Malls. Carmine tosses Tootsie Rolls into our bags as we wander into the back to browse through the selection of magazines. Joseph flips through a Superman comic book while Teresa and I skim the antics of Archie and Veronica.

"Teresa, Joseph, Rosie, let's go," Mama calls from the front of the store. We drop the books and hurry out.

We zigzag in and out of Ciccone's Pasty Shop, Aaron's One Hour Martinizing, and Mr. Petsky's Shoe Repair. For me, the only treat worth the stop is the chocolate éclairs from Ciccone's. Joseph trades me his éclair for the pennies Mr. Aaron pressed into the palm of our hands. Teresa sniffs a black heel Mrs. Petsky gives us for hopscotch.

"It's brand new," she says.

Outside of Harry's Cut Meats, Mama scribbles a note on a match cover and tucks it into my palm.

"Why do I have to go? I went the last time," I say, kicking pebbles with the tips of my sneakers.

"I'll go," Joseph says, taking the matchbook cover dangling from my hand.

"Both of you go," Mama says, shoving us toward the door.

Joseph and I creep into the store. Harry the butcher resembles Santa Claus in a dirty and unkempt way. His bushy eyebrows are corroded with dandruff, and his wiry mustache crawls over green teeth; cigar ashes litter a gray beard.

"What do you want?" he says, peering over the meat counter. "I'm closed."

The space is cluttered with boxes of wilting produce waiting to be stocked. Sawdust sprinkles the wood planks, absorbing the odor of the trimmed fat the butcher slices off the blood red meat and tosses on the floor.

Joseph dashes in front of me, anxious to be the beggar. His wide black eyes bear no shame, and his cheeks don't blush as I can feel mine are blushing. Two things I inherited from Daddy's Polish side of the family: needle-straight hair and fair, mottled skin.

"What's this?" The butcher snatches the note from Joseph's hand.

"Can you please trust us a pound of bologna?" Joseph says, before the butcher reads the note.

He shakes his head back and forth, and a clump of ash floats onto his heaving chest.

"What kind of father sends his kids out to beg for food? You tell him I have bills to pay, too," he hollers as he loads an empty cardboard box with bread, milk, and eggs.

Erect like soldiers, our mouths drool as he slices bologna and cheese onto waxed paper.

"Get going, now." He sets the packed box in Joseph's stretched arms. "There's a package of cupcakes in there for you, too," he adds with a wink.

Above the cash register, invoices dangle from meat hooks. He plucks one off and marks it with the pencil he keeps behind his ear. Mama says that's how he records what we owe him. There are about one hundred invoices. I don't feel so bad knowing we're not the only family that borrows food, promising to pay it back. When you're hungry, you promise anything.

At home it's dark and damp. Mama lights the pilot with a match and opens the oven door. The three of us dump the contents of our bags onto the table, careful to keep our treasures in individual piles.

"Get your pajamas on," Mama says. "You're not eating a bit of that candy until after supper."

We scoot into the bedroom. The glass pane is broken since Joseph batted a hardball through it. For months we found glass crystals beneath and on top of our bed. I even found one that looked like a diamond in my sneaker. Daddy taped cardboard over the smashed pane, but it's mushy from rain and doesn't do a very good job keeping the cold air and rain out. Shivering, we change into our pajamas and hurry back to the kitchen, where a pot filled with water clamors from the steam.

Sorting through the pile of Hershey's bars, Mounds, and licorice, we trade our least favorites with each other, toss unwrapped candy into the garbage, and build a bridge with the nickels, dimes, and quarters.

Mama demolishes the bridge and swoops the coins into a glass jar. She counts under her breath. Clearing her throat, she says, "Too bad it's not enough to pay the rent."

Satisfied with our treats, we reload the marked bags and set them under the table, eyeing them occasionally to be sure they don't disappear. Mama layers slices of bread with cheese and toasts it on the oven rack. She pours milk into three glasses, saving a drop for her morning coffee. She doesn't eat with us. She stands at the window, peeking out of the torn shade and lighting one cigarette with another. After our meal she permits us one chocolate bar each, helping herself to a pack of Spearmint Gum.

Savoring each bite, we finish three games of Go Fish. Joseph wants to play another, but Mama says it's time for us to go to bed. From the bedroom we drag the mattresses off the twin beds and haul them into the kitchen in front of the stove. On one of the mattresses I squeeze between Joseph and Teresa. Mama lays on the other, still dressed in her dungarees and nylon turtleneck.

Teresa is asleep the instant she closes her eyes, but Joseph wiggles around like a worm, kicking my shins and elbowing my chest. I'm anxious for him to fall asleep so I can talk to Mama. Finally, he relaxes. The glow of Mama's Pall Mall assures me she's still awake. Leaning on my elbows, I see flames flickering on Mama's tear-streaked skin.

"Mama, are you still up?"

"Why ain't you sleeping?" she says, wiping her nose on her sleeve.

"Mama, when's Daddy coming home?"

"He'll be home soon."

"But that's what you said yesterday," I say.

"Rosie, go to sleep before you wake everyone up."

Sleep is the last place I want to go. I lay on my back, staring at the ceiling, conjuring images of the grand castles we visited that afternoon. I imagine sitting for supper at a mahogany dining table, eager to devour meat and potatoes, lulled by the radiators rattling off steam. I wonder whether the girls who live in the mansions sleep in fluffy pink beds, canopied in white lace.

Our home doesn't even have hot water or a toilet that flushes, and it hurts when I hold my business until I get to school. If the pain is really bad, I have no choice but to squat over a box in our bathroom and toss the stink in the backyard where the weeds are taller than I am. To erase that image from my mind, I blink three times and fall asleep.

———

I'm the last one to fall asleep and the first to wake. Overeating candy has caused my stomach to cramp. Stretching up, I glance over at Mama asleep on the mattress, hoping Daddy's there too. But she is alone. I elbow Joseph and Teresa.

"I don't want to wake up," Teresa groans.

Joseph jumps up and relieves his bladder on the back porch.

"I'm going over to Peter's house to watch *The Little Rascals*," he announces, pulling dungarees up over his pajama pants.

"You can't go out unless Mama says so," Teresa says, yawning.

"I want to come, too," I say, wiggling out of the tangled sheet.

Glancing at the empty space next to Mama, Joseph says, "Daddy didn't come home again."

"So," I say, shrugging my shoulders, as if his return weren't the only thing on my mind.

"I'm going to wake Mama and ask her if I can go to Peter's," Joseph says.

"You better not—you're going to get in trouble," Teresa says.

Teresa thinks she's the boss of us just because she's older but Joseph ignores her. He taps Mama's shoulder.

"Can me and Rosie go to Peter's to watch *The Little Rascals*?"

Mama's eyes flutter and her words slur, "No."

Joseph stomps. Mama's snoring again.

"Hey, I have an idea," Joseph says, crinkling his nose again.

"What?"

"I'll put on a magic show for you and Teresa," he says, tying the crepe cape around his neck.

Teresa and I sit cross-legged on the mattress. Joseph circles the speckled wand around his head and says, "Joseph the Great will now perform the greatest trick of all."

Teresa and I applaud Joseph, poised in the center. When he scowls to look mysterious, the freckles splattered on his cheeks draw together in a puddle. He slowly squeezes a red silk scarf inside his clamped fist. Circling the wand, he chants, "Abracadabra." He taps his fist and flexes; the scarf has vanished. We gasp but don't move a muscle. When Joseph is confident he has our full attention, he repeats, "Abracadabra." One by one, his fingers crawl open, and the red scarf flows like a stream of blood.

We clap and chant, "Again, again, again."

Joseph bows.

"What's wrong? What happened?" Mama pops up like the jack-in-the-box Joseph finally tired of after playing with it for two years. The twist bobby-pinned on the back of her head has loosened, and curls bounce on her shoulders.

"We're just playing," I say, rolling my eyes to the back of my head.

Mama gets up, slips into her slippers, and lights a cigarette.

"Put the mattresses away."

"But I have one more trick I want to do."

"I said put them back."

The three of us do as we're told without another word. Mama sprinkles cornflakes into three bowls she has set on the table.

"Mama, can we have candy after we eat our cereal?" Joseph says.

"Yeah, can we?" I say, although I've had my fill of candy.

"Someone's knocking," Teresa interrupts.

"Your father probably forgot his key," Mama says, fixing her hair and wiping the black mascara from under her eyes.

"Daddy's home, Daddy's home," I say running toward the door.

Mama's eyes glint as she unlatches the chain and swings the door open. Two nuns dressed in black habits and a middle-aged man wearing a tie and a trench coat shadow the threshold.

"Mrs. Scarpiella?"

"Yes, sisters, can I help you?" Mama says, closing the door a sliver.

"We're from the Catholic Charities...."

Mama slams the door and presses her back against it. The way her black eyes bulge and her chest heaves triggers an alarm inside of me. Tears as round as olives spill down her confused face.

"What is it, Mama?" I scream, wrapping my arms around her waist.

"Hide," she says, shoving me into the kitchen.

"What's wrong?" Teresa asks, dropping her spoon on the floor.

"Take Joseph and Rosie and hide in the attic closet," Mama says.

But we're unable to escape the nuns bolting through the door. To me they resemble cartoon characters, cloaked in black from their heads to their steel-toed shoes, their stout faces blotchy.

"Mrs. Scarpiella, we're here to help. We've come to take the children to a safe place."

"No," Mama screams, "I don't need your help."

I duck under the kitchen table and watch Joseph and Teresa as if they're not real, like characters on a television show. They cling to Mama's waist as if they can't stand on their own. Mama's unable to support their weight and staggers into the table.

"I want Daddy—I want Daddy," Joseph cries.

"We'll be good. Mama, help me. Don't let them take us," Teresa sobs. Bewilderment clouds her eyes the same as when the scarf reappeared in Joseph's fist.

The women are not deterred by our howls. One of them peels Teresa's fingers from Mama's arm. The man lifts Joseph, and they're whisked away. Just as I catch my breath, the table flips over. The two nuns hovering over me shackle my ankles and wrists with their calloused hands as strong as Daddy's. Their garbled words don't make sense to me. "Everything is going to be fine, dear. We're going to take you to a safe place."

They carry me outside as if I'm on a stretcher and shove me into a van where Teresa and Joseph are huddled in the backseat. Tears stream down their cheeks. I bang on the glass window, screaming for help. Our neighbors are on their porches in their housecoats and slippers.

Mrs. Pirelli looks away and continues to sweep the sidewalk. Mr. Meyers peers out from under the hood of a junked car; the whites of his eyes glow against his greased face. Joseph's best friends, Peter and Gerry, stop pitching pennies and stare at the ruckus with their jaws drooping. All ignore our pleas for help.

The van lurches forward. Mama chases it. She is twirling her hair around her fists, pulling it out of her scalp. Her eyes stretch to the sides of her head. The van screeches around the corner. Through my tears I see her eyeballs roll behind her head as she falls to the ground. And then, like Joseph's magic scarf, we're gone.

CHAPTER TWO

The walls of the shelter are painted lime green, my least favorite color in the crayon box. The combined smell of borax and applesauce nauseates me. The three of us are on a single cot, our arms interlocked, our fists clenched. A lanky man, with skin as dark as a Mounds bar, rolls a table into the room. His uniform is the same lime green as the walls. He points to three pints of milk and steaming bowls of SpaghettiOs. His dark skin accentuates white teeth when he speaks.

"Jerome wants you to eat your lunch, and later I'll bring you some Oreo cookies, you hear."

Staring blankly at the man addressing us, we tighten our grip and say nothing.

"Once your bellies are full, everything will seem a whole lot better," he chuckles, swinging the door open and disappearing into the corridor.

Our stomachs growl, but we don't budge, and we don't speak. We're trembling and sniveling on each other's shoulders. The light shifts from the single window in the room, and shadows dance on the walls. I'm relieved when Jerome returns and switches on the lights. Slinging three white cotton nightgowns, specked with blue, onto the cot, he glances at the crusty SpaghettiOs.

"You children have to eat if you want to stay strong," he says.

"We want our Mama and Daddy," Joseph croaks, squeezing my hand tighter.

"We'll have to see about that tomorrow," he says. "I want you to put these gowns on and hop into your own cots so you're comfortable. If you want, I can even wheel in a television for you."

We don't utter a single word between the three of us.

"By the way," Jerome adds, "the bathroom is down the hall on the right. I'll be back in a minute with the TV."

"I really have to pee," Teresa whispers.

"Me, too," Joseph says.

"We'll go together," I say.

Sliding off the cot, we stagger to the door. We step into the fluorescent-lit hall. The cold, scuffed linoleum floor stings my toes. Nurses sitting behind desks at the end of the hall peer up from their work, nod, and point to a door. We rush into the bathroom and pee, one at a time. Without washing our hands we scoot back to the room. Jerome follows behind us, wheeling in a television. He plugs it into a socket and switches on *The Carol Burnett Show*.

"Is this okay," he says.

"It's good." Joseph is the only one who responds. He loves *The Carol Burnett Show*.

"Here're those Oreos I promised you," Jerome says, dropping a sleeve of cookies onto a tray.

"When can we go home?" Teresa asks.

"We'll see about that tomorrow," Jerome says. The door slowly closes behind him.

Joseph is engrossed with the blinking television, Teresa can't stop crying, and I'm just about to doze when a whiff of a Pall Mall and Spearmint Gum seeps into my nostrils. Teresa and Joseph smell it, too. Leaping off the bed, we trip over one another, but I reach Mama first, jumping into her arms, resting my legs on her narrow hips. I cup my hands on her face and trace her cheekbones with my thumbs. Powdered makeup is clumped on her skin, but it doesn't do a good job of concealing the deep lines that shatter her skin. Her thick, wavy hair rests on top of her head, twisted into a bun; not even a curl dangles on her wide forehead. She is still wearing the clothes she slept in the night before. Teresa and Joseph dance around us.

"Mama, you came to take us home," Teresa says.

"Where's Daddy?" Joseph asks, jumping up and down.

I slide down Mama's leg, and she kneels on one knee, opening her arms for Teresa and Joseph's embrace. We sob and hiccup.

"Don't cry, my big boy. And you, too, Teresa, you have to be brave; you're the oldest."

"I don't want to be brave; I want to go home," Teresa says.

Mama fends us off with her purse and snaps it open, pulling out a single bent cigarette. She strikes a match. Smoke flows out of her wide nostrils and pursed lips. In front of a mirror hanging above a sink, she applies pink lipstick. I coil my arms around her waist, clasping my hands together at the arch of her back. My head rests on her soft belly. I can hear her stomach growl.

She unclasps my fingers. I fold my hands, prayer-like.

"Mama, was I a bad girl?"

"No, no, you're not bad. It's just that…." She turns away.

"Was I bad?" Joseph says, folding his hands, too.

"Was I?" Teresa says. Bubbles of snot stuff her nostrils.

"No one was bad. Daddy can't take care of us right now."

Mama isn't making any sense, but I don't care. I just want to go home. Tugging on her arm, I say, "We promise not to be bad ever again."

"Rosie, stop it," she says, yanking away. She straightens and clutches her purse in the crook of her arm.

"Tell you what. I'm going to get us some ice cream. I'll be back in a minute."

"I don't want ice cream; I want to go home."

"Me, too," Teresa and Joseph scream.

"You are coming home, but first Mama's going to get us some ice cream."

She moves fast, and before I can grab onto her, she's gone. The scent of Spearmint Gum and sulfur is all that remains.

I swing the heavy door open and run into the corridor. The chatter at the nurse's station ceases. I wail as loudly as I can. "Mama, come back."

From behind I am scooped up and held down on a cold metal surface. My arms and legs thrash, and two nurses hold my ankles and wrists to prevent me from swatting the needle aimed at my arm. Their voices are in the distance now, replaced by shards of memories floating in the air like soap bubbles: me crying the first day of kindergarten, Mama teaching us how to jump rope with the clothes line, Daddy sticking Joseph's drawing of yellow fuzzy chicks to the refrigerator with a wad of gum, Teresa sneaking a scissor to her curls. And then, I'm bouncing in an ocean. The salty water swells beneath me and rises to the bridge of my nose, tickling me into a giggling fit, until the fist of a current yanks me down into an eerie silence.

I wake, tangled in a sheet, and realize I'm alone. When I hop off the cot, the cold tile stuns my bare feet, and my toes point upward; goose pimples pop up all over my skin.

"Teresa and Joseph, you're not funny," I say.

My head is heavy, as if it were loaded with rocks during the night, and I want to lie back down. I don't want to play their game. But when they don't answer, I get on my hands and knees and peek under the bed, where a paper kite and blue crayon are smothered under an inch of dust.

"Come out, come out wherever you are." I say what I think they want to hear. Just then the door swings open, and I expect Teresa and Joseph. But it's Jerome, carrying a single bowl and one pint of juice on a tray.

"Good morning, Rosie," he says.

"Where're Joseph and Teresa?" I say, jumping onto the cot, covering my bare legs with a sheet.

"I brung you a bowl of oatmeal and orange juice," he says.

"Where're my brother and sister?"

The door opens. The man who barged into our house and hauled us away floats in; a strange woman tails behind. Her shoulders are square like Daddy's, and she towers over the balding man. But for the hairnet, she could be mistaken for a man.

"Good morning, Rosie. I'm Mr. Waxman. Remember me. I'm your family's caseworker. And this is Mrs. Finch," he says, pointing to the manlike lady.

"Where're Teresa and Joseph?" I draw the sheet over my head.

Mrs. Finch treads toward me as if trying not to spook a cat. She pulls back the sheet. Her eyes shine like clear glass. Pronouncing every syllable as if I'm deaf, she says, "Joseph and Teresa have been taken to foster homes, and you'll be coming with me to my house."

"I want to go home," I say, skidding back into the metal headboard.

"I know it's hard for you to understand, Rosie...." Mr. Waxman says.

"I want Teresa and Joseph."

Mrs. Finch sits on the edge of the cot and strokes strands of loose hair behind my ears, as if she's done it a hundred times before. Her fingers smell like onions.

"You're not my Mama—don't touch me." Spit flares off my tongue.

"This is a temporary situation," Mr. Waxman continues. "You'll all be together again, but for now you have to live with someone who's capable of taking care of you. Until your mother and father can. Do you understand?"

"No. Mama can take care of me. She was here last night. She's coming back for us."

The room begins to expand, and Mrs. Finch, Mr. Waxman, and Jerome shrink like balloons leaking helium. The ache in the pit of my stomach is worse than any hunger pangs I've ever known. I want to run. I'm trapped.

CHAPTER THREE

In the backseat of Mrs. Finch's station wagon, I curl my knees to my chin. The car is littered with half-eaten sandwiches and empty Coke bottles, and it smells like the cabbage Mama simmers in the oven for hours on Daddy's birthday.

Still wearing my nightgown, I trace the blue veins beneath the pale skin on my bare arms; they're squiggly like the worms Joseph and I use to dig up to feed the lizard at the house of Salvatore, Daddy's friend. Before Daddy and Salvatore had a fight, we used to visit him on Sunday afternoons, so Daddy could watch the football games. I enjoyed the visits because we'd get to tease Salvatore's poodle, which growled when we got too close, and feed the black pink-eared rabbit through a wired crate. Joseph liked feeding grains to the yellow fuzzy chicks that lived in a hatbox.

One afternoon, Joseph asked, "Can we keep one of the chicks?"

"If it's okay with your dad."

I glanced at our father, gnawing on a hanky, cursing at the glowing tube. He had been to the barber for a shave and haircut and reminded me of Teresa's Ken doll. His skin was soft and white like a wet bar of Ivory soap, his nose just a dot between emerald eyes. His front teeth overlapped, but when he smiled wide, all you really noticed were his dimpled cheeks.

"I don't need any more mouths to feed," Daddy said. "Besides, you should be in here with the men watching football—never mind playing with those chicks."

Joseph blushed, and his lower lip quivered.

"But it's little. It won't eat that much," Teresa said, petting the chick's head.

"Pretty please, can we keep him," I said.

"We'll see," Daddy mumbled, trying to focus on the game. But at half-time Daddy said it was time to go.

"Have a dish of pirogues before you go," Salvatore said, jabbing a fork into the pan.

"Antonette had gravy on the stove when we left. She'll be pissed if I don't eat at home."

"You're missing out," Salvatore said, swallowing a pirogue whole.

Joseph teetered near the hatbox; uneven teardrops, similar to the kernels of corn, zigzagged down his cheeks and flowed together at the square of his chin.

"You keep acting like a sissy, and I swear I'll smack you on your ass right here in front of everyone," Daddy said, raising his hand.

Joseph ran outdoors, and we chased after him. He was kicking stones on the sidewalk. Stepping off the porch, Daddy whistled for us to follow.

"Joey," Daddy said, "there's a card trick I want to teach you at home."

Joseph ignored him, and Daddy pretended to punch him in the chest.

"Snap out of it, Joey. You got to toughen up."

Joseph flinched and then punched Daddy in the arm. They pranced around each other on their toes, swinging their fists in the air. Daddy hooked Joseph's head in the crook of his elbow and knuckled his curls. Joseph giggled.

"You sound like a girl," Daddy said.

Joseph shoved Daddy away.

———

As the station wagon lurches to a sudden stop, I roll off the seat. Mrs. Finch flings the rear door open.

"We're here, Rosie," she says.

I grip the chrome handle, but I quickly learn Mrs. Finch is too strong to fight. She yanks me out of the wagon with one hand. I kick her shins.

"I want my Mama."

"Stop it and come inside with me. We have to get some clothes and shoes on you."

"No, I want to go home."

Mrs. Finch lifts me up and coddles me in her arms. I feel as tiny as the baby chicks at Salvatore's.

"Rosie, you have to be more cooperative," she says. "Make the best of the situation."

"We're here," she says, kicking the door open.

There is chatter in the adjacent room and glasses clanking, but I can't see anyone. Mrs. Finch sets me down in a dank foyer. She removes her coat and hangs it in the closet. I stand still, scanning the space. In the living room a television is backed into a corner next to a stone fireplace. On the mantle a huge photograph of a young man, dressed in a blue uniform with gold buttons like the badge pinned to his chest, requires dusting. Paperback books, boxes of shredded envelopes, and a basket of yellow yarn swarm the coffee table.

Mrs. Finch takes my hand. "Come along and meet everyone else of the house."

I don't resist when she guides me into a formal dining room. At a round table a teenage boy and girl about the same age as Teresa dip forked bits of pancakes into gobs of syrup. I hide behind Mrs. Finch's wide frame, feeling exposed in my nightgown.

"Tracey and Kevin, I'd like you to meet Rosie Scarpiella."

The boy and girl barely utter hello. A burly fellow, slightly resembling the man in the photo above the fireplace, rises and pours a glass of orange juice. Curly black hairs protrude from the V-necked T-shirt stretching across his jutting stomach. The armpits are soiled.

"What's all the fuss about?" he says.

"Oh, she'll be fine in a couple of days," his wife says.

"Join us for pancakes," he says, pointing to an empty chair.

"I don't think now's a good time," says Mrs. Finch. "I need to find her something to wear first."

Because Mrs. Finch rescues me from that moment, I don't resist her tug up to the attic, where she points to a cot centered between the eaves, covered with a yellow and pink knitted blanket. On the other side of the room is a twin bed, neatly made with a dark green army blanket.

"This is your side of the room; that's where Kevin sleeps. And in here we should be able to find something that fits you," she says. Opening a drawer stuffed with clothes, Mrs. Finch tugs a purple dress stitched with white daisies. "The last girl who stayed with us was about your age," she adds, smoothing out the wrinkles in the dress.

"I want to go home. I want my own family," I say, sitting on the bed, struggling to breathe through my stuffed nose.

"I know. Everyone feels lost at first. You'll get used to us." She rubs my shoulder, and I jerk away.

"I don't want to—I want to go home."

Mrs. Finch sighs and walks to the door. She hesitates, as if she's searching for just the right thing to say.

"When you get yourself settled, come downstairs and eat something."

I clutch the purple dress and tug at the collar until it tears. Gripping it in my fist, I climb underneath the layers of blankets. Punching the pillows, I imagine all the ways I could hurt my Mama. I envision her arriving at the Finch's, eager to take me home. I'll hide in a closet, pretending to have run away. I'll peek at her worrying and pacing. I won't reveal myself until she promises all the saints she prays to that she'll never leave me again. I fall asleep with these thoughts. When I wake in the dark of the night, I stumble from the bed to pee and step on a plate of biscuits, buttered and jellied. I'm starving, but I push the plate away. With only a single light on in the hallway, I manage to find the second-floor bathroom I spotted on my way up to the attic. The house is quiet. I relieve my bladder and return to my bed.

On Monday I learn the routine of the Finch's household by its sounds. Kevin bolts out of bed the instant the alarm buzzes. Peeking over the blanket, I watch him slip on wrinkled jeans and a gray sweatshirt before he stomps down the steps. Mrs. Finch calls Tracey twenty times before the bathroom door slams shut.

When they're off to school, Mrs. Finch ducks her head into my room to inform me I'll be registered at school by Wednesday. I ignore her because I know I have no intentions of getting out of that bed to go anywhere but home.

I doze again. When I wake, there's a bowl of oatmeal and a glass of orange juice on the dresser. I am so thirsty and hungry I think I might faint, but I roll over so I can't see it. I can hear Mrs. Finch clanking dishes and vacuuming. When she's finished with her chores, she taps on the door before she enters. "Rosie, you can't stay in bed all day," she says.

I roll over to face her. "I want to go home." I grit my teeth, pinching my tongue.

She is holding a plate with a sandwich and cookies.

"Please eat something," she says, removing the bowl of oatmeal from the dresser and replacing it with the sandwich plate.

I turn over and fall back to sleep.

The house comes alive again that afternoon when Kevin and Tracey return from school. Books slam, the television blares, a Partridge Family album skips. Tracey calls Kevin a jerk for not attending to it, and he counters with "stupid head"—the same names Joseph and I throw at each other like hardballs. It isn't too much different than our house, except for the television.

When Mr. Finch hollers, "I'm home," the arguing stops.

The television channel switches. A soothing voice says, "Good evening, I'm Roger Grimsby, here now the news."

I imagine them sitting down to the meat and potatoes I smell roasting. My stomach spasms, but I refuse the overstuffed plate when Kevin delivers it on a tray. He doesn't utter a word to me, but in the middle of the night I hear his angry fists slam the wall while his muffled sobs cause the mattress springs to squeak. I think of Joseph and Teresa sobbing into pillows, and it makes me cry, too.

Tuesday morning, after Kevin and Tracey are off, I overhear Mrs. Finch talking on the telephone. She's saying she doesn't know what to do to get me to eat or bathe. I haven't bathed or changed my underwear. And I don't intend to. My underwear is all I have. Mama bought a package of panties for Teresa and me to share. Each has one of the seven days of the week embroidered on it; I am still wearing "Friday."

My heart thumps when I hear her say she isn't sure whether it's a good idea for me to stay there with them. When she's through with the call, her heels click up the steps. She enters the room and switches a lamp on. She sits on the edge of the bed; the mattress sags, and I roll toward her.

"Rosie, you can't stay in bed forever. You have to eat or you'll get sick."

I tug the blanket over my head.

"I have an idea. How about we call your brother at the foster home where he's staying."

Pulling the covers down, I reveal my eyes.

"Would that make you feel better?" she asks.

I coddle my knees to my chest. "What about Teresa? Can I call her, too?"

"Unfortunately, I don't have a number for her, but I did get one for your brother from Mr. Waxman."

Tasting bile on the edge of my words, I say, "I'd very much like to call him."

"Please come downstairs and eat something first."

"I'm not hungry. I want to talk to Joseph." The voice that carries my words sounds as weak as the flesh that protects my bones.

"Okay, but promise me you'll eat after you talk to him."

"Promise."

Mrs. Finch smiles and hugs me. She's warm and soft, and I linger for a while in her embrace.

"Come on," she says, getting up from the edge of the bed, "let's get you a robe."

She disappears and returns with a thick white terry cloth robe and wraps it around me. It's as soft and warm as she is. My legs are stiff when I climb out of the bed, and my head throbs.

"Here, put these on your feet," she says, grabbing a pair of wool socks from the dresser drawer. I put the socks on and follow her downstairs into her bedroom. It is shaded with orange and brown plaid drapes, and the bed is big enough for four people to sleep in. On each side of the bed there's a nightstand. On one of the tables, beside the Bible, is a telephone. She lifts the receiver, dials seven numbers, and hands it to me. A woman answers the line on the third ring.

"Hello, is Joseph there?" I say in a high-pitched voice that doesn't sound like my own.

"Is this Rosie?" the strange voice asks.

"Yes. I'm Joseph's twin sister."

"He's been waiting for your call. Joseph, Rosie's on the phone."

There is a knock, a door creaks open, and rubber soles shuffle.

"Rosie, is it you?"

I can't form words. Only sobs erupt when I open my mouth. Joseph speaks in the squeaky voice that means he's scared. Licking tears, thick as syrup, I manage to ask, "Are you okay?"

"I want to come home."

The side of my face is soaked with perspiration as I switch the receiver to the opposite ear.

"Me too."

"Where are you?" Joseph asks.

"I don't know, really," I say, curling the cord around my finger.

"Do you think Daddy's sick again?" he says, hiccupping between sobs.

"I don't know."

There is rustling; then his sobs float away.

"Rosie, Joseph's too upset to speak right now. Try calling again tomorrow," the woman who answered, says.

Mrs. Finch hears me wailing and barges into the room.

"What's wrong? Did you speak to your brother?" She removes the receiver from my trembling hand.

"I want to go home," I cry into Mrs. Finch's pillow.

She lies down beside me and pulls me into her arms. I don't resist as she rocks me back and forth. I hold onto the strange woman and cry until my ribs ache and my throat swells and I can't cry anymore. When I'm calm, she stands and dials the telephone.

"May I speak to Mr. Waxman please?"

CHAPTER FOUR

Mama leans on a lamppost, puffing on a cigarette. Mr. Waxman double parks the van in front of the apartment building, where Joseph and I had often raced to the entrance to be the first one to push the doorbell, eager for our Nona to buzz us into the vestibule so we could pet the tabby cat lying curled in a ball in the corner.

Mama flicks the cigarette butt in a pile of leaves when I hop out of the van. Her dungarees hug her hips, and thick curls bounce on the shoulders of a fire red turtleneck.

"Come to Mama." She stretches her bony arms. Sweat beads bubble on her nose as her almond-shaped eyes flit to avoid mine. When I don't budge, Mr. Waxman nudges me. Mama grows impatient and leaps forward, folding me into her arms, where everything feels warm, familiar, and safe. My head nestles between her breasts. The palpitations of her heart beat in rhythm with my own, and the weight of her sadness flows through me.

"I missed you so much, Rosie," she whispers.

My heart wants to melt inside of hers, but my arms are rigid at my sides. I push her away. Glowering at her, I say, "I want Joseph and Teresa."

"They'll be home real soon, too," she says, tugging me back into her embrace. Tears splatter on my head. "Let's go see Nona; she's waiting for us."

As the superintendent, my Uncle Carmen is provided with a two-bedroom apartment that he and my grandmother share. Mama and I climb the steps. When we reach the sixth landing, we see Nona stooped in the opened doorway. She makes the sign of the cross. Her fine graying hair is pinned in tiny wheels around her head, revealing the sagging skin she tries so hard to hide beneath thick powdery makeup.

"Little one, come," she says.

Falling into her short, stubby arms, I inhale the odor of burnt garlic on her black housecoat. Sinking deeper into her belly, as soft as a feather pillow, I begin to relax.

"Come," she says, "You're skin and bones. Nona make you fat, like her."

In Nona's efficient kitchen a large pot steams over a low flame on a four-burner stove. It's a typical routine of my grandmother to prepare the evening meal immediately after clearing the breakfast dishes. When she removes the lid from the pot, the aroma of beef and potatoes makes me feel famished.

"Mangia," she says, ladling the stew into three bowls.

After Mama sets them on the round table, the three of us sit. I reach for the hot loaf of panella, buttered and sprinkled with bits of garlic.

Mama and Nona chat. Nona says Uncle Carmen is worried the landlord will find out we're staying there and throw us all out. She says we have to be careful not to make any noise.

"Why can't we go home?" I ask.

"We're going to stay here for a while," Mama says.

"But what about Daddy and Joseph and Teresa?"

Their lashes flutter, but neither responds to my inquiry. My instincts tell me not to ask again.

Just as the church bells chime at noon, Uncle Carmen saunters in. The chatter ceases. His hands are greasy like his black hair. He heads to the sink, nodding in our direction. The back of his head is bald, and he is almost as wide as he is tall. He rolls his sleeves up before scrubbing the grease caught in his fingernail with a toothbrush. He dries his hands on a dish towel, then pours a glass of red wine from a jug collecting dust on the countertop.

Nona ladles the hearty stew into a large spaghetti bowl.

"Hey Rosie," he says, easing into his chair.

"Hi," I say, diddling with my bread.

Uncle Carmen's voice is soft like the flab that pours over his belt. I don't understand why Mama seems so frightened of him.

After chugging a glass of wine, he says, "Don't play with your food."

"Rosie, eat before it gets cold," Mama adds, bulging her eyes out at me.

"You have to behave while you're here," he says, tearing bread.

"I will. I promise."

"And you," he says, glaring at Mama, "I don't want that husband of yours coming around here."

Mama lifts her eyes to meet his. "He's out of my life for good."

"We'll see—I've heard this story before," Uncle Carmen responds.

I had also heard Mama say this and much more to Daddy when he'd come home with empty pockets and dark stubble, a shadow of shame on his face. His clothes would be stiff and wrinkled, as though they could stand on their own when he stripped them from his broad, muscular frame. At first sight of him, she'd trick him with her silence, and I'd hold my breath in anticipation of the surprise attack; she would not disappoint. She'd lunge at him when he least expected her, hissing and clawing at his back until she tore his shirt off him, shouting curse words that she warned us never to use. He'd bend over and hide his face in his hands, accepting the punishment just like Joseph did when he got caught crossing the street without Mama's permission.

"Well, I mean it this time," she says to Uncle Carmen, picking at her food with a spoon.

"You better mean it," Uncle Carmen says, his voice rising.

"*Basta, basta*," Nona says, and her son and daughter stop squabbling.

After lunch, Uncle Carmen leaves to resume the dismantling of plumbing parts in apartment 2B. Mama fills the tub and sprinkles bath beads in the water. I haven't taken a bath or brushed my teeth in almost a week, so I eagerly strip off the jumper I wore home from the Finch's and splash into the tub. Since the hot water stings my skin, Mama adds more cold. I soap up a rag and scrub my face, arms, and legs. Mama gobs my head with Purel and rinses it with clean water from the faucet.

"You're all clean again," she says, pulling the chain on the stopper.

She holds my hand as I step out of the tub and into a terry cloth towel. She gives me one of Nona's flannel nightgowns. It is way too big but feels good against my clean skin. I comb the tangles from my hair as Mama rinses the jumper in the sink and stretches it over the radiator to dry. She swats my behind.

"Go rest on the couch," she says.

"Where're you going?"

"I'll be right here. I want you to get some sleep. You look awful."

In the parlor a pillow and two blankets are spread out on the gold damask-fringed sofa. I snuggle beneath the layers, sniffing bleach. Mama pulls the shades while I curl up and fall deeply asleep. I don't wake until noon the following day.

"Hey, sleepyhead," Mama says, standing over me.

My eyes flit around the parlor, confirming that I am safe at Nona's. Gurgles roar in my stomach, jolting me off the sofa.

"You hungry?" Nona asks as I shuffle into the kitchen.

"Yeah."

Mama butters toast while Nona cools a soft-boiled egg under cold water. She cracks it on the edge of the sink, spoons out the yolk, and scrapes the egg white off the shell into a bowl.

Mama watches as I devour the eggs and toast. When I'm finished, she cleans up. Nona slumps in a cushioned chair in the parlor to rest her arthritic legs.

"Go put your clothes on; we have to go out," Mama says.

"Where're we going?"

"Home."

CHAPTER FIVE

The distance between Nona's apartment and our house is three blocks. As it is a school day, no children play tag or pitch pennies on the sidewalks. Only delivery men are out and about, unloading crates of milk, bread, and cakes to refill the empty shelves at the local stores.

Mama's pace is quick; I have to skip to keep up with her. So many questions roar in my head that I'm afraid to ask out loud. Is Daddy waiting for us at home? Are Teresa and Joseph coming home too? Is Mr. Waxman coming back?

Jaywalking across the street to the house I was certain I'd never step foot in again, I notice steel chains looping the door handle. Darting my eyes toward Mama, I see she's pursing her lips the way she does before having a fit about something. She bolts to the back of the house, and I follow. Another chain bars the back door.

"Son of a bitch." Mama picks up an empty Coke bottle and throws it at the window.

The crash prompts Mrs. Pirelli to bob her head out the window.

"Anything wrong, Antonette?"

Mama snubs her, so Mrs. Pirelli busies herself, clipping bleached undershirts and boxer shorts onto the clothesline.

Using a shoe, Mama dusts the shattered pane off the sill, then slips an arm through the gape, unlocks the latch, and lifts up the window. She interlocks her ten fingers and cups her hands. "Rosie, climb inside and stuff whatever you can in pillow cases."

I'm motionless. Tears erupt and scald my skin as they roll down my cheeks.

"Come on."

"I'm scared."

"There's nothing to be scared about." She grits her teeth. I can feel the burning behind her angry eyes.

After I place a foot on her cupped hands, she boosts me toward the broken windowpane.

"Watch out for the glass," she says.

Sniveling and trembling, I manage to grip the sill and haul my legs over to the other side, landing on the mattress Joseph, Teresa, and I had shared the night before we were taken away. The floor is splattered with Halloween candy. Joseph's glittery wand lies next to a broken chair. Bending to pick it up, I begin to cry.

I tug the cases off the pillows and hurry to our room. I stuff dungarees, hooded shirts, and long-sleeved sweaters into the sack. When it is full, I go to the parlor and empty the box filled with Mama's polyester slacks, turtleneck tops, and Daddy's socks and underwear.

"Rosie, hurry up," Mama yells.

Wiping my snivels on my sleeve, I tuck the wand into the pillowcase.

———

The first day back to school, I beg Mama not to let me go. She warns if I don't Mr. Waxman will come and take me away again. Since I'm more petrified of Mr. Waxman than I am embarrassed to confront our classmates' questions about what happened that morning outside our home and the whereabouts of Teresa and Joseph, I dress.

Walking to school reminds me of my first day of kindergarten, when excitement overcame my fear. I had been anxious to see the inside of a classroom with its vast blackboard and rows of wooden desks. There were so many questions I needed to have answered—like why birds fly and fish swim and why the sky is blue and the grass green. Amused by my curiosity, Mama teased that I should have been there when God created the world, so I could have had a say in its design. I'd imagine myself by God's side, my knees sinking into a spongy cloud with a box of crayons at my fingertips, shading the sky green and the grass in blues.

Joseph's sole interest in kindergarten was to meet friends; he had a knack for drawing attention. Our classmates shoved and fought to sit next to him, offering to give up their snacks. He entertained huddles of boys and girls, even the older ones, with ghost stories he plucked right from his imagination.

"Rosie, stop daydreaming and pay attention to where you're going," Mama says, stopping in front of the familiar building.

"I don't want to go without Joseph and Teresa," I say, pleading with my eyes for her to change her mind.

"You'll be okay," she says, nudging me toward a line of boys and girls marching indoors. "I'll be here when you get out."

Swallowing the lump that prevents me from taking a breath, I scoot to the end of the line, clutching a brown bag containing two slices of buttered bread and biscotti that Nona prepared for my lunch.

The first day is difficult, but the weight of my loneliness lightens when the last bell rings and I skirt outdoors. Mama is leaning on a parked car, lighting one cigarette with another. Offering me a stick of gum, she says, "Was it bad?"

"Can Mary Jane come over and play tomorrow?"

"Don't be inviting anyone over Nona's. You can see her at school."

Rather than go directly home to my grandmother's, we visit Mama's best friend, who lives in a house on the block between school and Nona's. Adele Matthews greets us with a smile that could melt icicles. No matter how gray the skies outdoors, the sun always shines in Adele's kitchen the color of yolk.

Dropping my books in the mudroom, I kick off my shoes; the promise of treats lures me into the kitchen. On top of a gold icebox is a basket stuffed with Devil Dogs, Oreos, and several small bags of Wise potato chips.

"Just for you, Rosie," Adele says, removing the basket from the refrigerator. She doesn't even have to stand on the tips of her toes.

"Only one," Mama says.

"Oh, let her have what she wants." Adele places the treats in front of me.

Like Nona, Adele owns a console television that her husband, Roger, surprised her with on their fifth anniversary. Once my stomach is full, I flop on the carpet with a sofa pillow, lying as close to the tube as I can get, settling in to watch *Dark Shadows,* even though I'm scared of vampires.

Adele and Mama whisper in the kitchen. My eyes are fixed on the television, but I'm listening to their conversation.

"You can get a job," Adele says, rummaging in the refrigerator.

"I don't know how to do anything but raise kids." Mama snaps her gum.

"You can go back to school to learn typing."

"And then what?"

From the living room I can see Adele tying an apron around her waist so as not to soil the mint green pleated skirt that matches her eyes. She rolls up the sleeves of her white blouse, stretches a hair net over her teased bleached hair, and begins to peel and chop potatoes.

"And who's going to take care of the kids?"

"I'll help, and your mother can, too," Adele says, peeling and chopping.

Mama's heels click the short distance from the table to the pantry where the stove is wedged between a built-in cabinet piled with dishes and Roger's fishing gear. Click, click back to her post at the table.

"My mother can't take care of three kids; she couldn't even take care of me and Carmen. You know how sick she's always been," Mama says.

"They're in school all day. Get something part time."

"Part-time work isn't going to pay the rent and feed them. I'm so tired of worrying about them. I wish I never had them. That's what I wish."

Mama's words hurt more than the time she hauled a shoe at Daddy and hit me in the chest, knocking me off my feet. I couldn't find my breath or feel the ground beneath me, but I could hear everyone around me screaming. That's how I knew I wasn't dead.

"Who do you have to blame for that?" Adele's shoulders broaden.

Mama's chair screeches on the linoleum. "Rosie, time to go."

I jump to standing position. Mama is already at the front door, holding my books.

Wiping her hands on the front of her apron, Adele says, "Don't go mad; please stay for dinner."

Mama mumbles something as she pushes me outdoors.

The sun is setting, shading the sky in powdery pink. The cold air stings, but not so much as Mama's words. I turn to wave goodbye to Adele, but she has already closed the door. Mama unzips the jacket she borrowed from Uncle Carmen's closet and drapes it over my shoulders. I shrug it off and skip ahead.

CHAPTER SIX

Christmas morning: the aroma of lasagna baking in the oven and meat pies cooling on the counter arouses me from sleep, but I lie there with my eyes shut tight. We are planning to visit Joseph tomorrow, and I just want to sleep until then.

"Get up, Rosie; it's Christmas." There is no energy in Mama's words; they are stale like day-old bread. I pretend to sleep, but she scampers in and tugs the blanket.

"It's late; we have chores to do."

"I don't want to."

She rips the blanket off me. It's cold.

"Come on—help me put the bed away," her voice rises, and I do as I'm told.

We stuff the cot back into the sofa and fluff the pillows. I dust the furniture while Mama vacuums the carpet.

"Go get dressed. And comb your hair."

Adele splurged on a red velvet jumper and black Mary Janes at Bamberger's for me. But I'm not in the mood to dress up and pretend I'm merry just because it's Christmas.

"Why do I have to?"

"Do it now, Rosie Scarpiella."

The jumper fits just right. Not having the energy to deal with the tangled mess, I pull my hair into a ponytail. Uncle Carmen whistles when I enter the kitchen to help set the table. Nona is sitting with her legs propped up on a pillow.

"Come here; let me fix the collar."

I nuzzle between Nona's legs. She straightens the collar and reties the ribbon around the waistband.

"There, that looks much better," she says.

Under her supervision I set six places with the ivory gold-rimmed dishes and the silverware that belonged to her mother. Adele and Roger are joining us for dinner, and Nona's effort to create a special day and Mama's weepy eyes make me sleepy.

Sneaking away, I switch on the television and curl in a ball on the sofa. *March of the Wooden Soldiers,* Joseph's and Teresa's favorite movie, is on. I switch it off. There is only one place I can go to be alone. I wait for Uncle Carmen to bathe and shave. When he exits the bathroom, I lock myself inside. The speck of a room smells like Old Spice and talc. I wipe the foggy mirror with my hand. M-shaped bangs crawl onto my lashes. The tip of my tongue curls between the spaces in my front teeth. My pale skin barely conceals squiggly veins and purple flesh sagging under my eyes.

Crouched on the tiled floor, I gaze at an unframed print of a ballerina tying the laces of satin slippers around her ankles. The doorbell rings. Chatter fills the apartment. Adele calls my name and then Mama does. Ignoring them, I climb into the bathtub to distance myself more. Lying down, I position a towel between my neck and shoulders. The tub is still damp and warm from Uncle Carmen's bath. Turning on my side, I bite into the terry cloth and wail, kicking the basin walls.

"Rosie, what're you doing in there? Adele and Roger are here," Mama says, pounding the door.

Once I start, I can't stop. She bangs harder, demanding I come out, but my body is unwilling. I'm not even scared when Uncle Carmen shouts for me to open up. There is so much commotion on the other side of the door; the only way I can escape it is to sleep. I'm just dozing when Uncle Carmen dismantles the lock and trips inside. He lifts me out of the tub.

"Rosie, are you all right?"

Mama and Adele are crying. "Is she okay?" Mama says.

Resting my head in the nook of Uncle Carmen's neck and shoulder, I can smell the dried speckles of blood from his shave. He carries me to Nona's room and lays me on the bed.

"Look what you've done," he says, glaring at Mama. She shoves him and sits on the edge of the bed.

"Rosie, you're scaring me. Does something hurt? Is it your tummy?" she asks.

I can't explain what hurts because I don't know whether the pain is in my stomach or my head or my arms and legs. I just know I hurt. Everywhere.

"I want to sleep," I say, rolling on my side away from her cigarette breath. "I'll feel better tomorrow."

———

It is two months since our separation, and we are both anxious to see Joseph. Standing when the driver lurches at the stop, we trip forward. Before stepping off the bus, Mama pauses to tighten my ponytail. She licks her finger and wipes a smudge of jelly off my cheek.

We trot on the sunny side of the street to keep warm, but by the time we reach the address my toes are numb.

"Here it is, Mama," I point to a steep flight of stairs that lead to a red brick duplex.

I dash up the stairs and press my thumb on the bell. Mama is coughing behind me. When the door flings open, shock registers on her face as a woman with spotted skin as wrinkled as Nona's introduces herself as Doris Welles.

"I'm Antonette Scarpiella, Joseph's mother."

The woman's shoulders don't round forward, and she doesn't limp when she walks, but her fingers are gnarled and purplish like Nona's.

"You must be Rosie." Her smile reveals a gold tooth.

"Yeah."

"Come in."

The kitchen is larger than the single bedroom we shared in our previous home. The Formica countertops are uncluttered, and the ceramic floor shines as if it's wet. To the right of the kitchen is a den; the walls are paneled in pine, and the floor is covered with shag carpet specked with yellow and orange. A console television glares in front of an oversized recliner, upholstered in brown plaid, from which Harold Welles peers over a newspaper long enough for me to glimpse his black-and-white mustache and round, cratered nose. He mumbles hello and resumes reading.

"Would you like a cup of tea?" Doris asks, filling a teapot at the sink.

"No," Mama blurts. She wrings her hands together. They're as red as raw meat.

"I'll get Joseph for you then. He's next door playing with my grandson," Doris says, placing the teapot back on the stove; she then disappears through a side door.

40

"She's nice," I whisper to Mama, curious to know what she thinks.

"Maybe a bit too nice," Mama says.

Mama has often joked that Joseph and I were as tiny as wet kittens the night we were born, just eleven minutes apart. She said Daddy was so proud to have two babies instead of one he kissed the nurses and hugged the doctor that delivered us. Mama said when we were placed in separate incubators we wailed until our faces curled up like a worn leather shoe. And now, nine years later, my twin and I stand, after two long months of separation, eyeing each other as though we don't know he prefers hard chocolate ice cream and I soft vanilla or that he sucked his thumb and I slurped milk from a bottle until we were forced to give up the childish habits the day we began kindergarten, or that I took the blame for his bedwetting.

"What happened to your hair?" Mama asks Joseph, but she's glaring at Doris.

Joseph's curls are sheared close to his scalp. With his dark eyes and olive skin he resembles the Puerto Rican boys who lived in the six-family building across the street from our last home more than a Polish-Italian.

"It had to be cut," Doris says. "It was loaded with dead lice scabs."

Mama doesn't deny that she had to wash all our heads with medicine to kill the bugs that caused itching worse than mosquito bites in July.

"Where're Daddy and Teresa?" Joseph asks, slicing the mounting tension. The brushed denim Levis he wears are creased down the center of each leg; the collar of a Yankee blue shirt is starched over a sleeveless red wool sweater. The only thing familiar about him is the dimple on his right cheek, which mimics Daddy's.

"Your father couldn't get off from work," Mama says.

On the ride there she briefed me on what I was allowed to tell Joseph. "They'll come next time," she adds.

"You want to see my room," Joseph says.

"Sure."

"Joseph, come give me a hug first," Mama says, stretching her arms. Joseph practically falls into Mama's embrace, and she smothers his face with kisses.

If envy can be seen, I hope Joseph doesn't notice it oozing out of my pores and dripping onto the plush carpet. My eyes flutter and shift from the four-drawer wooden dresser, where baseball cards are neatly stacked in one pile and sticks of stale gum in another, to the glossy posters of Mickey Mantle

41

and The Great Houdini pinned on the walls. A wooden bench is at the foot of a twin bed. Joseph brags that he built the bench all by himself in workshop and proves it by turning it over to show me his carved initials.

"Come and feel how strong it is," he says.

I shuffle over and pound a fist on it to make certain the legs don't wobble before sitting. Joseph kneels in front of me, racing two miniature cars.

"Do you want to try?"

One car smashes against the wall, flipping over, and the other crashes into the wooden leg of the bed. I retrieve both of them and imitate Joseph's movements, revving the engine before releasing them to spin out of control. As we play, Joseph gushes about the friends he met at his new school and how on Saturdays they walk to the bowling alley together. His cheeks get all rosy when he tells me about the royal blue Schwinn the Welleses surprised him with for Christmas. His enthusiasm for this new life terrifies me.

"Mama got me a puppy for Christmas," I say, releasing the red car. It doesn't go very far, and I try again with another.

"What's its name?" Joseph says, revving up a racecar. I can tell he's pretending not to be so interested.

"We didn't name it yet. I wanted to wait for you to come home." I watch my car go a distance before smashing into a chair leg.

"Is it a boy dog or a girl dog?"

Hoping to guess which he'd prefer, I blurt, "A boy."

His eyes widen and his dimples deepen, the way they do when he's confident he has a better idea than I do. He's clutching a car in each fist. "How about Snoopy?"

"That's a good name, but we'll wait for you to meet him first."

"Okay," he says, feigning interest.

Attempting to keep the subject on his coming home, I say, "Can you teach me how to bowl when you come home?"

"Yeah, it's really fun. Maybe Daddy can come with us, too."

"Yeah, he'd really like it, I bet."

Doris calls for us to join Mama and her in the kitchen for lunch. There are four bowls of tomato soup and saltine crackers in a plate in the center of the table. Joseph sits beside Doris, and I take the chair next to Mama. Mama doesn't touch a spoonful of soup.

"Joseph, are you being a good boy for Doris and Harold?" Mama's voice is sugary.

"Um um." As Joseph slurps the soup, I'm reminded how annoying he is to eat with.

"He's an exceptional boy," Doris says, crumbling saltines into her soup.

"Am I coming home today?" he asks for the first time since we arrived.

Mama clears the phlegm in her throat. "Next time, baby."

"Now, run along," Doris says, scooping the bowls off the table just as I was hoping she'd offer a second helping.

Joseph and I return to his room and settle our knees into the plush navy carpet for a game of Chinese checkers. Joseph sighs as if preparing to say something and then shrugs it off.

"What's wrong?" I say, setting up the board.

Tears stream down Joseph's cheeks, and I'm almost glad he's crying.

"What is it?" I slide the game out of the way and crawl over to him.

Wiping the tears away quickly, he says, "How come you and Teresa get to be with Mama and Daddy, and I have to stay here?"

I often wonder the same thing but am afraid to bring it to Mama's attention. "I don't know." I fiddle with my shoelace.

"They like you and Teresa more than me," he says, flipping the game over. He stands, walks over to his dresser, and shoves a few slices of gum into his mouth.

"That's not true. Teresa's not with us either," I say, jumping up and going over to him.

"Where is she?" he asks.

I help myself to a stick of gum. Its hard edges cut into my tongue.

"I don't know where. But that's why she didn't come today."

"See, Mama and Daddy like you the best," he says, bouncing on his bed.

"No, they don't. Daddy doesn't ever even talk to me like he always talks to you. He doesn't teach me any card tricks," I say, sitting on the bench.

"Then how come you get to be with them?" Joseph is staring up at the ceiling, his hands behind his head.

"Well, if you have to know, I'll tell you," I say, rising to me feet. "The family I stayed with was really mean."

"How so?" Joseph says sitting up.

"They made me eat worms."

"Did you swallow them?" he says, with a smirk that says he hopes so.

"Yeah, and they had to take me to the hospital. That's when Mama came to get me."

"We're you scared?"

"Not really," I say, rolling onto the carpet.

"I want to come home, too," he says.

"Aren't Doris and Harold nice to you?" I sink into the plush carpet.

"They're okay, I guess. But then Doris asks a lot of questions, though."

"Like what?"

"Like if Mama and Daddy spank me often. And why my teeth are rotted." Joseph pauses and shrugs his shoulders. "Doris buys me a present every time we go to a store, so I really like that."

"You're luckier than me. You have your own room, and I have to sleep on the sofa bed at Nona's between Mama and Daddy—and you know how Daddy snores all night."

Joseph giggles at the thought, and his smile dulls the guilt I feel for lying.

"Hey, maybe if I eat worms, I can come home, too." Sitting up, he crosses his legs. And then we laugh until our bellies ache.

The hours pass so fast, and we dread saying goodbye. We cling to each other in the entry foyer, sobbing. Mama pulls us apart, gently. Joseph steps back and leans into Doris.

"We'll see you soon," Mama says, pretending not to notice how comfortable he seems to be with this stranger. Doris shuts the door behind us.

On the bus, I ask, "Why does Joseph have to stay there? Why can't we get a new house? Where's Daddy? Why can't we see Teresa?"

"Joseph is better off where he is right now. He has his own room and a hot meal on the table every day," Mama says, peering into a compact mirror, clearing mascara from the corner of her eyes with her pinky nail.

"I want him to come home," I screech louder than I intended.

Shifting my eyes from Mama, I squint at the bus driver's black bushy brows twitching in the rearview mirror. Across from us, a woman cradling an infant changes her seat while a black man seated in front of us cocks his head and mumbles. Mama pinches the skin on my hand. I shoot up and take a seat behind her, kicking the back of her chair.

As the bus halts, Mama rushes for the exit. For a moment I consider staying on the bus, but when the doors squeal open and she steps down, I bolt after her and grip her hand.

———

Nona slouches at the stove. When she smiles, her lips sink into her hollow mouth. I tilt my head toward her to accept a kiss.

"Are you hungry?" she says, turning back to a large cast-iron pot.

Quickly, I wipe the sticky saliva off my cheek. "Is Mama home yet?"

"Not yet."

"Oh," I say, opening the refrigerator, pulling out a jug of milk.

"Can you wash and set my hair before supper?" she asks before slurping a spoonful of lentil soup.

Unable to descend or climb six flights of stairs because of her knees, my grandmother hasn't left the apartment in more than five years. Mama grocery shops, lugs the laundry down to the basement where everyone in the building shares the machines, fetches Nona's medicines at the pharmacy, and washes and sets her hair once a week.

"Oh, goody, finally I get a chance to do it," I say, kissing her wrinkly arm.

Nona bends over the bathroom sink, and I wet and lather her hair, kneading her scalp with the tips of my fingers. Her head is as small as a doll's. I rinse the soap and pat her head with a towel. In the living room, she sits in a winged chair, cradling the bucket of rollers and pins.

I comb the fine strands of gray, parting them in sections, then curling just a few strands around my finger into a wheel and pinning it with a bobby pin. Nona, passing the pins, chats only during the commercial breaks of *One Life to Live*. She meshes Italian with English. Sometimes it is difficult to understand, so I really have to concentrate.

"I was twenty-nine when your grandfather proposed," she says.

"That's how old Mama is now," I say.

"That's right, but she has three children. I didn't have my first until I was thirty-one. The doctor told me I was too old to conceive, so when we discovered I was pregnant with Uncle Carmen, your grandfather threw the biggest block party our neighbors ever saw."

"Did you have a party when Mama was born, too?" I say, pinning a curl.

"Your Mama came years after Uncle Carmen. Times had changed by then. Money was scarce, but your grandfather was still very happy when your mother came home from the hospital."

Tilting her head toward me, she adds, "Did you know your grandfather helped build the turnpike?"

"No." The only thing Mama ever said about my grandfather was that he had ruined her life. If it wasn't for his old-fashioned thinking, she could have been a model for Sears, Roebuck's catalog.

"Well, he did. He was strong in those days. He worked all the time and never complained. He was a good man. God took him away too early." She snivels into the hanky crumbled up in her tiny fist.

"How did he die?" I ask.

"His heart gave out." She sways her head back and forth.

"Hold still, Nona."

"Sorry. Maybe it's for the best," she continues. "His heart would be breaking now, to see his grandchildren suffer."

"Mama says Grandpa ruined her life…is that true?"

My grandmother sighs, then gnaws on the hanky—a habit she says soothes her gums.

"Maybe if she listened to him she wouldn't have ended up with your father."

One Life to Live resumes, and the opportunity to ask another question is gone for the moment. I hold my thought until the next commercial.

"Is my Daddy bad?" I ask.

"He comes from mixed blood," she says.

"What does that mean?" I ask, certain I have the same blood he does.

"His father and his brother were lowlife conmen."

"What's a conman?" I say, twirling the last strand of hair.

"Shh…Rosie, my show is on."

CHAPTER SEVEN

My eyes pop open as if I'd been stung by a bee. Jumping from the bed, I stub my toe but don't stop to fuss over it. I unhook the receiver from the shiny black cradle that rests on the lamp table. The number is burned in my memory. Joseph answers on the second ring.

"Happy ninth birthday."

"Happy ninth birthday to you, too," he says.

Mama rolls to the edge of the bed and pokes through the butts in an ashtray under her pillow.

"I'm still older than you," I say, curling up on the floor, coddling the telephone.

"I grew two inches," he says. "I bet you I'm bigger than you."

"Big deal," I say, pulling lint off the carpet.

"Rosie, guess what?"

"What?" His voice rises, and I straighten my back because I think he has a secret to tell.

"Harold and Doris are taking me to New York City, today." He is practically screaming.

"What for?" I cross my legs and twirl the cord around my finger until it pinches.

"We're going to a real live magic show."

"Oh."

Joseph rambles off a list of gifts he's received. His birthday is already bursting with excitement. Harold surprised him with a Yankee jacket, and Doris bought him a real magic wand and a shiny black cape with white silk gloves and a top hat with compartments.

"Me and Mama are going ice skating," I interrupt.

"What about Daddy?"

"Yeah, he's coming, too."

"I wish you could come to New York," he says, lowering his voice.

"Me too."

A gruff voice interrupts Joseph's. He covers the mouthpiece and returns.

"I got to go now."

"But it's Sunday; we can talk longer." His angst jolts me to my feet.

"We're taking a train and can't be late; otherwise, we'll miss it."

"Okay, goodbye." I set the receiver in its cradle and lay back on the cot beside Mama.

"What's the matter," she says, leaning on her elbow.

"If Joseph doesn't want to come home, you'll make him, right?"

"Did he say he wants to come home? Does he like it there? Did he miss me?"

I answer yes to the questions thrown at me as quick as darts. "He's going to New York City to see a magic show."

"I heard." She stubs out the butt. It smolders in the ashtray. She disappears into the bathroom.

Adele and Roger come to celebrate my birthday. Nona bakes a rum cake and decorates it with whipped cream and almonds. Mama scribbles "Happy Birthday Rosie" in pink icing. Uncle Carmen lights ten candles, one for each year I've lived and one for good luck. My dwindled family sings. Squinting, I blow out the candles on the cake that should have Joseph's name on it, too.

Mama asks, "What'd you wish for?"

"If I tell, it won't come true," I say, already feeling the disappointment when I open my eyes and Joseph and Teresa aren't surrounding me.

After two heaps of rum cake, gifts are stacked on the table. Mama gives me a Snow White and the Seven Dwarfs nightgown and a new package of panties the color of a rainbow after a spring shower. Adele and Roger give me a much-needed winter coat. It is fuchsia pink with white fur as soft as a rabbit's tail edging the hood. Nona embroidered a white laced handkerchief with my name in red. After Uncle Carmen plants two shiny quarters in my palms, he pecks the top of my head, and says good night. He's off to join his *Pisanos* at the Italian American club, where Nona says they drink pots of espresso, smoke cigars, and reminisce about their precious Italy.

Adele hugs me good night and Roger pinches my cheek. When they're gone, Mama rinses the plates, gives Nona a sleeping pill, and helps her to bed.

I change out of my dungarees and into the Snow White nightgown, then prepare the sofa bed, layering it with extra blankets.

Mama switches the television on to *The Ed Sullivan Show*. I am sleepy but determined to stay awake until Ed Sullivan tucks Topo Gigio snugly into his bed. A whistle pierces my eardrums, and Mama springs up. She lifts the window, a gust of wind hurls in, flipping the pages of the *TV Guide*.

"Go to the door," she whispers.

"Who's there?" I ask.

"Shh. It's Daddy; go buzz him in."

At the intercom I hold my finger on the button until I'm sure he's had enough time to enter the building. Mama combs her hair with her fingers, pinches her cheeks, and licks her dry lips.

Daddy enters, balancing wrapped boxes with pink bows in his arms. Mama takes the packages, tips forward on her toes to peck his lips, and shuts the door with her foot. Daddy hauls me on top of his shoulders and twirls around, singing in a whisper.

"Happy birthday, Rose Petal."

I start to cry. "I missed you." Not until this moment do I realize how much I missed my father. Mama had given me strict orders not to breathe his name since we've been staying with Nona and Uncle Carmen.

"I missed you, too," he says, tickling my toes.

Sitting on Daddy's shoulders, I'm able to tap the ceiling. When I look down, my stomach somersaults, but I feel as safe as a sparrow nesting on a sturdy branch at the top of a tree.

"It's Joseph's birthday, too," I say, massaging his head.

"I know." He sets me down.

"I want to see him and Teresa," I say, staring up into his eyes.

"Rosie, Daddy's hungry," Mama interrupts, unwrapping sliced salami and provolone she grabs out of the refrigerator.

"Are these presents for me?" I ask, touching the wrapped boxes Mama set on the table.

"Shh, you'll wake Nona," Mama says, stuffing a roll with the cold meats.

"They sure are, Rose Petal." Daddy slings a leather jacket on the back of the chair, the sleeves skim the floor.

Mama touches the jacket, "Where did you get this?"

Patting her backside, he says, "I won it from some guy."

Mama slams the plate on the table. The sandwich topples over.

Ignoring her outburst, Daddy says, "Open the big one first."

He bites into his sandwich, and I tackle the neatly wrapped gifts, carefully untying a pink bow before tearing the paper away.

In the box lies a sleeping Thumbelina doll. A tuft of blond hair falls between blue eyes. I hadn't had a doll since the time Joseph tossed my Raggedy Ann out the window and it landed on Mrs. Pirelli's porch roof. Over time, I was forced to witness harsh winds, ice and snow, glaring sun, and overwhelming heat shred the doll.

"I love her," I say, coddling the Thumbelina.

"Isn't she getting too old for dolls?" Mama says, arching an eyebrow at Daddy.

"She's only nine. What else is she supposed to play with?"

The other packages contain a bottle, a rattle, and a pacifier. I stick the pacifier in the doll's mouth, swaddle it in a dish towel, and bounce it on my knees.

Daddy gobbles his sandwich and swigs the Coke. "Want to help me shave?"

Mama peeks in Nona's room to be certain she is asleep, and Daddy and I tiptoe into the bathroom and lock the door. I sit on the toilet seat lid to assist my father the way Joseph used to.

"Shaving cream, please," Daddy whispers, cupping is palms.

With both hands, I squirt a wad of dense cream into his hands. He lathers his square jaw and neck. Leaning into the mirror, he skims the cream with Uncle Carmen's razor, removing the stubble. Bending down, he splashes water on his face, rinsing the leftover cream. It splatters the mirror and the sink.

"Towel, please," he says.

I hand him the towel. He pats his face dry before splashing on Uncle Carmen's Old Spice.

"Give me a kiss for good luck." He bends down to dot cologne behind my ears.

I peck his cheek; his skin is smooth and shimmers like Nona's nylon stockings drying on the towel rack.

"Now go tell Mama to come in here; I have to talk to her about something," he says, swatting my butt.

Snuggling in bed with my doll, I count the thumping sounds coming from the bathroom. There are twelve before my parents emerge, flushed and perspiring. Daddy blows kisses at me in the dark. Mama locks the door and slips into bed with me. She smells like a wet rag that's been left in the sink.

"Mama, where does Daddy sleep?"

"At a friend's," she says, yawning.

"Are you getting married again?"

"We never stopped being married," she chuckles.

"Is Daddy going to bring Teresa and Joseph home?"

"Yep." She pulls the sheet over her shoulders.

"When?"

"Soon. Now go to sleep."

"I hope Joseph had a good birthday," I say, rubbing her arm in the dark.

Mama rolls on her back and stares at the ceiling.

"Don't mention to anyone that your father was here."

"I won't."

———

Two weeks later, Nona is asleep, and I am filling the tub for Daddy. Over the gushing water I hear Uncle Carmen shout, "What the fuck are you doing here?"

I turn the faucet off and rush into the kitchen. Nona shuffles behind me.

"I'm just leaving," my father says, pecking Mama's cheek.

Uncle Carmen blocks the doorframe. My father towers over him, but that doesn't seem to frighten my uncle.

"How dare you come into my house?" he says, poking my father's chest with greasy fingers.

Daddy doesn't flinch. He raises his hands as if to surrender. "I don't want any trouble. I just stopped by to see Rosie."

"Antonette, I told you I don't want this scum in my house." Uncle Carmen spins around to face my mother.

"Shh…the neighbors will hear," Nona says.

It feels as though the walls are crushing us. I clutch Mama's waist. She's trembling.

"Rosie wanted to see him. He won't come again."

Stepping out of the way, Uncle Carmen rasps, "My father was right about you and your lowlife family."

And then my father is gone without a glance back. But the tension is still smothering us in the tiny kitchen. Uncle Carmen glowers at Mama. "So you took him back again, eh?"

Mama rolls her lips into her mouth and begins to clear the dishes off the table.

"You're a fool to believe his lies over and over again. He'll never amount to anything."

Mama spins around so quickly I think she's going to fall. "And what have you amounted to. You're thirty-five years old, and you live with your mother. You can't even find a wife."

"And you're an unfit mother."

Mama raises her hand, but Uncle Carmen catches her wrist.

"Papa warned you what would happen if you got involved with that piece-of-shit mixed breed."

"Please stop shouting," Nona says, taking a seat and tugging on Uncle Carmen's arm.

"I want you out of here," Uncle Carmen says, before stomping away. He charges through the living room, and I can hear all Nona's precious knick-knacks rattling in the glass cabinet.

CHAPTER EIGHT

The following morning, Mama folds the bits of clothing we own into a Bamberger's shopping bag. I don't want to ask questions that might upset Mama anymore than she already is, but I am afraid Mr. Waxman is going to barge in and take me away.

Crying at the door, Nona tucks a nylon sock into Mama's hand. I recognize it as the one where she stores the few pieces of jewelry she cherishes.

"Take this," she says.

"I can't." Mama fends it off with a swat of her hand.

"What am I going to do with it?" Nona says.

Mama hesitates, then takes the sock and squeezes it into her purse. Nona wiggles the gold wedding band off her gnarled finger and presses it into Mama's palm. They hold each other like one is attempting to catch the other before a fall.

The day is sunless; only gray clouds mill around in clusters. Shivering in a light windbreaker, Mama zips my jacket and tucks my hair inside the hood. Glancing up and down the street, she decides we'll go left. She clenches the bag of clothes, whitening her knuckles.

Drifting into the center of town, I worry that mama's going to send me back to the Finches. We zigzag in and out of the drug store and coffee shop before stumbling into a pawn shop. I had visited a pawn shop on another occasion with Daddy. This one is similar, cluttered with brass tea sets, sterling silverware, and a rack of fur coats. Mama empties the contents of the sock onto a glass counter. A bald man with a beard as long as my ponytail stands erect behind a counter. Blubber hangs over a red, white, and blue striped belt as if gasping for air. He picks through the specks of gold and silver and examines them under a bright bulb belted to his head. He tosses the pearl broche

Nona's parents had given her for her twenty-first birthday into a heap of metal. His breath is heavy, and when he exhales, dandruff flakes flutter on his brow.

The man examines the jewelry and switches off the light. He takes two twenty-dollar bills from the cash register and offers them to Mama. Without hesitating, she snatches them, and we head out of there.

The constant gurgles in my stomach inform it's noontime when we knock on Adele's door. Adele answers, biting into a tuna fish sandwich.

"Hey, what a surprise," she says, waving us in.

"I figured you'd be home for lunch," Mama says.

"Rosie, why aren't you in school?" she says, walking and talking over her shoulder.

"It's a long story," Mama says, darting a look at me.

In the kitchen Mama pours a cup of coffee. Still shivering, she sips it black.

"You don't look good, Antonette. What happened?"

Mama blurts out a short version of the argument with Uncle Carmen and Adele listens as she prepares two more tuna sandwiches.

"Well, you just have to stay here with Roger and me," she says, leaning her back against the refrigerator.

"I'm so embarrassed. What'll Roger think?"

"He thinks you married a loser, but that doesn't mean he won't help you and the kids."

Mama flinches but doesn't argue.

"Just for a few weeks," Mama says. "I promise."

"I'll call Roger at the office right now."

Pacing, Adele curls the telephone cord around her fingers. The conversation is spaced with silence, but she hangs up with a smile and opened arms.

"See, I told you he wouldn't mind."

"I have to get back to work. I don't like the stylists answering the phone at the shop. They screw up everyone's schedules," Adele says. She grabs her coat and purse off a rack in the mudroom.

"Thank you," Mama says. "I'll have supper ready when you get home."

"Great. There's ground beef defrosting in the fridge."

"See you later," I say, gulping the last bit of sandwich.

That afternoon Mama makes up the bed in the spare room Adele uses for sewing. She empties a coffee can full of loose multicolored threads and stashes the money she was paid for Nona's jewelry along with the pawn ticket in it. She tucks it on the closet shelf behind a blanket.

"Don't tell Adele we pawned Nona's jewelry."

"I won't."

"After we save enough for our own place, I'll get it all back."

––––––––

I enjoy being fussed over, without a twinge of guilt. Adele prepares all my favorite meals: fried breaded veal cutlets, spaghetti with meatballs, and grilled mozzarella sandwiches. When she shops, which she does often, she always returns with a surprise for me: an Etch-a-Sketch, my first Barbie doll that I can't wait to show Teresa, and plastic high heels.

On Saturday Mama and I visit Adele at the beauty parlor. Sitting on a rolling chair behind the desk with Adele, I pretend to answer the telephone the way she does. Mama slumps over the counter, and they share a cigarette and gossip about the women sauntering in and out. We learn that our old neighbor, Mrs. Pirelli, came home from morning mass to find her husband sitting on the toilet seat, his head between his knees. She tapped his shoulder, thinking he had fallen asleep, and he rolled onto the floor dead. Mama and Adele laugh, but I cringe at the thought of the staunch Mrs. Pirelli walking in on such a sight.

One evening Roger is working late, so just the three of us are sitting down for dinner when the doorbell rings.

"Who could that be now?" Adele wonders, maneuvering an oversized roasting pan onto the square speckled Formica table. "Antonette, go see."

In the foyer Mama eyeballs the peephole.

"Who's there?" she asks, cracking the door a smidgen. A male voice mumbles a few words.

"He's not here, and I don't know where he is," she says, slamming the door. Her cheeks flush, and her nose sweats.

"Who is it?" Adele asks.

"Go inside, Rosie," Mama says, wringing her hands.

I'm piling potatoes onto my plate. "But I'm hungry."

"Go watch television for a few more minutes," Adele says.

Obeying, I withdraw to the living room. Turning the volume down, I still have to strain to hear them.

"If Roger finds out, he'll go crazy, Antonette. I can't have those kinds of people milling around here."

"I'm sorry. I'll take care of it," Mama says.

"Why would a bookie come here looking for him?" Adele says. A cabinet door slams, and Adele's heels click back and forth on the linoleum.

"I don't know why. It won't happen again," Mama whispers.

"They're dangerous people, Antonette—I don't want them near my home." Another cabinet opens and slams shut.

"I'll take care of it; please, let's just drop it. Rosie, come and eat," Mama calls to me.

Adele's ivory skin is blotched with anger—or maybe it is fear—and I wonder whether she knows about my father's brother, Joe. He was a bookie, and Mama said he gave Daddy the gambling disease, too. She said he dragged Daddy to the racetrack and taught him how to play poker and shoot pool.

None of us swallows a morsel; there's too much tension in the air. Adele swipes her uneaten dinner off her plate into the garbage. She retreats to her room without saying good night. Mama tidies the kitchen and grabs her coat from the closet.

"Go to bed, Rosie; I'll be back in a little while."

"No, I want to come with you," I say, squeezing my feet into a pair of worn Keds that remind me of pumpkin seeds.

"Shh, come on then."

Fine drizzles swagger under the glare of the streetlamp, and the sidewalks are slick like olive oil. I manage to keep up with Mama's pace until we reach Paolucci's, where my father delivers pizzas. We've been visiting him after school to collect his tips to save in the coffee can.

The heat exuding from the fired brick ovens and the aromas of hot dogs and potatoes restore my appetite.

"Can I have a slice of pizza?" I ask, tugging on Mama's sleeve.

"Not now."

Behind a stainless steel counter a petite man, dressed in a uniform as white as the flour he dusts onto a wooden block, speaks into a telephone, jotting notes onto a pad. I stare at the bald spot on the back of his head, imagining a set of eyes, a nose, and a smile on the illuminating skin.

"Can I help you, lady?" The man hangs up and wipes his hands on a soiled apron.

"Yes, I'm Antonette Scarpiella; I'm here to see my husband."

In one swift move the man leaps over the counter.

"That son of a bitch." Saliva sprays Mama's face. "If I get my hands on him…." His harsh words startle the mix of teenage boys and girls devouring gooey slices of pie. I'm embarrassed by their stares.

"I'll beat his brains in. That bum stole all my money. He better never come back here." The man flaps his arms in circles, as if he's trying to keep from flying.

"I'll call the police on him."

Mama yanks my arm almost out of its socket. We scramble out of the pizzeria as the crazy man chases after us, shouting in Italian. We run and don't stop until his insults fade in the wind.

Roger's Cadillac is parked at the curb. The porch light is on, but the rest of the house is dark. The floorboards creak as we tiptoe into the spare room. We strip off our wet clothes and change into pajamas without switching on the lamp. The rain sizzles on the roof shingles like eggs in bacon grease, muffling Adele's and Roger's voices.

"Temporary," Roger says.

"Keep it down."

"They're not *our* responsibility, Adele," he adds, clicking the door shut.

Although they can't see me, I duck under the pillow to hide the shame burning my face. Mama sits up and lights a cigarette in the dark.

"Where's Daddy?" I ask, burrowing into her side.

"I don't know."

"Is he ever coming back?"

"Stop asking questions I don't have answers for." She stubs out the cigarette.

After school, we stop at the bakery to pick up a French loaf for supper. When we approach Adele's, Daddy jumps off the stoop. Mama lets go of my hand and lunges at him. He blocks her clenched fists, which aren't strong enough to kill a fly, never mind hurt my six-foot father.

"What did you do, you bastard."

"Antonette, calm down."

"Mama, the neighbors," I say, glancing around at the staring strangers.

Mama steps back and unlocks the door. We follow inside.

My parents scamper into the bedroom. In the hallway I press an ear to the door.

"Antonette, I'm in trouble."

"I know all about it. You're bookie came by, and your boss told me you stole his money."

"It's bad, Antonette."

"It's always bad." The dresser drawers open and close; Mama is searching for a cigarette.

"I felt lucky," my father says.

"All you have is bad luck. I'm tired of hearing about it, and so are your kids."

"I tried to stop. I wanted to, but I kept chasing one bet after the other," he rambles on.

Mama swings the door open and rages past me, covering her ears with her palms. He chases after her into the living room.

"All I could think of is getting the kids back."

"You don't care about me or them. You're a loser, and everyone knows it." She picks up a glass ashtray and hurls it at Daddy, nicking his ankle.

"This is different. Shut up and listen to me."

Daddy grabs Mama's shoulders, forcing her to be still. He looks into her eyes and says, "If I don't come up with three thousand dollars by Friday, I'm a dead man."

It's as if Mama has stopped breathing. All the twitching in her body ceases, and her eyes look like two black marbles. When Daddy seems certain she's calm, he let's go, and she steps back, bumping into the coffee table. "Three thousand dollars?" she repeats over and over again, sitting on the edge of the sofa. She buries her face in her hands and sobs. With the sleeve of her jacket, she calmly wipes her nose.

"Please, Antonette. You got to talk to this guy for me. He owns Wrigley Tavern on Fifth Avenue. Take Rosie with you. You can explain why I needed the money. 'Cause of the kids and all."

Daddy kneels down in front of Mama and takes her hand; they're eye to eye. The grandfather clock chimes, and Mama jumps up. I know she's worried Adele will be home any minute from the beauty parlor.

"Antonette, this is the last time. I promise. Get me out of this jam, and I promise I'll get the kids back."

"Tomorrow—I'll go tomorrow," she says.

———

On a subway bound to Wrigley Tavern, Mama and I bounce as if we're on a roller coaster. She doesn't speak to me during the whole ride, but I know she's worried because she is biting the cuticles off her fingernails. I massage her arm, but she nudges me away.

The two-story red brick building constructed on a corner is bordered on two sides by parking lots. A lit sign flickering in the window illuminates the grime and smudges.

We tiptoe into the dank bar as if we're trying not to wake the haggard men perched on stools, coddling whiskey shots and puffing cigars. Several sets of eyes, the color of urine, dart in our direction when they hear the creaking door—more out of habit than interest I suppose.

The sole bartender nods. "Can I help you, lady?"

"I'm looking for Scraps," Mama says.

"He'll be back in a minute. Take a seat if you want," he says, pointing to a wooden table.

"We'll wait outside for him."

"He said he'd be back, but I can't make any promises." The bartender wipes a beer mug with a wet cloth that looks like a diaper. "I'm not his keeper," he sputters.

As we turn to step out, the door flings open. The glare of the sun exposes the torn leather stools.

"Hey, Scraps, this lady here wants to see you."

"Me?" A gray-haired man dressed in a black suit and red tie around a starched white collar pokes his chest.

"My name's Antonette Scarpiella." Mama's words are jittery like my legs feel.

The patrons' muttering ceases; the heat from their beady yellowed eyes sears the back of my neck. Mama arches her back and straightens her shoulders.

"Can we talk in private?" she whispers, squeezing my hand.

"Sure."

Scraps guides us through a red-and-white checkered curtain and into a dining area. Round and square tables are covered with green plastic tablecloths. Ashtrays, salt and pepper shakers, and grated cheese center each table. Black-and-white photographs hang, scattered, on the paneled walls. I recognize Marlon Brando, Humphrey Bogart, and Bette Davis from old movies I've watched late at night with Mama at Adele's.

Scraps removes a charcoal gray cap and tosses it like a Frisbee onto a hook. On a wall between the ladies' and men's rooms is a jukebox. Scraps inserts several coins and punches in his selections. "Can't Take My Eyes Off of You" sounds from the box. Taking a seat, he motions for Mama to join him. Standing behind her, I can just about see over her teased hair.

Just like the song that plays in the background, I can't take my eyes from Scraps' face. He looks like I imagine God would. His head forms a perfect circle, and although he appears to be Nona's age, the lines in his skin are not so deep and harsh. Bushy gray brows accentuate the bluest eyes I've ever seen. He is as short and slender as Mama, and I wonder how my tall, husky father could be so afraid of such a gentle man, with a face like God's.

"You're here about the money your husband owes me?" Scraps starts the conversation.

"Yes." Mama crosses her legs, uncrosses them, and then recrosses them.

"Has he sent you to pay his debt?" Scraps leans in and folds his hands on the table.

"Well, I came to ask if you could give him a little more time to pay you."

"Did he tell you how much he owes?" he asks. Arching thick brows, his eyes rest on mine. His brows soften.

"What's your name?"

"Rosie."

"We got three kids. I promise he'll pay you every cent he borrowed. Just give him some time," Mama pleads.

"He should have thought of his kids before he borrowed money he can't afford to pay back," he says, knuckling the wooden table.

"He has a sickness; he can't help it. He's really a good man; he just doesn't know when to quit."

"His sickness is selfishness. *Good* men don't send their wives and kids to save their asses," Scraps says, picking lint off cuffed trousers.

"Please, for my kids." Mama tilts her head in my direction, as a reminder that I exist.

Scratching the shiny spot on top of his head, Scraps sighs. The jukebox pauses, selects another record, and music replaces the silence.

"You look familiar; what's your family name?" he asks.

"Minnelli."

"I thought so. You're Dan Minelli's daughter; your brother's Carmen." Scraps removes a pack of Marlboros from his pocket and offers it to Mama.

"My father died years back." She snatches a cigarette from the opened pack.

Scraps flips open a glittery lighter.

"I'm sorry to hear that; he was a hardworking man," Scraps says, tapping the lighter on the table. "He did a couple of favors for me years ago." His chair screeches back and Mama twitches.

"Tell you what I'll do. I'll give your husband ninety days to come up with the money. But I do that for you," he says, pointing a finger at Mama. "As a favor to your father."

"Thank you, thank you." Mama bounces off the chair. I have the notion she is going to embrace him, but she steps backward rather than forward, knocking the chair into my knee.

"Remember, ninety days," he says. Standing, he pinches the creases in his trousers.

We back away.

"Wait a minute," Scraps says, peeling a twenty from a wad of bills.

"For Rosie."

I don't dare snatch it without Mama's permission. I stretch my eyes to their corners, anxious to glimpse the *yes* sign.

"Let her take it," Scraps says.

Mama nods, and I thank him as he folds the bill into my palm.

Exiting the tavern, I feel a thousand pounds lighter than when we arrived. We stop at the grocery store to purchase a loaf of bread, milk, Pall Malls, and candy cigarettes for me.

Daddy's pitching cards on the side of Adele's house.

"How'd it go?" he asks, slouching to pick up the cards.

"You have ninety days," Mama says.

"That's it?"

"You're lucky he gave you that much time. How are you going to come up with that kind of money?" She swings her arms in the air.

"I'll figure something out."

"You better get out of here before Adele comes home," Mama says, peering up and down the street.

Daddy hugs us goodbye and struts away.

———

Sauntering into the kitchen, wiping sleep from my eyes, I am surprised to see Mama, nibbling a slice of rye toast between glances at a newspaper. I recognize the dress she wears. It is one of Adele's: navy with white polka dots. She wobbles in heels and balances pink rollers on her head.

"You look silly," I giggle.

Mama pats the wide rollers and smiles. "I'm going job hunting. So your sister and brother can come home," she says, tucking the paper under her arms before reaching to pull the rollers out of her hair. Pins fall onto the floor, and I bend to pick them up.

"Are they coming home today?" Tiny needles prick at my brain, numbing my head.

"No. When I find a job, they can come home."

"Is it hard to find a job?" I ask, throwing the pins into a tin can on the table.

"It's very hard." She rolls the paper and swats my butt with it.

"But you'll find one—right, Mama?"

She points to a bowl. "Eat some cereal."

In front of Adele's cosmetic mirror, Mama teases and twists her hair into a loaf as I slurp every last Cheerio from the bowl I purposely overfilled. When she is through, she dabs her cheeks and lips with coral lipstick.

"Can I have some lipstick, too?"

Switching the bright bulbs off, she says, "Don't be silly."

"You let Teresa wear lipstick."

"Let's untangle that head of yours, before you're late for school."

She wets a comb under the tap and tugs it through my knots, then licks her finger and wipes my cheek.

"You always look like such a mess."

Glowering at her, I stagger out.

"Walk home from school in a group today," she hollers.

Spinning around, I ask, "Aren't you going to be waiting outside?"

"I'm going to be gone all day looking for work. I'll see you at home for supper."

———

It is suppertime, and Mama is not home like she promised she would be. Recognizing my panic, Adele distracts me with questions about my studies. I can't concentrate on anything else but why Mama is not home. Crouching on the sofa arm, I stare out the living room window and count to one hundred, one hundred times. Not until I glimpse Mama's petite frame do I relax.

"She's back; she's back," I say, clapping my hands.

"Of course she is." Adele unlocks the door before Mama inserts the key.

"Any luck?" we both ask as the door flings open.

"Let me come in first, and I'll tell you all about it." Mama removes the raincoat Adele had also loaned her. Plopping on the sofa, she kicks off her heels. Adele lights a cigarette and gives it to Mama.

"So, what happened?" Adele asks.

I massage Mama's stocking feet. They are calloused and sweaty.

"The manager at the pastry shop asked me to come in tomorrow to meet with the owner."

"That's fantastic," Adele says, patting her friend's arm. "Let's celebrate. I'll treat you to roast beef sandwiches at the pub."

"Adele, I didn't get the job yet," Mama says, yawning, stretching her arms above her head.

Adele pulls Mama off the sofa. Without heels, the top of Mama's head is even with Adele's shoulder.

"Don't be so gloomy all the time," Adele says.

Mama glances down at me, grinning as widely as I am. Tugging me up to my feet, she says, "Come on. Let's go celebrate."

———

Mama isn't offered the job at the pastry shop and continues searching for work. While I'm in school, she applies for the cashier opening at Leo's Deli, the waitress position at Kresgee's lunch counter, and as a receptionist for an insurance agency. At the end of the day she's wearing the same navy blue dress and face of despair she wore in the morning.

One afternoon while I'm heading home, light drizzle shifts to heavy rain. I stack my history and geography books on top of my head and sprint to Adele's.

Mama's shoes are in the foyer, and her raincoat and purse are slung over a chair. The lights are out, and as I move about the house, switching on the lamps, I whisper, "Mama, Mama. Are you home?"

The bedroom door is closed. I enter without knocking. Mama lies on top of the bedspread; the pleats on her navy dress are flat.

"What's the matter—are you sick?" I ask, lying down next to her.

"I have a headache," she says, sitting up, shouldering the headboard.

I catch a faint scent of Old Spice. "You smell like Daddy," I say.

She nudges me away. "You're soaking wet; get out of those clothes and dry your hair."

Shivering, I strip the soggy jeans and blouse off and welcome a warm pair of pajamas.

"Did you get a job today?"

"Either I don't have the experience or the position has already been filled. That's all I hear day after day."

"You can try again tomorrow," I say, towel drying my drenched hair.

"Rosie, get my cigarettes for me. They're in my purse."

I return to the living room with the hope that Mama has a pack of gum in her purse, too. Rummaging through the bottom, I find bobby pins and tubes of lipstick. I notice a bulge in the inner lining and unzip the pouch. Mama's pantyhose are knotted into a ball.

"Rosie, what are you doing," Mama shouts from our room.

I shove the pantyhose back into the purse and grab the half-empty pack of cigarettes.

"Go do your homework until Adele gets home." Mama snatches the pack from me.

"I don't have any."

"Well, then, go read or something," she says, lighting a cigarette. "And close the door."

Adele balances a grocery bag on each hip, and I rush to relieve her of one. "Is your mother home?"

"She's lying down," I say, setting the bag on the counter.

Arching her pencil-lined eyebrows, she asks, "Did she have any luck today?"

I shake my head no.

"Start unpacking," she says. "You know where everything goes."

It's an hour before Mama and Adele emerge from our room to prepare dinner: Campbell's chicken soup with stars and hamburgers on toasted buns. There is little conversation during supper. Before I take the last bite of burger, Mama collects the condiments and puts the ketchup in the refrigerator and the salt and pepper shakers on the stove next to the egg timer.

We say good night and go to our room without even watching *The Newlywed Game*. Mama tells me to sleep because we have to get up extra early in the morning, but I lie awake, counting the ceiling tiles instead of sheep. The refrigerator humming, the clock ticking, the furnace switching on and off, and the rattle in the back of Mama's throat can't make me stop thinking that I'm never going to see Joseph and Teresa again or whether I'm even safe here with Mama. Every time there's a tap on the door I expect Mr. Waxman and the black habit nuns to barge in and take me away again. I get the chills thinking about them and roll over, ducking my head under the covers.

Morning comes. Adele calls work to say she's sick, and Mama says I don't have to go to school. In Adele's Plymouth we drive downtown to the Welfare Department. The three of us sit in front of a metal desk, piled with folders stuffed with papers. The woman behind the tower of files has round cheeks that are caked with red rouge; her neck is thick like Daddy's, and the fat on her arms jiggles as she pens a clipboard.

"How long have you been separated from your husband?" the woman asks.

"Six months."

"Do you have any communications with him at all?" The woman presses the pencil eraser against the tip of her nose.

"No," Mama says, shifting on the wooden chair.

"Have you seen your Daddy?" she asks, pointing the pencil at me.

"No," I say, fully prepared to answer.

She jots down Mama's answers and slides the clipboard across the desk.

"Sign at the red X."

Mama signs, and we all stand. The woman shakes Mama's hand so hard I half expect it to snap off. She explains that she'll submit the application and that Mama should hear back from her in a few weeks.

During the drive home, Mama snivels into a handkerchief the entire time.

"It's not that big a deal, Antonette. No one has to know," Adele says, adjusting the radio.

"And you don't know how this feels; so, please, don't say anything," Mama says, grinding her teeth.

"Fine," Adele snaps, turning up the volume.

CHAPTER NINE

A customer at the beauty parlor informs Adele of a two-bedroom apartment available for a cheap rent above a confectionary store on the avenue. Mama and I strut to the address jotted on a matchbook.

The number twenty-two printed on the tattered striped awning is barely visible, but my keen eyes don't miss it. Plastering the glass window, cardboard signs written with a black marker advertise "Cigarettes Sold Here," "Homemade Jam," "Coca-Cola," and "Food Stamps Accepted."

When we enter the store, a bell chimes overhead. I scan a clutter of opened boxes stacked in a corner, loaded with thick bars of dark chocolate, plastic bags of granulated sugar, and rolls of cellophane. The counter is crammed with glass jars overstuffed with cherry shoestring licorice and vanilla taffy.

"We're here to inspect the rooms for rent," Mama says.

"And you are?" the man behind the counter asks, peering over bifocals.

"My name's Antonette Scarpiella, Adele Matthews' friend."

The man shuffles to the front of the store and leads us outside to a separate entrance on the right side of the building. He fumbles with a key chain dangling from his belt loop.

"How many kids you got?" He pauses at the door, waiting for her answer.

Mama darts her wide eyes at me. "One," she says. We had rehearsed on the way there.

Stepping into a dank parlor, paneled in pine, we both sigh. Built-in bookcases stand behind a chenille sofa, and I imagine squeezing into the small spaces during a game of hide-and-seek with Joseph. In the tiny kitchen four vinyl chairs surround a metal card table. The two bedrooms are on opposite sides of the bathroom. In my mind I choose the larger of the two. The walls are marked with black and red crayons, but the oak floor shines like the school gymnasium's wide planks do. Bunk beds butt up against the double-hung window, overlooking a park across the avenue. Mama whispers in my ear, "Swings."

"Can we go to the park today?" I ask.

"We'll take it," Mama says, spinning around, her cheeks flushed and her eyes moist and bright.

"Rent's due now and every first day of the month," the landlord says, extending his crooked fingers.

"I have it right here," Mama says. Her fingers tremble as she snaps open her purse.

We had stopped at the bank to cash our first welfare check before venturing to view the apartment. Stacking the bills in the landlord's hand, she counts aloud. He recounts, removes a key from a chain, and drops it in her open palm.

Securing an apartment of our own warrants a celebration, so Adele nourishes us with a Thanksgiving-style dinner. For dessert I have two helpings of warm apple pie topped with vanilla ice cream.

"You're going to get a bellyache, and you won't be able to sleep," Mama warns.

I sleep soundly that night without even getting up to pee. The bellyache comes in the morning. But not the kind from overeating—it's the type kids wake with the first day of school.

Mama and I pack the few possessions we have accumulated during the months we lived with Adele and Roger Matthews. Although having our own place means we are a step closer to Teresa and Joseph coming home, I'm going to miss three meals a day, hot baths, and steaming radiators.

Adele surprises Mama with a bulging box wrapped in shimmering paper. Mama wipes the tears away before they plop onto the white linens, blankets, and bath towels splayed in the overstuffed box. Mama hugs Adele and thanks her for all she has done for us.

"For nothing," Adele says, blowing her nose into a hanky.

"I'll make it up to you somehow," Mama says.

"Just stay away from that bum once and for all."

After hauling us and our baggage to the apartment above the confectionery store, Adele seems pleased roaming the four rooms, nodding and smiling. She sits on the sofa to test its comfort, and I plop down beside her.

"This is great, Rosie," she says.

"Isn't it," I say, bouncing up and down.

Before leaving, Adele tours the apartment one last time.

"I'll stop by tomorrow," she says, dangling keys. "I have to get to work now."

"Goodbye. Thanks again," Mama and I say.

Mama gets busy scouring the bathtub, toilet, and sink with bleach and Comet, and I make up the bunk beds in my new room with the sheets Adele has given us. Mama decides it is time Joseph has his own bed, since he is a boy, and I don't make a fuss. I say he can have the top one because I think that's what he'll like.

The single cabinet above the sink is stacked with odd plates, cups and saucers, and bowls. Mama empties the cabinet, scours the shelves, and then rearranges everything. She snaps a plastic liner over the metal card table and sets a bouquet of silk flowers in the center.

The single window overlooks a neighbor's yard. Mama pulls the worn shade down, and the string snaps off.

"We'll have to get a pretty curtain at Kresgee's," she says.

In a festive mood after settling into our new home, Mama and I strut to Bond's and split a grilled cheese sandwich and a Coke. She squashes her after-meal cigarette in the plate and asks the waitress for change for a dollar. Sitting in the public telephone booth, she winks at me and closes the door. A dull light switches on, and she dials. She is telephoning Mr. Waxman to inform him of our new address. After a brief conversation, she hangs up.

"Did he say Teresa and Joseph could come home now?"

"It's not that simple, Rosie."

"But you said if we had our own place, they could."

"That's what I thought. But Mr. Waxman has to come see the apartment first."

"When is he coming?"

"Next month. We'll make it pretty and cozy."

For the first time since I've been reunited with Mama, I hop into my own bed and am excited at first. But I toss and change positions one hundred times. I wrestle out of the tangled sheet and blanket and creep into Mama's room. She has fallen asleep with the lamp on. Under its glow her olive skin shines like the satin wedding gown Adele bought for my Barbie. Her eyes flutter open.

"What's wrong?" she says, leaning up on her elbows.

"I can't sleep."

"Isn't your bed comfortable?" she asks, lifting the blanket.

"It's okay," I say, snuggling into her warm body. I wait a few seconds before asking, "What if Mr. Waxman doesn't like our new home?"

Tucking the blanket around me, she mutters, "Of course, he will."

Spearmint Gum, stale tobacco, and the rhythm of her pulse lull me into a deep sleep.

CHAPTER TEN

Winter coats, hats, and boots have been stored in mothballs in backs of closets. The clocks have been turned an hour ahead for daylight savings, and I relish the extended days easing the nights that are still as dreary and cold as March. When I try to visualize my brother and sister, their faces blur. I worry that one day they'll fade away completely, so I begin to conjure them daily.

In the mornings we skip to school together, chatting endlessly. On Saturdays we sit on the front stoop, poking fun at Mrs. Martone's flab jiggling as she hobbles to the fish market for the freshest catch. Mr. Fatima strolls by with his long-fanged German shepherd. Teresa is petrified of it, so when I see dog and master, I warn Teresa so she can hide. I become an expert at mimicking Teresa's throaty giggle and Joseph's habit of dropping the last letter of his words.

At bedtime I whisper stories to them. Their favorite is about a boy who lives alone in a mansion and befriends a mouse. The adventures of the boy and the tiny creature vary. Once I pretend the mouse is trapped in a shoe, which upsets Joseph. Teresa scolds me, but Joseph begs me to expound on the gory details.

One night Mama overhears me whispering under the covers.

"Who're you talking to?" she asks, tugging on my layers of blankets.

"I'm pretending to tell a story to Teresa and Joseph."

By a slant of light glinting from the bathroom, I see Mama smile. Her chin juts out past her pointed nose.

"Can I hear your story, too?" she asks, sliding into the lower bunk.

"Sure," I say.

"Where're Joseph and Teresa?"

"Right here." I point to the empty space between us.

Mama squeezes in the middle, shuts her eyes, and relaxes her jaw.
"Go ahead, Rosie; tell us your story."

———————

Daddy shadows the doorway of our new apartment, juggling boxes, large and small, square and round, shimmering in iridescent paper, tied with bows. In minutes I rip through the paper: a cradle for my Thumbelina, barrettes in assorted colors, and a hula hoop, which is impossible to disguise.

"Yeah," I say, spinning it around my waist.

Mama opens her gift last. The box is square and deep. Unlike me, Mama savors the surprise, loosening the bow first and peeling back the paper so as not to tear it.

She shakes the box. "It's as light as paper." Recently trimmed bangs dance on her forehead.

"Open it," Daddy says, more excited than she is.

Mama flips the lid. She gasps at the silky dress, the shade of a peach pit. Her eyes shine like a new dime, and she hops into Daddy's arms, clasping her legs around his waist, crinkling the dress between them.

"Try it on," he says.

Mama slides down his leg. "We can't afford this. You have to take it back."

"Don't worry about it," he says, massaging her cheek with his thumb.

"We have to save every penny we can," she says, folding the dress into the box.

Daddy tugs it out. "Come on, you haven't had a new dress in a long time. Just put it on."

Mama strips off her jeans and T-shirt and slips the dress on over her panties. The hem sways just above her knee; the neckline buttons in the back, showing off squared shoulders. Dragging a chair into the bathroom, she giggles like me. She steps onto the chair to view her figure in the mirror above the sink. Daddy whistles, and I try to, but only spit comes out.

"Rosie, go outside and play with your hula hoop for a while," Mama says, smirking at Daddy as he lifts her down from the chair.

Gloria Suarez, who lives across the street, next to the park, dashes across the avenue when she spies the hula.

"You want to try?" I ask, securing it around my waist.

"Sure, you can play with my jump rope," she says.

I'm more interested in the hula hoop, but I don't want to play alone, so I make the trade. In just a few minutes Mama hollers out the window, "Time for a bath. Daddy's taking us out to dinner."

"See you tomorrow," I say, taking my hula and disappearing indoors before Gloria can catch her breath.

Mama slicks her hair back into a tight twist; not a wisp strays. She buffs an old pair of black pointed pumps with a towel and slips into them. Even in heels, her head doesn't reach Daddy's shoulder.

I wiggle into the red velvet dress Adele had bought me for Christmas. I've grown, making it tight in the shoulders and too short. Mama uses a butter knife to pull down the hem and then irons it. She dabs lipstick on her lips, and I pucker for her to do mine.

"Just a little," she says.

"Look at my girls." Daddy tucks a white silky shirt into black trousers. "You're the prettiest in town."

We smile back at him. When he's through dressing, we switch the lights off and head out.

The restaurant is wall-to-wall carpeted. Its chairs are high-backed and cushioned in crushed velvet, the same cherry red as my dress. When I sip water, a bus boy rushes over to fill my glass to the rim again, each time gazing at Mama from the corners of his eyes. Our meal is served on china by waiters suited in black with white starched shirts and bowties. It's the first time I've ever tasted steak, and I suck every last drop of juice from the meat. Mama nibbles on hers. She squeezes Daddy's arm and giggles when he whispers in her ear.

"Are you going to live with us again?" I ask.

Daddy tweaks my nose, "You bet."

In bed that evening, conjuring Teresa and Joseph, I describe the restaurant with its white linen and candlelit tables. I fall asleep snuggled between them, serenaded by the sweet sounds of my parents' groans in the next room.

CHAPTER ELEVEN

Mama and I lug soiled sheets, towels, and all our dirty clothes to the Laundromat. It is mobbed with women, children, and infants wailing in carriages. To occupy the time, I sit on a chair, swinging my feet to the beat of the snaps and buttons scratching the walls of the dryer drums. To me, the scent of bleach and detergent is as soothing as hot chocolate simmering on the stove on a winter afternoon. When I'm bored, I get up to search the empty machines and dryers for coins forgotten in trousers and shirt pockets and am thrilled to find enough to buy a hot dog from the scooter man on the corner.

I'm assisting Mama with folding the sheets when I recognize Scraps from the tavern. He enters the Laundromat from a back door. He wears a baseball cap instead of the cap he had worn the day I first met him; he looks younger and more relaxed.

"Hey, what are you doing here, little Miss Rosie?" he says. I feel happy he has remembered my name.

Mama's back is toward him; she spins around. She drops the corners of the sheet onto the sticky floor.

"What a surprise," she says, bending to pick it up before it smears with dirt.

"I own the place. My grandson usually stops by to fill the dispensers and clean up, but I gave him the day off," he says, jiggling bunched keys.

"Oh, we come here all the time," Mama says, pointing to the unfolded laundry. Sweat is dripping between her breasts.

"You live around here?" The fluorescent light reflects in his bright blue eyes.

Mama shifts her stance and refolds the sheet. "A block away."

Scraps bends to pick up an empty pack of Lucky Strikes. "Well, I got to clean this place up. Why don't you and Rosie stop by the tavern one afternoon for lunch? We have the best pizza in town," he says, winking at me.

"Sure," Mama says, wiping the sweat off her chest with the clean sheet.

Inching closer to Mama, Scraps softens his voice to almost a whisper. "Where's your husband been?"

"He's around." Mama is steady at her task of folding. She keeps her eyes down. "He's been working really hard." Mama's tone is as strained as her smile when she looks up.

"You might want to remind him he has about thirty days left to pay off his debt." He sings this like a tune.

"Sure, I'll remind him." Mama stacks the sheet on top of the counter along with my denims and gym uniform.

"Well, I got to get busy with my chores," Scraps says, pinching the tip of my nose.

I don't want him to go, and I hope Mama has something else to say, but she turns away. I can see the sweat has also soaked the back of her blouse.

"See you soon," he says to Mama's back.

"See ya," she says without turning around. Then he disappears.

———

Mr. Waxman arrives on Friday, soon after the postman delivers the welfare check. Mama offers him a cup of coffee.

"Too hot for coffee," he says, wiping his forehead with a handkerchief. It's only nine o'clock in the morning, but the June sun is already beating through the windows, stifling the air in the apartment. Mr. Waxman's cheeks are rosy, as if he just came in from the cold. He loosens a red, white, and blue tie, wiggles out of a wrinkled damp jacket, and slings it over the arm of the sofa. The ivory shirt he's wearing looks as though only the front has been ironed.

"We were planning on buying a few fans before summer, but the heat just snuck up on us," Mama says, looking all worried.

"Hmm."

With a glass of water Mama fetched for him, Mr. Waxman roams the apartment. In the bedrooms he inspects each window, opening and closing the screens, testing the locks. In the bathroom he runs the tap and flushes the toilet. I am holding my breath the whole time because I can't tell whether he likes it or not, and I know his opinion will determine whether Teresa and Joseph can come home. He strolls into the kitchen, places the empty glass in the sink, and tucks his hands behind his back; an occasional grunt falls off his lips.

Mama smoothes the curtains we bought on sale at Kresgee's. The chipped and scratched Formica counters are polished and the floors scrubbed. Finally, Mr. Waxman returns to the sofa and opens his briefcase. Mama perches beside him, and I kneel on the floor under her heels.

"What do you think," she says, crossing her legs and folding her hands in her lap. Her skirt rises above the knee, and she pulls it down.

"You've done a good job with what you had to work with," he says, fumbling with papers that are as wrinkled as his clothes.

Mama looks embarrassed, like when she's counting out the food stamps at the store and people are staring at her.

"There are some other requirements before the children can return home," he says.

"What do you mean?" she says.

He stops fumbling and stares back at her. In a tone similar to the one my teacher uses when she is instructing the class on our daily assignment, he says, "Your husband must attend recovery meetings for gamblers."

"What is that?" Mama asks, wringing her hands in her lap.

"There is an organization for men with similar problems." He delves into his valise and pulls out a booklet. It is yellow with black blocked letters. He slides it on the coffee table. Mama plucks it up before I can read what it says.

"There are scheduled times and locations listed in the back. He must attend the meetings once a week."

"Okay." Flipping through the pamphlet, she adds, "I'll make sure he goes."

"I suggest you attend the meetings with him," Mr. Waxman says, zipping his leather bag closed. He stands and tightens his tie. He swings his jacket over his shoulder.

"Very well, then," he says, extending his hand to Mama. It is so hairy it looks like a toupee is flopping on it.

Looking relieved, Mama rises and accepts his hand. I can tell she's afraid to ask what we both need to know.

"Can Teresa and Joseph come home?" I blurt out.

Mr. Waxman moves closer to me, and I step back. I'm afraid of him and despise the power he has over my family.

"Yes. I'll arrange it for after the school year. There's no sense in dragging them out of school again. They'll finish up where they are." He walks toward the door, hesitates, and turns around.

"I'll forward you the dates the children will be returning home in the mail."

And then he is gone. Not until the sounds of his heels have faded does Mama let out a breath. She lifts me under my arms and swirls me around. The lines on her skin seem to have run off her face with the sweat.

"Come on; let's celebrate," she says, grabbing her denim purse off the chair.

"Where are we going?" I ask.

"Shopping."

Mama and I hike twelve blocks to Main Street to the community bank. It's air conditioned, and my sticky body craves the armless leather bench. Lying on it, I eye the jar of hard candies on the ledge of the teller's window. As the woman behind the window counts the cash, Mama scoops out a handful of candies and winks at me.

With a hefty purse Mama's posture broadens, making her look a foot or so taller. Hand in hand, we stroll to the five-and-ten. Like best friends, we browse the housewares aisle and pretend we could afford the items displayed to entice us.

"Which patterns do you like best, Rosie?" Mama points to a selection of plate sets, one colored with roses, the other a bushel overflowing with bright red apples. When she asks my opinion, I feel grown up and important.

"I like this one with the roses," I say, sniffing the plate of scattered petals.

"When we get our own house, we'll buy everything new." She carefully puts the plates back on the display.

"Are we going to buy a house?" I ask, skipping to keep up with her as she tears down the next aisle.

"One day," she says. Pausing at a sale rack in the children's department, Mama pulls a blue-and-white sailor dress off a hanger.

"Do you like it?" She's acting like we can afford to buy anything I desire.

"I hate dresses." I've grown two inches in a year, and I despise my scrawny legs, which are as crooked as bare branches. I dread exposing my knobby knees.

Tugging bunched short sets off the sale rack, she says, "It's summer. You'll smolder in long pants." The empty hangers dangle on the rod as if dancing, and I touch them to make them stop.

In the fitting room behind curtains, Mama instructs me, with a low but stern tone, to remove my jeans and put on the shorts in layers.

"Why do you want me to do that?" I'm suddenly frightened.

"Just do it," she says, folding the matching shirts into small squares and stuffing them inside her bra.

"Why do I have to?" I say, refusing to budge.

"Because I'm tired of you looking like a beggar." She unsnaps my long pants and yanks them down to my ankles.

I kick off the pants swimming at my ankles and somehow manage to wiggle four pairs of shorts on, one on top of the other. When I pull the dungarees over them, it is impossible to snap them, and Mama stretches my shirt down over my bulging waist.

Mama pinches my elbow. "Just act normal."

We saunter out of the dressing room and glide past a sales woman as if we are in no hurry at all. Sweat is dripping beneath the layers, and I wonder how no one notices the uneven slopes on my body.

Once safely outdoors, Mama ushers me quickly around the corner. She rummages through a receptacle and finds a plastic bag. In a parking lot bustling with women and children, I duck behind a silver Cougar to remove the stolen clothes. I'm trying to hurry as Mama says to, but the shorts get tangled at my feet. I trip and fall.

"Jesus Christ," Mama says, tugging the shorts away from my sneakers. She shoves the clothing into the bag and helps me up. The pair I'm left wearing is the color of a lime's skin. Sunflowers are stitched on the front and back. The shorts clash with the red-and-white striped shirt I'm wearing.

"Can I put my jeans back on?" I ask, trying to pull the shorts down past my wobbly knees.

"You look fine," Mama says, grabbing my hand and rushing me along.

"Mama, is God going to punish me for stealing?"

"No. God doesn't punish little girls. Just say a prayer."

CHAPTER TWELVE

Strolling to the Presbyterian church where the meetings Mr. Waxman said Daddy must attend are held, I feel proud as we pass other pedestrians, certain they are admiring our closeness. Mama and Daddy loop arms, and I lag behind, stepping on their shadows.

By the time we reach the square dull building, my bangs are soaked, plastered to my forehead, and my eyes sting from the salty drops of sweat dripping into them. There is a note pinned to the door. "Meeting in basement. Enter from the back."

I follow my parents around the building and down the cinderblock steps, leading to a windowless room crammed with men milling around alone and laughing in groups. It takes me a second to notice how similar they all look. Thick black mustaches crawl over their lips, caps shadow their eyes, and pockets conceal their hands. Rows of metal chairs in the center of the room are lined evenly toward a small platform like our school stage.

A man approaches us smiling. His teeth are as yellow as corn, and when he speaks, spit flies from his mouth. His body parts look like they don't belong together as if they have been temporarily borrowed. Short, pudgy arms dangle from broad shoulders, and his legs are long but skinny like Mama's. A thick bulge struggles to escape a tight leather belt.

"You don't look familiar. Is this your first meeting?" he says, extending a hand toward Daddy.

"Yes, my first time," my father says, with a chuckle, shaking the man's hand.

Mama stands a step behind Daddy, and I'm a step behind her, peering out at the stranger. He glances over Daddy's shoulders and points to a back door. He says, "Your family can wait in the room across the hall with the other families. They can't stay for the session. It's private."

I can see by the way Mama pinches her full lips together in a single line that she's annoyed. The room is filling with smoke, and the voices are becoming louder. Daddy whispers something, but I can't hear it. I grip Mama's hand as the men step aside to let us pass. We exit through the back door and step into a dimly lit hallway. There are noises coming from another door, which we open without knocking.

The space is smaller, but there are high windows letting in the last of the day's light. Young women are chatting, and several toddlers are tromping around in T-shirts and diapers. Two grandmotherly ladies sit side by side, one crocheting a handbag, the other playing solitaire on her thighs as thick as oak planks.

Only one boy appears to be close to my age. He's moping in a corner as if he's being punished. I mosey over to strike up conversation, but as I get closer, I notice his pants are soiled. The stench propels me away from him and straight to Mama, where she has settled on a chair in the corner, away from the chatting women. Clipping a cigarette between her fingers, she rummages through her purse for matches. A young pregnant lady leaning against a wall offers Mama her lit cigarette. She accepts it and nods thank you.

Squeezing between Mama's bare knees, I say, "I have to go to the bathroom."

I don't really, but I can't get the boy's smell out of my nose. It's worse than Joseph's sopping pajamas when he wets the bed.

Mama nudges me away. "You just went before we left the house."

I shift legs and prance around in a circle several times to prove I really have to go, but all I want is to get rid of the boy's stink, which I swear must be stuck in my nose hairs.

"I can go by myself. It's one door over. I saw it when we came in." I back away from her slowly, until she gives me permission.

"Go ahead." She crosses her legs and swings one like she does when she's waiting for Daddy to come home at night.

The corridor is creepy, but I'm relieved to escape on my own. In the bathroom I switch on the light and lock the door. It consists of one toilet and a large crucifix hanging over a sink instead of a mirror. I fill my cupped palm with cold water and inhale through my nose. It stings, and I cough and sneeze the boy's germs straight out into the sink. I dry my face on a sandy paper towel and saunter out.

Gliding past the room where we left my father, I hear voices roaring, but I'm unable to put words together. Peeking through the cracked door, I can see the men settling into their seats, their backs toward me. Slithering in, I squat down behind a long table draped with a white cloth set up with cookies, a coffee urn, and Styrofoam cups and plates. I cannot see anyone, and I hope they can't see me.

The sea of men applauds, and my heart pounds with the palms of their hands. The group becomes quiet, and I recognize the voice of the man who approached us when we arrived.

"Please, welcome several new members who have come here tonight to acknowledge the disease."

More applause. The familiar voice continues: "Newcomers, please feel free to share your misgivings. We don't judge anyone here."

All the men rise, clapping and whistling. The entire room rumbles, and I'm suddenly amazed at the number of people who suffer from the same illness as Daddy. I panic, thinking the disease could spread to me, too—like the poison oak that ravaged my skin one summer. I hold my breath to block their germs from entering my body, but once the meeting begins, the obsession of their contagion peels away, and I am swept into the stories of their lives.

Their faces are not visible to me, but I can feel the weight of their guilt in my head and up and down my spine, as though a large foot were pressing down on the nape of my neck. A metal chair screeches, and heels thud. A voice shouts out, "My name is Tom, and I'm a gambling addict."

The crowd applauds. The man's words rumble out like thunder. "I had my seven-year-old kid climb into his grandfather's home—to steal the old man's Purple Heart that he treasured from the war. I had a hot tip, and I promised myself I'd get the thing back. But I lost every cent." The man begins to sob and gag, just like Joseph did when he was caught stealing nickels from Mama's purse. Even though I understand the man did something wrong, I feel sorry for him and wish he'd stop crying like a baby. Finally, he calms down and continues. "The worst part of it." His words are strained now, and I can hear him take a deep breath before exhaling the last of his confession. "When my kid told his grandfather he had taken the Purple Heart for me, I beat him until he was black and blue."

I cringed, thinking of the little boy all bruised, and now I hated the man for doing such a thing.

"Do you want to change your life?" several men shout.

"Yes. That's why I'm here."

"Then start by quitting gambling right now," everyone in the room shouts several times. When they finally stop, a different man speaks. His words are strong and steady.

"My name is Gerald, and I'm a gambling addict. It's been five weeks since I've made a bet. I keep busy tending my garden and go to bed early. That seems to help." Rubber soles squeak on the asbestos floor as the man plops back into his chair.

The familiar man's voice shouts from a distance: "Would a new member like to get the devil off his chest?"

A few chairs screech, and then a new voice speaks—younger than the others, softer, too. But his words are clear. "My name is Theodore, and I'm a gambling addict. My parents tossed me out of the house on my ass when they found out I bribed my five-year-old sister to knock on strangers' doors to sing and dance for money, promising to buy her Tootsie Rolls. Instead, I took her to an all-night poker game."

There's grumbling in the audience, and someone hollers out, "Quit gambling now, and they'll forgive you."

Another chair screeches. Heels thump then stop in the front of the room.

"My name is not important," the voice says, "but I am a gambling addict. I don't get why I do it. It's like poison flows through my veins instead of blood. The only time I feel really alive is those few seconds before the dice rolls or the horses finish at the line. It's like I have hope of something good happening. And when I've lost every cent, I regret it but know if I had another buck or two, I'd bet it all over again."

My knees ache on the slab; trying not to make a sound, I shift onto my feet. Crouching, I stretch my eyes for a peek at my father. But I can't see him as he continues to speak.

"The truth is, when I'm watching those ponies, I ain't thinking about nothing else. Not my wife, my kids. Nothing. All I care about is scoring big."

I cover my ears and start counting in my head, but it doesn't drown out the rest of what he's saying.

"Sure, I lie to myself that I need to make the score so I can feed my family and put a roof over their heads, but I do it for me. To keep *me* up."

A part of me wants to run out of there as far away from him and his diseased friends as possible, but then I know in my heart I want to know my father better. I stay glued in place.

"How do you feel when you're not gambling?" someone yells out.

"Bored. Resentful. Guilty."

"What is it you resent?" another voice yells out.

My father doesn't pause to think about his answers. It's as if he's rehearsed them.

"That I have a wife and kids depending on me. I wish I had the guts to walk out on them. But I can't do it."

Salted drops puddle in the corners of my mouth, and I can't tell whether they're sweat or tears. I cup my palms over my ears, but it's not enough to stop the words from seeping in like hot oil burning my eardrums.

"That's because you really do care about them. Make amends to your family and quit gambling. Eventually forgiveness will follow," the man leading the meeting shouts.

"I can't make amends to my dead mother," Daddy says. His tone is angry, unrecognizable to me.

"She was gone two days before I found her. I knew she was sick and that I should leave the poker game to check on her. But I didn't. I stayed in the game—lost every cent and the chance to say goodbye to my own mother. How am I supposed to say I'm sorry to her? You tell me."

"Pray," the sea of men sings out like a church choir.

Without another word, Daddy steps away and takes his place in the audience.

Just as another man stands to admit his crimes, I slip out of the room. My bones feel as stiff as my heart, and it hurts when I stand. I return to the waiting area to find Mama chatting with a woman about her age who is bouncing a toddler on her knee. Mama seems relieved to see me.

"What took you so long?" she asks, gritting her teeth.

"I want to go home—I don't feel good," I say.

"What's wrong?" she asks, standing to feel my forehead. "You don't have a fever."

"My stomach hurts," I say, tucking my head in the pit of her arm.

"I guess we don't have to wait," she says.

Looping my fingers through hers, I feel safe and warm again.

At home she helps me undress and tucks me into bed.

"You'll feel better tomorrow," she says, switching off the light.

"Can I sleep with you tonight?" I say, trying to focus on her expression under the glimmer of light coming from the hallway.

She places her hands on her hips. Arching her brows, she says, "You're getting too old to sleep with your mama."

"Just for a little while."

"Okay. Just until you fall asleep."

In my parents' room Mama changes into a nightgown. She fluffs a pillow, pulls the chain on the lamp, and lies down beside me. I snuggle into her side and tuck my head under her chin. Her breath is cool on my head. In the dark, between her breaths, I whisper, "Mama, does Daddy like us?"

I feel her stiffen under the light sheet covering us. "Don't be silly; he loves us."

"Does he love Joseph and Teresa, too?"

Rolling away from me, she curls her knees up to her chin and wraps her arms around her legs. "Of course he loves them, too."

"Mama, how did Daddy and all those men get the gambling disease?"

"They were born with it. Like a birthmark."

"Can I catch it from Daddy?"

"No, you can't catch it. Now quiet—I'm tired."

Relieved, I fall asleep to the rhythm of Mama's snores.

The aroma of bacon sizzling arouses me from sleep. I wake in my own bed without a memory of Mama removing me from hers. At the stove Daddy flips French toast on a griddle. Bacon sizzles in a second pan. He sprinkles the golden slices of bread with sugar, stacks them on a platter, and sets it on the table.

"Come on, eat up." Bits of crisped pork are snared in the spaces between his teeth.

My hunger is stronger than my anger. I decide to put aside the mean things he said about us last night at the meeting. I sit at the table, anxious to bite into the greasy bacon.

Mama joins us. She is dressed in a yellow-and-white polka-dotted summer dress that accentuates her dark eyes and long neck. Her hair is taut in a twist, raising her cheekbones. An unlit Pall Mall dangles between her pursed lips. When she bends to light it over the gas jet, her dress strap rolls off her shoulder.

"What's all this?" Smoke flows out of her nostrils like the steam off a hot bath.

"French toast and bacon," I say with my mouth full.

Mama pours two cups of coffee, offering one to Daddy. She leans against the sink, smiling at him and rubbing her bare foot up and down his leg. They remain on their feet, leaning over the table, picking at the food with their fingers.

Daddy rinses his hands in the sink and wipes his mouth with a dish towel. He crushes an empty pack of cigarettes and says, "Do you want to come with Daddy to get cigarettes and a paper?"

"No." Now that my belly is full, my anger reemerges.

"Suit yourself," he says, buttoning his shirt and then slicking back his hair with his fingers.

Mama nibbles on the crusts left on my plate. "Go ahead with your father," she says.

"I don't want to," I say, stuffing another forkful of bread into my already full mouth.

"Slow down," Mama says, "before you choke to death."

Daddy kisses my mother's cheek and leans down to kiss mine, but I turn away.

"I'll be right back."

"Make sure of it," Mama says, dousing her cigarette under the tap water.

In my room I lie on the bed, staring at the ceiling. The images of Daddy and all the men keep flashing through my head. To stop from thinking about it, I conjure up Joseph and Teresa.

"Hey, let's make a tent," I say.

"How?" Teresa asks.

"It's easy," Joseph says, pulling the sheets from the bed.

Draping the sheet over the top bunk, the edges hang down, and we tuck them between the posts. I slither underneath the tent on my belly like a snake in the dirt.

"Come on in," I say.

Teresa and Joseph crawl behind me, and we sit cross-legged in a circle, pinky fingers linked, anxious for the storytelling to begin.

"Make it real scary," Joseph says.

"No, just a little," Teresa begs.

And so I begin. "Once upon a time there were a brother and sister lost in the woods for three days and three nights. For warmth, they huddled between two huge rocks, and to keep from starving they dug the dirt for worms and ate them for breakfast, lunch, and supper. On the third night, they lay face to face. The sky was black like mud, and they couldn't even see the whites of each other's eyes. The boy heard a sound like thunder under his feet. Looking up, he spotted the silhouette of a bear. It was bigger than all the trees in the forest. They screamed and begged the bear not to hurt them. And then the strangest thing happened. The bear bent forward and opened his furry paw. Suddenly, the little boy and girl were no longer scared. They walked onto his paw, and he carried them all the way home."

"I want to tell a story," Joseph says.

"I'm hungry; let's eat first," I say, lifting the sheet to slide out.

Mama is dozing on the sofa. I tap her head.

"We're hungry."

Mama's lashes flutter, then her lids pop open. Sitting up, she scans the room.

"Who are you talking to?"

"Teresa and Joseph."

"Rosie, stop that nonsense now." She shuffles into the kitchen.

"I thought your father would be back by now," she adds, as she butters the last of the two slices of bread in the cupboard.

"Eat," she says, slamming the sandwich onto the table without a plate. She glances at the radio clock. Her brows twitch back and forth as if they're dancing. She ignites the pilot beneath the morning coffee.

"He better be back soon if he knows what's good for him."

"Do you want half of my sandwich?" I ask, tearing it in two with my fingers.

"You eat it." She reaches for a cigarette and an old issue of *Homes & Gardens* magazine she reads daily like a newspaper.

After lunch I return to the tent. Teresa toasts marshmallows over the imaginary fire we built with pencils and scraps of paper. Joseph is out fishing for trout to roast on the open fire. But before he returns the fire is petering out, and I decide to scout for more kindling.

On the dish rack the gleam of a knife catches my eye. I carefully remove it and kneel on the floor to chop the invisible tree trunk I found in the forest.

Axing the log, I slice through my index finger. Blood gushes, and I scream. I can't look at it; I just cradle it to my chest.

Mama bolts in, shouting before I can even answer: "What did you do?" Blood flows out of the cut onto my pajamas.

"It burns—it burns."

My mother remains calm. She whips a dish towel out of the drawer and ties it around my hand. Pressing down on the gash firmly, sweat beads on her nose and forehead. Her hands tremble. I squeeze my eyes shut when she warns she's going to take a peek.

"You need stitches," she says, rewrapping the finger.

"I don't want stitches." The throbbing in my hand and the buzzing in my head harmonize. She lifts me to my feet. The weight of my flesh seems to have tripled, like when I saw the butcher chop a chicken's head off, and I fell backward into a glass refrigerator.

"Come on; I have to get you to the hospital," she says, draping a sweater over my bloody pajamas.

"I don't want to go to the hospital," I say, pulling away.

"You need stitches," she says, dragging me by the arm.

Planting my feet onto the floor, I cry, "I want my dolly."

Mama lets go, stomps into my room, and returns dangling the Thumbelina Daddy had surprised me with on my ninth birthday. I fold the doll in the crook of my arm, under the sweater.

Outside, it's beginning to rain. Hovering close to the buildings, we dodge the fine drizzles that quickly turn to pellets. At the bottom of the hill we turn left onto Jefferson Street and walk the path leading to the church where the gamblers' meetings are held. Mama taps twice. A minister slithers out. He is dressed in black trousers and a black buttoned-down shirt. His cheeks are as fiery as the tight curls on his head.

"Can I help you?"

"I need to get my husband out of the meeting."

"The meeting ended hours ago," the minister says. He glances down at the towel blotched with red and winces.

"That bastard," Mama says.

"Can I help…?" The minister's voice trails off as we hurry away.

Mama drags me back up the hill to Henry's Fish Market. The entrance to the cellar is in the back of the building. I gag from the stench. Mama knocks, shouting, "It's Antonette Scarpiella. Is my husband in there?"

"No," a raspy voice hollers back.

"Mama, my hand doesn't hurt anymore. Let's go home; it'll be all right," I say.

And it's true. I'm not even making it up because I'm scared to death of hospitals. My hand is numb.

"You might need a tetanus shot," she says. "We're going—and that's it."

From Henry's we skitter between the raindrops to the One Hour Martinizing. All I want to do is to lie down and sleep, but Mama tugs at me to keep on walking. The stairwell of the dry cleaners wreaks of urine, more potent than the stench of dead fish scales at Henry's Fish Market. Mama doesn't knock this time; she barges in, shocking the men huddled on their knees, their jaws drooping.

"Seven out," shouts a man aiming a yard stick at the dirt floor.

The ceilings are low and cobwebbed. Shivering, I scan the cellar and spot Daddy, crouching beside the coal furnace; embers snap and crackle in the pit, illuminating his face. Although he had a clean-shaven face that morning, his jaw is dark and stubbly. Strands of his carefully gelled hair lie flat like bangs on his forehead. Clutching loose bills in his fists, he leaps to his feet when he realizes the intruders are Mama and me.

"What the fuck are you doing here?" He rages toward us, hunching over so as not to bang his head on the low beams. His green eyes are black, as if they've been turned inside out.

Mama lifts my limp hand to show him the towel streaked with blood.

"Ouch," I say, pulling away.

"She cut herself deep; she needs stitches." Mama's tongue is flapping like a fish out of water.

Daddy circles us, raising his hands in the air. "So take her to the hospital."

"We can't walk that far. She's in a lot of pain."

Daddy's shadow looms over us. He doesn't even inspect my injury, which stings more than the cut itself. "I can't leave right now. It's my turn to roll the dice."

"Ask one of these degenerates to take us." She swings her hands in the direction of the disinterested men.

"C'mon, Antonette. She's all right. Aren't you, Rose Petal?" he says, winking at me.

"Yes, it feels better already," I say, staring up at my parents, trying to hold back the tears.

"See—she's okay," he says. His eyeballs bulge as if he's hanging from a tight rope.

"You're a rotten son of a bitch." Mama screeches like the stray cats that sleep in the alley below my bedroom window.

"You're a fucking jinx, Antonette," he shouts. "Get the fuck out of here."

"Don't bother coming home." She spits in his face.

Trudging through the alleyway and back onto the avenue, Mama removes her jacket and drapes it over my already sopping head. The air smells fresh, as if cleansed by the shower.

"It's only a few blocks," Mama says. "You can do it; right, baby?"

"Yes, Mama."

The steady flow of automobiles swishing through puddles splatters our shoes and ankles. Waiting for the light to change at the crosswalk, a car pulls close to the curb. Mama tightens her grip on my shoulder. A horn honks, but she ignores it. Then I hear a familiar voice.

"Antonette, what are you two doing out in the rain?"

Mama recognizes the voice too. It's Scraps'.

She lets out the breath she was holding and lifts my hand. "She cut her finger; I'm taking her to the hospital. I'm pretty sure she needs stitches."

Scraps leans over to unlatch the passenger door.

"Get in; I'll drive you," he says.

Mama doesn't resist his offer. I slide in the middle of the black Cadillac; it's as long and wide as a hearse. My doll is crunched between my legs.

"Does it hurt bad, Rosie?" Scraps asks.

"Not really."

"We'll be there in a minute." He offers me a stick of gum over his shoulder. "Chew on that, Rosie; it'll take your mind off your hand for a while."

I unwrap the gum with one hand and place it in my mouth. It's Juicy Fruit, and it tastes delicious.

Scraps slows at a stop sign and then accelerates, turning left into the hospital's emergency entrance, swerving into a vacant spot reserved for medical personnel. He scoops me up and carries me in. He smells of rain, Ivory soap, and cologne. Tucking my head into the crook of his neck feels like a natural thing to do.

At the reception desk, Mama struggles to answer the questions the nurse darts at her.

"We're on welfare…I left in a hurry…. No, I don't have my card; I say we left in a hurry."

"Have a seat; we'll be with you in a minute." The nurse shoos Mama away as if she were an annoying fly.

"How long will it take? The rag is soaked with blood," Mama says, waving my throbbing hand in front of the woman's sagging face.

Scraps sets me on my feet, delves into his trousers' pocket, and pulls out a wad of money strangled by an elastic band.

"Get a doctor to see her now." He slams the wad on the counter.

Blushing in response to the stranger bullying her, the nurse rises from her station and sashays down the corridor. The white dress drooping on her petite frame glows under the fluorescent lights; thick bluish veins are transparent through her pantyhose.

Minutes later she veers round the corner pushing a wheelchair. She assists me into it and rolls me into a cubicle draped with a gauzy curtain. Mama is beside me the whole time. There's a cot behind the curtain, and Mama helps me onto it. I lie on my back, mesmerized by the effort of two flies to escape the confines of the florescent light.

"Are you scared?" Mama asks, pushing my bangs off my forehead.

A doctor enters the cubical, crowding the small space. He's dressed in the traditional white knee-length jacket. His black eyes slant downward, and he speaks with an unusual accent. I'm guessing he's Chinese.

"I am Dr. Tao; what is your name?"

"Rosie."

"What happened here?" he asks, unraveling the dish towel.

"Do you have to give me a needle?"

Wincing, he says, "Yes, but Dr. Tao's needles do not hurt."

"I don't want a needle." I turn away from him.

"You need stitches. They'll hurt a lot less if you let me numb your hand first."

"Please, don't make it hurt," I say, squeezing my eyes shut.

"How old are you?" he asks. As he cleanses the gash, the cold cotton swab sends a shooting pain up my arm.

"Nine.'

He jabs the needle between my thumb and forefinger.

"Ouch."

"You won't feel a thing in a few minutes."

I feel tiny pricks as if mosquitoes are flitting about under my skin; then everything is numb; the pain is gone.

"Rosie, how did this happen?" he asks, rolling his black slanted eyes toward Mama.

"My brother and sister and me were pretending to be on a camping trip."

"Oh, I see," he says, "Where are they now?"

"At home."

"Alone?" the doctor asks.

Mama rolls her eyes. "She has an active imagination," she says. "She's an only child."

Snipping the last stitch, the doctor says, "There, you'll be as good as new. But you'll need another shot to prevent infection."

At this point all I want is to go home. Cringing at the sight of the second needle, I cover my eyes with my free hand. "Just hurry," I say.

"It'll only hurt for a second," he says, rubbing my right forearm with a cotton ball again. And just as he promised, he withdraws the needle before I can say ouch. He wraps gauze and white tape around the injury. He scribbles a prescription for penicillin on a notebook and hands it to Mama.

"She'll be all right, then?" she asks, tucking the prescription in her purse.

"She's already great." He pulls three cherry lollipops from his jacket pocket.

"One for you and for your brother and sister, too."

"Thank you." Mama holds me under the arm as I slide off the cot.

"I'll see you back here in a week to remove those stitches."

"Thank you. Bye." I wave the lollipops.

The waiting area is more congested than it was when we arrived. We're heading toward the electric doors when I see Scraps' white head peering over a newspaper.

"Mama, Scraps waited for us." I point to the man I think not only resembles God but also must be God.

Scraps stands, folds the paper under his arm, and tops his head with a black cap.

"You didn't have to wait," Mama says. "We can walk home; she's fine."

"Nonsense. I'll see you home safely."

"Hey, look what I got," I say flailing the lollipop. "Plus I got two needles and three stitches, and I didn't even cry," I add.

"Wow," Scraps says, pinching my cheek. His fingers are slick and warm.

Lying down in the backseat, I can only see the tops of Mama's and Scraps' heads as they chat. The radio is blasting the news, but I hear Mama say, "You can drop us at the pharmacy, so I can fill her prescription."

"I'll wait for you," he says, pulling to the curb.

"It might take awhile. We're only a block away; we'll be fine," Mama says, opening the door.

"Nonsense. I'll wait."

Mama helps me out of the backseat.

"It's not even dark out yet. We'll be fine." Mama's voice is firm. She slams the door shut.

Scraps tips his hat. "Just one more thing."

Mama bends to peer through the opened window.

"Tell your husband I expect to square things away with him in a few weeks," he says in a tone that sounds like he's smiling. But he's not.

"Sure, thanks again," Mama says.

"Rosie, you take care of that hand," Scraps says, winking at me.

We wave goodbye as he speeds away.

My parents' screaming and cursing, accusing each other of their misery, wakes me early the following morning. Lying still, I roll a pillow around my ears to muffle their rage. My finger throbs, and my head aches. Not until they've stopped do I shuffle into the kitchen. They are both sitting at the table, sharing a cigarette. I ask Mama for a glass of water and an aspirin. Without looking at me, she gets up, fills a glass from the tap, and takes an aspirin from the bottle. Handing it to me, she says to Daddy, "I told you a hundred times. The man says he wants to square things away. Did you think he was going to forget you owe him three thousand dollars?"

"We can ask him for more time," Daddy says. "I need more time."

"I'm not asking him for nothing." Mama recaps the bottle and walks out, leaving Daddy with his head in his hands. I follow her.

CHAPTER THIRTEEN

It's the Fourth of July. My parents and I are getting ready to pick Joseph up from the Welles' to take him home. I can't sit still for another second. Hopping off the toilet lid, I nag Mama to quit fussing with her hair. She twists and sprays it until it could withstand a tornado.

"Let's go Antonette," Daddy hollers, ducking his head in the door. His face is smooth, and his blondish hair looks much darker with all the gel he's used.

"We'll go when I'm ready to go." She bangs the can of Aqua Net on the vanity.

"Rosie, go wait outside. It's hot in here, and you're crowding me." She fans her face with her hand.

Sporting white shorts, a midriff, and sandals Mama has polished white, I do what I'm told. It is only morning, but the sun is already scorching. It's too hot to pass time jumping rope or trying to balance the hula on my hips, so I duck inside the confectionery store to stay cool. The landlord doesn't seem to mind my milling around; he even offers me a handful of Tootsie Rolls. I gobble two and stick one in my shorts' pocket for Joseph.

Stepping out of the store, I recognize a black Cadillac idling in front. The windows are rolled down.

"Hey, Rosie, I was hoping to see you," Scraps says.

I rush toward the car. "Hi."

"You forgot your doll in the backseat," he says, dangling my Thumbelina by the arm.

Stretching my hand through the window, I say, "I've been looking all over for her."

"How did you find me?" I add, remembering that he dropped us off at the pharmacy not at our home.

"How's that hand?" he ignores my question with his own.

"It's all better. It didn't even hurt when I got the stitches out," I say, cuddling the doll to my chest.

"Great. How're your parents?"

"They're good. Do you want me to get my Mama for you?"

"No. Just let her know I stopped by. Okay, you take care now." He shifts gears. The car jumps forward a bit.

Stepping back onto the curb, I say, "Thank you."

"Take care of yourself," he says, gliding away.

Minutes later my parents finally emerge. Mama is slim in a light pink sleeveless cotton dress Adele had grown bored with. Daddy gripes about sweating in the black trousers Mama pressed for him.

"Look, I found my doll," I say, holding her up so Mama can see.

"Where'd you find it?" she asks as she licks her finger and wipes the chocolate off the corners of my mouth where I can still taste Tootsie Roll.

"Scraps dropped it off. I forgot it in his car the night we went to the hospital."

Mama's steel smirk warns me I've done something wrong.

"When? How does he know where we live?" Daddy shouts at me, and now I'm sure I've done something I wasn't supposed to. But I don't know what.

Mama steps in front of Daddy. "What did he say?" They are both hovering over me, and I start to cry.

"What did I do?"

"Nothing. Stop crying and tell us what Scraps said," my father says.

I sniffle and wipe my nose with the back of my hand. Darting my puffed eyes from Mama's to Daddy's, I can't tell whether they're angry or frightened.

"He just came by to bring me my doll," I say, scraping stones with the tip of my sandal.

"Just forget it," Daddy mumbles as he walks away. "Let's get going."

The three of us head east to gather Joseph, his bike, racecars, and mountains of clothes he had acquired during his stay with the Welleses. Despite the incident with Scraps and humidity that could stop a freight train, the day holds the promise that something grand is happening.

At the bus stop, I twirl around in an effort to rally a breeze, envying a group of shirtless teenage boys thrusting in ice-cold water thundering out of the fire hydrant. It's tempting, but I choose not to ruin my outfit; I'm deter-mined to remain tidy for Joseph.

The bus offers little relief from the hot, stagnant air swishing through the opened windows. When the driver stops to scoop up young women, cod-dling infants, and white-haired ladies who take forever to maneuver grocery carts up the steps, it's unbearable.

My lungs are sore from the endless chain-smoking of my mother, and my drenched underwear is wedged between my buttocks. Just as I think we're never going to get there, Daddy tugs the cord. We exit at the next stop.

"It's that one." Mama points to the only house framed with shutters.

Skipping ahead, I dash up the steep steps. At the landing I press my thumb on the bell; my heart chimes as loudly as it does. Heels click on tile; there's a pause before the door swings open. Doris is erect, dressed in a pleated navy skirt and yellow buttoned blouse, as taut as her teased hair. The blood orange lipstick smeared on her lips exaggerates a frozen smile.

"We're here for our son," Daddy blurts before allowing Doris to welcome us in.

"Yes, of course. He's waiting for you. Please, come in."

Harold stands at the sink plopping ice cubes into tall glasses. He and Daddy have never met. Harold extends a hand my father ignores.

"Where's Joey? We got to get going."

"I'll fetch him," Doris says, fleeing the room.

"This heat is oppressive. Just mixed up some lemonade. Want some?" Harold asks, filling four glasses.

My parents fidget in the presence of the stranger who's been raising their son. The house is air conditioned, but I'm still parched from the trip, and I hope Mama accepts his generous offer.

"No thanks," she says.

With that, Joseph emerges, pausing in the doorway; his arms idle at his sides.

"Joey." Daddy takes a giant leap forward.

"My boy," Mama coos as if Joseph is a toddler.

Leaning into Mama, I will my rigid brother to embrace us.

Joseph's gaze is blank. His black lashes coil upward like Mama's when she uses the eyelash curler. His legs are long and lanky like Teresa's. His freckles have darkened with summer, and his ears protrude out from the short hair-cut.

"Joseph, say hello to your parents and sister," Doris says, nudging him toward us.

"Hello." In a corpse-like stance, Joseph resembles a stuffed soldier, dressed in creased army shorts and a green short-sleeved polo shirt.

I'm uncomfortable in the sandals, which last year belonged to Teresa. They swim on my feet, and the shorts are so tight I'm unable to snap the clasp; I hope Joseph doesn't notice.

Daddy cups Joseph's cheeks and pecks the top of his head. It's been nine months since our separation, yet I feel the distance of years between us. I think we all do.

"Are you ready to go?" Daddy asks. His tone is soft like a breeze.

"Can we talk to you about something?" Harold interrupts.

"About what?" Daddy looks up at the strange man and places his hand on my brother's shoulder.

"Joseph, why don't you and your sister play in the yard so the grownups can talk," Doris says, pointing to a side door.

"Yes, Mother," he says.

Suddenly, I have an urge to spit in Doris's ugly lined face. I'd like to kick her in the shins and tell her she has no right to talk to my brother as if he were her son. I can't see Mama's expression, but her body seems to exude heat as if she is suddenly racked with fever. I inch away for relief.

"Go on." Daddy nods that it's okay.

The fenced-in yard is crammed with a swing set, charcoal grill, and a round table with chairs shaded by an umbrella. A basketball hoop is attached to the house. Without a word I settle on a swing while Joseph bounces a ball on the patch of macadam. The swing set is cemented into the ground facing the kitchen window above us. A faint breeze flaps at the plaid curtains. It looks as though they're inhaling and exhaling.

I think of something interesting to say, but what stumbles off my tongue is to the point.

"Why are you acting like you don't know me?" My voice quivers.

"Do you want to play a game?" Joseph asks, averting my eyes and question.

"I don't know how to play," I say.

"I can teach you." A flicker of recollection illuminates his face.

"Okay," I say, hopping off the swing, trying to prove I'm a good sport.

Joseph bounces the ball a few times and then tosses it in the air. As though the hoop were a magnet, the ball swooshes through the net.

"Now you try," he says.

I take the ball and bounce it like Joseph had. After several unsuccessful attempts, my arms tire, and I quit. Sweating, I drop onto the grass and pluck the dry blades, one at a time.

"How come you called Doris 'mother'?" I blurt out.

"'Cause she wants me to, I guess," he says, shrugging his shoulders.

"She's *not* your mother. You hurt Mama's feelings."

"So, I don't care; I like Doris better." He covers his own mouth as if a bad word slipped off his tongue.

"Joseph, don't say that."

He slumps on the grass beside me. We're quiet, and I can hear the adults' voices rising. Then there's a slam and the sound of glass shattering onto the linoleum. Crawling on my hands and knees to the window, I imagine Doris's face splattered with lemonade.

"Joey, Rosie, let's go." Daddy pokes his head out the window, sweat trickling over his bulging veins.

"Joseph, come on," I say, getting to my feet.

Trotting up the back steps, I hear Harold say, "You can't provide for him...." He pauses when we enter. Doris is sponging up broken glass and spilled lemonade.

"It's none of your goddamned business what I'm able to do for my kids," Daddy says. "They're *my* kids and...."

"Rosie, wait for us on the front stoop. Joseph, you stay here a minute," Mama interrupts.

"But I don't want to," I say, fear constricting my breathing.

Daddy gapes at Mama as if she has stripped her clothing, exposing her naked body.

"We're going now," he says.

"In a minute," Mama says. Narrowing her eyes at me, she points to the hallway leading to the front door.

From the porch I listen to their voices rising, falling, rising, falling. A few minutes later, the door swings open. My parents stagger out.

"Where's Joseph?" I ask. My heart is pattering.

Ignoring me, Mama assists Daddy down the steps as if he's had an accident and is incapable of such an ordinary task.

"Mama, where's Joseph?" I shout after them.

From over her shoulder she says, "He wants to stay until the end of the summer."

"No, he can't stay; he has to come with us." I stomp my feet. Tears roll down my face.

"Come on; we're going home," Mama shouts from below. The sun is glaring on her face and she looks headless.

Spinning around, I heel the door and jam my thumb on the bell. But no one answers.

"Rosie, stop it," Mama yells. "The summer will be over before you know it."

I don't relent. I kick and scream for Joseph. Mama dashes up the stairs, two at a time, I've never seen her move so quickly. She twists my hair and drags me down the steps.

"I don't want to go without Joseph." I grip the railing.

"Rosie, if you don't quit it, we'll leave you here, too," Mama warns. "Joseph wants to stay for now," she adds.

On the journey back to our apartment I sit rows behind my parents, trying to avoid breathing the same air as they do. Mama caresses Daddy's back and rests her head on his shoulder. He gazes out the window, muttering, "Let's go back. Let's go back."

———

In the weeks that follow it isn't difficult to avoid my parents: Mama sleeps most of the time, and Daddy stays out. In the night I drench my pillow with sobs. When I wake in the morning, the face in the mirror is unrecognizable to me. My round eyes resemble half moons, and my lips puff out like a sponge.

During the day I wander alone to the park and lie on my back beneath the unrelenting sun, naming each of the clouds. The two puffs that float side by side I call Adam and Eve. A web-like cloud with a swirl of blue is how I visualize the Mother Mary and Baby Jesus. I imagine God to be all the blue in between.

Wandering into far-away neighborhoods, I begin to recognize the people who reside there as much as I do my own neighbors. An old man crouches on the corner with a cup, his wrinkled trousers supported by a telephone cord. He spits tobacco on the ground and coughs a lot. Identical twins, men about the same age as Daddy, strut at an even pace. They're dressed in Budweiser T-shirts and bell-bottomed Levis.

Sometimes I stay out past dark, envying the gleeful boys and girls who live on our block above other storefronts and in the four- and six-family dwellings, kicking balls and playing tag in the streets. The scene reminds me of past summers when Mama allowed us to sit on the front stoop of the house we were evicted from, Teresa and I in baby-doll pajamas and Joseph in cutoff jeans and a Superman cape.

The memories fill my nostrils with yeast that used to exude from the chimney of Ciccone's Bakery, where Joseph, Teresa, a group of our friends, and I huddled at the rear entrance of the building, gaping at the bakers, kneading dough, their trousers and shirts as white as the flour that doused their black mustaches. The men would toss us hot sesame seed rolls, and we'd scurry back to our respective porches, gobbling the goods. Older teenagers would entertain us, harmonizing a capella. There were many occasions when Daddy joined them, and we'd clap our hands to their music until our palms were raw and itchy.

One afternoon, I'm trapped indoors, listening to the rain spatter the glass panes. It sounds as though the birds are pecking to come inside. Images of Joseph bouncing the ball at the Welles' place, acting as if I were a stranger to him, tug at my heart. Without him, the world appears slanted, as if my head has been glued to an axle.

I decide to telephone him. I swipe a fistful of change from Mama's purse. Latching the door very gently, my heart thuds with my feet down the steps to the confectionery store.

In the public telephone booth, which is hot as a coal furnace, sweat trickles down my back and buds on my scalp. The coins slip from my slimy fingers. The space is littered with chewed gum, cigarette butts, and candy wrappers. Retrieving my coins, I wipe them on my shorts and deposit them.

The firehouse whistles, announcing it is noon. I can almost see Joseph, munching grilled hamburgers and gulping ice-cold lemonade out on the Welles' patio. Dialing the number I had memorized, hoping Joseph answers so I'm spared Doris's gooey hello, I take a deep breath. Three rings and a series of beeps precede a recording announcing that the number I dialed is no longer in service. I hang up, retrieve the coins, and redial, slowly and carefully. But again, after the third ring, a series of beeps and a recording confirm the number's been disconnected.

Tripping out of the phone booth, I bump into the landlord.

"Slow down," he says, adjusting his bifocals.

I dash out into the rain. I feel as though I've been split in two and my legs are chasing my arms. I stomp up the stairs and run into Mama's room. Shaking her shoulder, I'm out of breath, crying, "Mama, Mama, wake up."

"Leave me alone," she mumbles.

Kneeling on the bed, I tug her arm.

"I tried to call Joseph, but the number's disconnected."

"What are you talking about?" she says, popping her eyes open. Week-old mascara clumps her lashes.

"I called Joseph from the pay phone, and a recording said the number's disconnected."

"Are you sure you dialed right?" She's off the bed now.

"I tried two times." I gulp air, relieved I have finally got her attention.

"Son-of-a-bitch." She flings off her nightgown and dresses hastily in a denim skirt, a paisley halter top, and flip-flops.

The rain is still pounding as Mama ducks into the confectionary store to borrow an umbrella from the landlord. Under its wings I cling to her as we jaywalk across the busy avenue. The black macadam steams under our feet as the rain pounces down on it.

We scurry past the park, the Laundromat, and the fish market. At the corner, Mama hails a bus. Huffing, she snaps the umbrella closed, and we hop on. It's crowded, so we stand the entire ride. By the time we reach the stop, the rain has completely stopped. The skies are brightening as though the angels have lit candles behind the clouds.

Scraping the metal tip of the umbrella on the sidewalk, I traipse behind Mama. She gasps and halts in her tracks. I bump right into her. Looking up, my legs buckle at the sight of a "For Sale" sign posted on the front lawn of the Welles' home. Glancing at the bare windows, I know no one will answer our knock.

The door is unlocked, so we stagger into the foyer and roam the vacant rooms. I peer into Joseph's bedroom; not even a sock is left behind.

"What did we do? What did we do?" Mama collapses on the hardwood floors, and I lie down beside her. We're crunched up, side by side.

"What's happened? What does this mean?" I ask.

She can't seem to form words. She just grunts and sobs, and we lie there until the sun sets and shadows boom on the bare walls. Mama gets up. She's stiff, and her hair is matted on one side. She holds out a hand to lift me up. We exit the house without looking back.

Daddy is lying down on the sofa, shaving a pencil tip with a knife.

"I have to talk to you," Mama says.

"In a minute," he says, peering up from his task.

"Now." Tears trickle down her thin skin like the rain on the glass panes.

In their room my father screams as if someone has taken an axe to his arm. He pants and curses, but his words are garbled. I sit on the floor, my back leaning against the wall across from their bedroom door. Daddy quiets down, and Mama begins to wail. When she stops, he begins again. I fall asleep listening to them.

CHAPTER FOURTEEN

In the First Ward, August 17th is celebrated as Salt Water Day. Men, women, and children who believe in miracles travel south with empty glass jars to fill with the blessed ocean water, hoping to make their dreams come true. For us, it means Teresa is returning home.

Mama fries meatballs and layers lasagna noodles, ricotta cheese, and sauce in a Pyrex dish. It's hot and humid; with the oven on, the window fan doesn't even cool us. I tidy the bedroom I'm to share with my sister and clear two dresser drawers for Teresa's things. When there is nothing left to do but wait, I slump over a chair, tilting my head out the opened screen. It's past noon, and the sun is playing hide-and-seek behind the clouds.

Mr. Waxman's van lurches to the curb. Teresa stumbles out, carrying a vinyl suitcase. It is ten months since we've seen or spoken to her.

"She's here; she's here." I hop off the chair. It topples to the floor.

Mama rushes to the window as I practically fly down the stairs to greet my sister. The Cheerios I had for breakfast somersault in my belly. We meet at the bottom. We're both smiling but wordless. At the top of the stairs Mama whispers, "My baby's all grown up."

Mr. Waxman tips his hat and says goodbye. I take Teresa's hand as we climb the steps side by side.

Under the kitchen's fluorescent light Teresa's black hair gleams like polished leather shoes. She's eleven years old and almost as tall as Mama. Nipples protrude through a cotton white blouse, and her lips are full and rosy as if she's wearing lipstick. I want to shout that I missed her, but the words bob in my throat, unable to surface.

"Hello, Mama."

"Teresa, we're going to have to get you a bra," Mama says, reaching for the suitcase rather than for her daughter.

Giggling, I cover my mouth while Teresa blushes.

"I'm not being funny. You're old enough for a trainer."

"I want one, too," I say, without taking my eyes off my sister.

"You're not quite ready yet." Mama cups Teresa's pointed chin in her hand. A tear bubbles in the corner of one eye. "Are you okay?"

Teresa nods. Her tears flow easily. "I missed you, Mama."

Mama embraces her. "I know, baby, I know."

Together they are slender enough for my arms to stretch around both their waists. Squeezing them, I inhale the fried garlic on Mama's halter top and Herbal Essence shampoo on Teresa's hair, which sways on her back, touching the top of her waist.

"I missed you, Teresa." My voice cracks.

Mama pulls back. She dabs the tears off all our faces with the terry cloth clipped to the waistband of her culottes.

"Go help your sister unpack. Adele and Roger will be here soon."

Teresa seems pleased with the way I've decorated our room. Mama had made a mess of a sale bin at Kresgee's, searching for the lavender lace curtains hanging on the window. Daddy painted the walls ivory, and I pinned a poster of Donny Osmond above the top bunk.

Teresa layers one of the two drawers I had cleared out for her with a navy-and-white pleated skirt, jean shorts, and two sleeveless blouses the exact same style and fleshy color. Bouncing on the edge of the bed, I watch her fold and refold underwear, a nightgown, and socks into the second drawer.

"How's school?" she asks.

"It's good," I say, swinging my legs. "I've read fifty-three books so far this summer," I add.

"Wow, that's a lot. I haven't read anything but the Bible."

"What for?" I ask. Except for Sunday school, I wouldn't dare think of opening the Bible.

She flops next to me on the bed, and her head barely misses the top bunk's metal frame. "Which bed do you sleep in?" she says, ignoring my question.

"I've been sleeping on the bottom. Mama says the top one is for Joseph."

"Where is Joseph?" Teresa jumps up and looks around as if she's going to find Joseph hiding somewhere.

"He's not here. Mama says he'll be home before school starts."

"Oh." She sits back down. She looks disappointed and sad. I want to say something that will cheer her up.

"Mama's gonna get us a puppy soon."

"When?" Her eyes are brighter now, and she's smiling again.

"As soon as Joseph comes home."

"Teresa, Rosie, what are you doing in there?" Mama calls from the kitchen.

Scurrying into the living room, we bump into Adele and Roger. Bundles of gifts fill their arms.

"Oh, my," Adele says, circling Teresa, "now this is model material."

"That's right. And I won't stop her either. You hear that Teresa? If you want to model, you're going to do it," Mama says, inspecting herself in the chrome toaster.

Teresa blushes as Adele sets the packages on the coffee table then hugs her. Roger is already in the kitchen, ripping a heel of bread from one of the loaves they brought from Ciccone's along with éclairs and cream puffs. He dips the chunky crust into the sauce pot.

"Now that's what I call the Italian style," he says, with a full mouth. Red gravy trickles down his chin.

"Is that a crack about my cooking," Adele jokes, setting her beaded pearl clutch on the counter.

"Of course not, dear, but you have to admit no Italian meal is better than when an Italian prepares it." Roger dunks another crust in the pot and gobbles it.

Mama swats his hand with the hot ladle. "That's enough for now."

"Let's open some presents," Adele says.

The adults lounge on the sofa and watch as we tear open their generous gifts. We're creating such a ruckus we barely hear Daddy shouting over the noise.

"Where're my girls?" he says, throwing open his thick arms. "Come give your old man a hug."

Daddy often jokes that he's old, but, unlike Uncle Carmen, he has a full scalp of hair and not one missing tooth, and his belly doesn't stick out past his chest like Roger's.

Teresa doesn't budge from the sea of torn paper and boxes.

"Hi," she mutters. It's the first moment since she's been home that she seems awkward.

"She needs time, is all," Mama says, gathering up the mess we made into a garbage pail.

"I'm starving," Adele says, standing and smoothing her canary yellow knee-length dress. High-heeled pumps enhance her muscular calves.

Daddy and Roger grip hands. Adele barely manages a hello. I worry an argument will spark between them and ruin the day, but Daddy ignores the snub. For the first time in a long while, our family gathers at the table, draped with a paper cover, imprinted with colored balloons and "Happy Birthday"; it was the only festive one we could find on sale.

During our meal the conversation ranges from before the day we were separated to the future, dodging the eleven months in between. I'm relieved when Mama gives us permission to leave the table.

In our room I lift the screen and climb out onto the fire escape. The heat smacks me in the face like a hot iron. Teresa follows me out. Leaning on the metal bars, we glance out at the world.

"There's the park I play in," I say, pointing to the small patch of grass and weeds across the avenue. "And there's where my friend Gloria lives," I add, pointing to the six-family building. The steps are loitered with teenage boys. "And our landlord owns the candy store downstairs; sometimes he gives me Tootsie Rolls for free."

Teresa is leaning over, breathing in the air. "Where's the church?" she asks.

I can't believe she's not interested in knowing more about the free candy. I shrug and say, "About four or five blocks away."

"Girls, time for dessert," Mama calls out.

After we devour the éclairs and cream puffs sprinkled with powered sugar, Adele and Roger say goodnight. Daddy pecks us on the cheek and follows them out.

"Why don't you girls get ready for bed; it's been a long day," Mama says, sweeping crumbs of food and specks of wrapping paper into a dustpan.

Teresa and I bathe separately and crunch together on the bottom bunk, nose to nose. The meatballs we devoured earlier linger on our breaths.

"What's it like where you lived?" I ask.

"Todd and Susan were their names. They taught me how to be a good Catholic."

"We're Catholic," I say. This is true, but except for an occasional sign of the cross and abstinence of meat on Fridays, we don't practice anything I learn in Sunday school. We hadn't even made our First Communion—another failure Uncle Carmen held against my parents.

"I know, but now I'm really Catholic. I made my First Holy Communion."

This information stuns me, and I'm curious to know more.

"What do good Catholics do?" I ask, leaning forward to rest on my elbow. Teresa does the same. Her eyes are wide, and the whites glow in the dark.

"We go to mass every day and read from the Bible a lot."

"Do you like doing that?" I'm crinkling my nose as if she's just passed gas.

"Of course I do. Did you know that anyone who doesn't believe in Jesus goes to hell when they die?" she says, lying on her back again.

"Really," I say, not sure whether she's teasing me. But she looks serious.

"Yes, it's true."

"Did they have any kids?" I ask, bored by the Catholic story.

"They used to have a daughter. A car ran into her one day when she was playing on the front lawn." Teresa darts her eyes toward me in the dark, no doubt wanting to gauge my reaction.

"That's so sad." I inch closer to my sister.

"They made a shrine of her on the fireplace mantle. Candles burned in front all day."

"Were you scared?" I say, inhaling the residue of the Ivory soap that we washed with.

"No, they were super nice. They wanted to adopt me," she says nonchalantly as she sits up and fluffs her pillow with a fist.

"Did you want to stay with them?" I hold my breath until she responds.

"No, I just like them; that's all." Teresa rolls onto her side away from me.

"What was their daughter's name?"

"Cindy." Teresa yawns and raises the blanket to cover her head. "Good night, Rosie."

"Good night, Tre."

It is difficult to fall asleep, imagining the little girl Cindy, sprawled on a lush lawn, giggling beneath a flowery tree, as she pours tea for her dolls, unaware of the car that is about to swerve into her. It makes me frightened for Joseph. What if something terrible happened to him? We'd never know.

———

It's early Saturday morning, and we're still in matching powder pink baby-doll pajamas, playing Twister. Daddy's asleep, and Mama's at the sink soaping dishes. A tap on the door jolts us out of play. Teresa and I stare at each other, seemingly without breathing. Mama rushes to the door and peeps through the hole.

"Just a minute," she says. She mouths for us to go to our room. I know she must see the panic on our faces because she adds, "It's okay. It's only the landlord."

Teresa and I scoot to our room. I shut the door but don't latch it, so I can peek through the crack to keep my eye on Mama.

"I'd like to talk to you," the old man says, stepping over the threshold before Mama invites him to.

"Sure," Mama says.

Pointing a finger that looks more like a crooked branch, the landlord says, "I thought you only had one kid. I've been seeing two around here."

"Why don't you sit down? I'll reheat some coffee." Mama steers him to the sofa. She disappears and returns with two coffee cups and a package of cookies balanced on top of the cups.

My view is of Mama, offering the landlord an anisette cookie. He accepts and dunks the sweet treat into the steaming cup. His back rounds forward like an owl's wings, and his bald head bulges with blue veins like those in Nona's legs. Their voices are garbled, but I can see Mama's constricted facial muscles easing and can hear the man's gruff tone slacken. He even chuckles at something Mama says.

"I was going to ask if my niece could stay here. You see, my sister is very sick, and she can't take care of her right now. I hope you don't mind," Mama says, loud enough for Teresa and me to hear.

Spooning coffee into his mouth, he asks, "For how long?"

"I'm not sure really. But I promise you'll never know she's here."

More slurping; then he shrugs his shoulders. "As long as they behave, I guess it's all right."

The landlord sets his cup on the coffee table. Mama swoops it up and takes it to the kitchen. I can hear water rinsing it. He stands, clutching the table for support. Mama is at the door, turning the knob.

"Thank you so much for understanding," she says.

Through the crack I can clearly see his gaze linger on Mama's legs silhouetted beneath Daddy's long shirt. He smiles, revealing black-spotted gums twice as thick as his teeth.

Mama pulls the door wide open. He rubs against her as he exits.

"Good day," he says.

It's the first week of school, and I've already read *A Suspenseful Search* three times. This is how I devise a plan to hire a sleuth like Nancy Drew to help me find Joseph. I am obsessed with money, as Daddy is with gambling, Teresa with religion, and Mama with smoking. To and from school my eyes scan the sidewalks for anything that shines. I scour each block for empty soda bottles to be redeemed for nickels. When Mama needs cigarettes, I jump at the opportunity to fetch them at the store and then keep the change. I am an expert at finding, stealing, and earning quarters, nickels, dimes, and pennies for Joseph.

In October our school requires that all students participate in chocolate and cookie sales to raise money. I volunteer to sell two boxes rather than the required one, strutting outside the designated blocks, knocking on doors, balancing the awkward box on my hips until every bar is sold. When the deadline to hand over the cash is due, I tell my teacher I lost all the money. I have to stay after school every day for a week dusting the classrooms to make up for it.

One Friday, at St. John's in the bingo hall, I'm fidgeting in a metal folding chair, bored out of my mind. Teresa is slumped across the banquet-sized table across from me, watching the women play. Some eye their cards without using chips to mask them while others curse the man who calls out the numbers.

Fidgeting one too many times, I draw a scowl from Mama. Scowling back, I get up and escape to the bathroom for a third time. Squatting over the toilet so as not to touch the lid, I spot a brown leather pocketbook strewn on the black-and-white tiled floor in the neighboring stall. Looping the handle around my sneaker, I drag it across the floor.

The main door squeaks open. Through the crack I am relieved to see Teresa moseying in. I unlatch the lock and whisper, "Teresa, come here."

"What are you doing?" Her brows are brimmed with curiosity.

"Look what I found," I say, waving the leather bag.

"What is it?" She's squinting to see.

"Come in," I say, pulling her by the elbow into the stall. I latch the door.

My heart pounds as I unzip the purse to inspect its contents. Inside is a vinyl cosmetic pouch filled with trial-sized tubes of red and pink lipsticks, like the ones the Avon lady drops off door to door. There is also a full pack of Kent cigarettes and a wallet with a snapshot of a black woman. A toddler boy bounces on her knee; his smile is so wide you can see the pink flesh lining his inner lips. Reaching into the bottom of the purse, I withdraw a wad of bills.

"Oh, my God, look at this."

Teresa's jaw droops. "Let's go tell Mama," she says, unlatching the door.

"Why?" I say, holding it shut with my foot.

"So we can find the lady in the picture," Teresa says.

"But I found it, and its 'finders keepers, losers weepers,'" I sing.

"It's a mortal sin to keep it. It's stealing," Teresa insists, folding her arms, tapping her foot. Her hair is pulled back into a high ponytail. I have an urge to yank it.

"Is not; I found it—I didn't steal it," I say, tucking the wad of bills into my sock.

"God's going to punish us if we keep it," Teresa says, tugging at my blouse.

I pinch the flesh on her hand, and she pulls away. "God, God, God. I don't believe in your stupid God, anyway."

Teresa gasps, and I shove her away from the door. I ram the pocketbook down a receptacle and return to the bingo hall.

Later that night, as I recount the three hundred and twenty dollars that had been folded inside the wallet, behind the snapshots, for the third and final time, Teresa kneels poised at the foot of the bed, praying aloud for Jesus and the Blessed Virgin Mary to forgive me. I think about taunting her but hold my tongue; I've insulted her God enough.

One day I'll explain that I kept the money to find Joseph. But for now, it's my secret mission.

CHAPTER FIFTEEN

The night before Christmas Eve an anxious storm blankets our region with eight inches of pure white snow. In the morning, from the window, the sun's glare stings my eyes. Teresa and I dash outdoors to roll around in the soft clean drifts. During the night huge trucks have plowed the snow into mountain peaks on almost every corner, wedging automobiles into parking spaces. On cardboard boxes we slide down the slopes, giggling until our lashes frost up and our butts are soaked and numb.

Mama has cocoa simmering for us when we return home, stiff like steel rods, to strip off our soggy jeans and sweatshirts. Our hands are as red as poinsettias and our cheeks chapped and tight. Daddy lies on the couch, reading the newspaper. Revealing his hidden face, he says, "Better warm up and get dressed; Roger's taking us to the farm to get us a big old tree."

My sister and I put on dry dungarees and shirts, gulp the cocoa, and rush outdoors just as Roger honks the horn of an army green pickup truck he borrowed from his workplace.

In the front seat Teresa squeezes between the two men while I bob on Daddy's lap, as wide and sturdy as a wooden bench. During the ride Daddy brags about a new system he has for betting on pro football. He's won five out of six games and plans to win many more.

"Hey, Roger, pull over at the corner store; I need to make a call."

After being gone only a second, Daddy returns with a pack of Bazooka. Teresa and I split it and blow bubbles the rest of the way.

The farm is as long as three city blocks, strewn with pines, Douglas firs, and spruces. Toddlers chase each other, slopping in gray mushy snow, as their parents ponder the depth, width, and height of the ideal Christmas tree. The freshly cut pines smell like the air freshener dangling on the rearview mirror in Roger's truck.

"Pick the biggest one you can find; I don't care what it costs," Daddy says.

We're patient in our hunt to find our dream tree, but, rather than choosing a tall spruce with bluish tips, we both agree on a short, stubby pine.

"That's a Charlie Brown tree," Daddy says, shivering and blowing hot breath into his hands.

"It reminds me of Santa Claus," Teresa says, spreading its branches.

"I love it," I say, walking around it, sniffing it like a dog would.

"Oh, well, suit yourself," Daddy says, pulling his collar up. I can tell he's too cold to argue.

Roger and Daddy haul the tree onto the roof of the truck and secure it with rope. While we head home, Teresa and I practice choruses from "Silent Night" and "Come All Ye Faithful"; we plan to carol door to door on Christmas morning.

At home, the fragrance of our tree dilutes the fish simmering on the stove for our traditional Christmas Eve dinner Mama and Adele are busy cooking. Teresa informs Mama that seven different types of fish should be served, each representative of the sacraments.

"Well, we can only afford shrimp for the spaghetti. Jesus will have to be satisfied with that," Mama says.

Slurping hot chocolate topped with mini-marshmallows, Teresa and I admire the rotund pine, tinseled in silver; its branches glowing under the red, white, and green strings of bulbs we have christened it with. I can't help but think of Joseph somewhere, celebrating Christmas with strangers, toasting marshmallows over a fire. It is at that moment Teresa interrupts my thoughts and asks, "Why isn't Joseph coming home for Christmas?"

Mama's and Adele's chatter ceases, and Roger and Daddy look away.

"He had the chance to go to Disneyland. He'll come home during spring break," Mama says, clanking dishes out of the cabinet.

"That's a long time from now," Teresa says.

So many nights when the two of us are alone in bed I am tempted to tell my sister about the day we went back for Joseph and he was gone. That we do not know where he is or how he is. The truth is lodged in my brain like a constant migraine, but I keep silent, massaging my head, hoping it will go away.

"Come help us set the table," Mama says, jiggling silverware out of a stuffed drawer.

"Why can't we call him to say Merry Christmas?" Teresa asks, wiping the table with a soapy sponge.

"I told you that the family he's with don't have a phone," Mama says.

"But why…."

"Enough, Teresa," Daddy says, "Help your mother set the table."

Sitting for supper, Teresa insists we say a prayer of thanks. Roger is already gobbling buttered bread, and Adele swats his hand when he reaches for another piece, nodding at Teresa to begin. Folding our hands in prayer, we bow our heads, just how Teresa expects us to. Rather than praying thanks for the meal, I pray for Joseph to find his way back home.

———

Christmas morning I wake to pee. On my way to the bathroom, two letter-sized manila envelopes grazing the candy canes and tinsel catch my eye. Ignoring my full bladder, I run back to our room and nudge Teresa.

"Wake up; there's a surprise for us."

Teresa's eyes pop open. She yawns and stretches her long arms. "What are you talking about?"

We had stopped believing in Santa Claus years ago, and it had been an eternity since our parents had surprised us with anything special.

"Two envelopes are pinned to the tree that weren't there last night," I say, so excited I can't even catch my breath.

Teresa rolls out of bed and follows me to the living room. The envelopes are still there. We dare not touch them, so we just stare, wondering what could be inside.

"What do we have here?" Daddy startles us so that we jump back, almost knocking into the tree. In boxer shorts and a Fruit of the Loom T-shirt he looks more like an overgrown boy than our father. Sniffing the envelopes, he smirks. "Doesn't smell like something you'd eat." We know he's teasing us.

"What is it?" I ask, bristling on the tips of my toes.

"You'll have to look inside," Mama says, joining us. She perches on the arm of the sofa, wrapping a sweater around her nightgown.

Daddy picks the envelopes off the tree, delicately, as if they're as fragile as glass. He hands one to each of us. I tear mine open while Teresa holds hers up to the light.

"Wow," I say, darting my eyes at Teresa, my parents, and back to Ben Franklin. "It's a one hundred dollar bill."

Mama giggles. "You can buy whatever you want with it."

"Why would we want to buy our own Christmas presents?" Teresa wonders, mildly disappointed.

"If you don't want it, give it back." Daddy has his hand out.

"No, I want to keep it," Teresa says, folding the bill into a tiny square.

"Well, stop complaining about it and say thank you," Daddy says, shuffling his bare feet into the bathroom.

Disappearing for a moment to stash the hundred dollar bill in a coffee jar hidden behind rusted paint cans in the closet, I rejoin my family clutching a shopping bag.

"What's this?" Mama asks when I dig in and pull out a small box wrapped with crepe paper.

"Open it up," Teresa says, kneeling down at the foot of the sofa.

Mama folds the paper away and lifts the lid. "How beautiful," she says, holding the multicolored wallet I beaded for her in art class.

"Unzip it and look inside," Teresa urges, patting the wallet.

With half a smile Mama unzips the pouch and empties it. A strand of rosary beads spills out.

"Now this is something I need for sure." Mama tucks the rosary strand between her breasts.

"What else do you have there?" Mama asks.

"It's for Daddy," I say.

"What's for me?" our father asks, on his way out of the bathroom. Shaving cream is caught in his ear, and his hair is slicked back.

I drop a plastic box in his palm. He tears off the lid.

"So you don't have to use matchsticks to clean your teeth," Teresa says.

"Good thinking. Give Daddy a hug."

I embrace his opened arms while Teresa stands on her toes to peck him on the cheek.

———

School break ends, and I am weary of *I Love Lucy* reruns and anxious to return to my routine of reading and studying. On the first day back I'm in history class, flailing my hand to respond to a question when I glimpse Daddy in the corridor. Clearing his throat, he whispers, "Excuse me, I'm here for my daughter, Rosie Scarpiella. We have a family emergency."

"Rosie, please come to the front of the class." The teacher's voice quivers.

The hardcover books piled on my desk thud to the floor when I leap out of the desk. Rushing toward my father, trying not to appear anxious, an untied lace causes me to trip, and several classmates chuckle. I feel my cheeks singe.

Daddy's pacing in the corridor.

"What's wrong?" I'm looking straight into his eyes, but I don't recognize them. They're cloudy and red-rimmed; his skin is gray like dirty bathwater.

"You have to come home. I need the hundred dollars…that I gave you for Christmas."

"What?" I say, stopping in my tracks.

"I need to borrow it for a little while," he says, shrugging his shoulders as if I'm supposed to understand.

"I spent it on a bathrobe, slippers, and a nightgown." This is not the truth, but I say it like it is because no one is getting a dollar of the money I'm saving up to find Joseph.

On his heels he makes a full circle then hovers over me again.

"You spent all of it?"

"Yes," I say, folding my arms behind my back, crossing my fingers.

"Someone's going to hurt me if I don't come up with the money I owe them," Daddy says, stomping a foot like an oversized child.

"I'm going to class." I turn away and don't look back. I wish that whatever he's afraid of will get him. Then I quickly make the sign of the cross and ask Jesus to disregard my thoughts. Teresa says this works.

CHAPTER SIXTEEN

On New Year's Eve Daddy hosts a poker game in our apartment, which sparks a weekend trend. The players participating in the games are charged a fee that Mama keeps so she can pay the oil man.

The men are noisy as they play, cursing and arguing with each other. It isn't uncommon for them to remain hunched in their places, through the weekend, as if minutes rather than days have passed, or for me to return from school on Mondays to find the shades drawn and them still at their posts.

The dread of my bladder bloating in the night taunts me, triggering the need to pee more often. At least three or four times I have to cut through the kitchen to get to the bathroom. I throw a wad of toilet paper in the bowl, stifling the tinkling; but I'm certain they can still hear.

Washing my hands, peeking through the gape in the door, I'm able to glimpse the entire circle of men. Their faces have become as familiar to me as my own parents'. Their names seem unusual and mysterious. There is Weasel (the Jewish man who owns the dry cleaners), Meat Man (the butcher we have a running tab with), Rathat (I assume this is his nickname because of the toupee flopping on his head), and Bean Man, who is the most mysterious because he never speaks. His legs are as long as my body from head to toe, and his clothes hang off his lanky frame as if they belong to someone else. It is rumored the reason for his silence is a severed tongue.

Bean Man empties and wipes the ashtrays and rinses the cups and saucers. At the stove he hovers over an aluminum espresso pot, and when the steam rises, he plops a black nylon sock filled with coffee grains into the boiling water. In an instant the aroma permeates the apartment.

Attending meetings with my father, I have learned many secrets gamblers harbor, but observing them in action, I am amused by their peculiar superstitions. The version of the game is up to the dealer. Most favor five

114

cards and deuces wild; few prefer the riskier game of "no peek." Weasel prefers not to inspect his hand until all cards have been dealt. Rathat crosses his heart before eyeballing his, and it is typical for Daddy to raise his bet without glimpsing the cards at all.

The marathon games end one Friday night, when Daddy gambles the money in the hat instead of giving it to Mama.

"You make your kids freeze so you can give these bums your money," her fingers slice through the air as if to clear the way for her anger. "Get out. All of you."

The men jump off their chairs as if a shotgun had sounded and skid out faster than the dealer shuffles.

"Who do you think you are? This is my house, too," Daddy says, spitting in Mama's face.

"I want you out." Mama starts tearing up the cards on the table.

Daddy grabs what's left to salvage of the deck. "I'll kill you, you cunt."

"You're nothing but a bum," she says, throwing the torn cards on the floor.

"And you're a lousy fucking mother. You can't even get up to make your kids breakfast," he says, slamming his fist on the table.

Mama lunges at him and claws his stubbed face with her painted nails.

"You bastard, I should have never taken you back."

They work their tongues like seasoned swordsmen.

"Get out. Go live in the sewer with the rats. That's where you belong," she says, clearing the table with one swoop of her arm. Cups and chips crash to the floor.

Ducking into our bedroom, Teresa and I dodge broken promises and splattering glass. Teresa clutches her rosary beads while I squish a pillow around my head, until the fight ceases and the door slams shut. *Don't come back,* I whisper.

I creep from the safety net of our room and am shocked to see Daddy inspecting the blood beads hardening on his scratched neck in the mirror.

"Where's Mama?" I say, maintaining a safe distance.

"She's gone, for good I hope. Now go to bed." He wets a towel under the running water and dabs the blood.

"Gone where?" My ears flutter, and I poke my fingers inside to get them to stop.

"I don't know, and I don't care, and you shouldn't either." He rinses the towel. The water turns pink as it swirls down the drain. I can't stand the sight of him, so I bolt away.

Teresa is already in bed, the covers tucked all around her.

"What's going on?" She sits up, bumping her head on the top bunk.

"Mama's gone," I say, slipping into bed with her.

Saturday morning Teresa and I eat Rice Crispies out of the box. There is no milk and no money to buy it with. To pass the time, Teresa reads verses from the Bible. When I can't stand listening to another scripture, I stack records on the turntable and fall asleep to Donny Osmond.

Daddy doesn't emerge from his room until sunset. He sashays into the bathroom, to shave, without requesting my assistance. Before he leaves for the evening, he shouts, "Lock up. I won't be late."

The hum of the refrigerator keeps me awake until Daddy tiptoes in past midnight. He rummages around in the cabinets for something to eat, and I want to go to him to ask whether he thinks Mama's ever coming back. But I'm afraid he'll say she's abandoned us for good, so I lie awake with the questions buzzing around in my head like flies trapped indoors.

On Sunday Teresa and I trudge five blocks, in a record-breaking April snowstorm, to pray for Mama to come home. Although I don't believe like Teresa does, I am willing to try anything so our lives can go back to normal. Without the aid of boots and gloves, our feet and fingers are numb as we ascend the staircase. An usher opens the wide double-oak door. When we step inside, I feel as though I've been swallowed up by an abyss of ice-cold marble, stained glass, and gilded crosses. Mimicking Teresa's every movement, I dip my fingers into a marble basin and genuflect, before slipping into a pew.

Above us, in the gallery, the choir bellows "Ave Maria," triggering a rash of goose bumps on my chapped skin. Men, women, and children, bundled in heavy coats, hats, and gloves, are crushed in the pews. All seem not to be offended that God decided to topple us with snow rather than the sweet scent of April showers.

The priest and his sermon bore me, so I'm relieved when mass ends. The entire congregation hurries out of the church—not even the priest lolls on the steps to chat with the parishioners.

As we rush home, the soft flakes harden and accumulate quickly. The balls of my feet are cold as if they are bare. At the crosswalk, waiting for the light to turn green, a navy blue sedan slows. I squint to see through the dense flakes building momentum. The driver rolls the window down, revealing a bald head and a mustache wider than his grin.

"Girls," he says, as though we know him. "I've been looking for you. Your mother's been rushed to the hospital. Hurry, get in the car; I'll take you to her right away."

"Dear Lord," Teresa says, darting toward the car. I tug her arm and jerk her away. Mama's relentless warnings not ever to go with a stranger ring in my ears.

"Hurry, get in," the man demands.

Gripping Teresa, I stare at the man, searching for a resemblance to someone we know. I notice he is tugging at something, and I look down. His hand is tucked inside his unzipped pants. Clutching Teresa's coat sleeve, we dash in front of the automobile, across the double-lane avenue. Horns honk, and we skid in the slippery snow, but we don't stop running until we are safely in front of our building. The landlord's nephew is shoveling snow off the walkway. I glance in the direction from which we ran. No one has followed us.

As we pant up the steps, burnt toast wafts in the hall. Opening the door, I am relieved to see it is Mama at the stove, safe in the confines of our four-room apartment. She's scrambling eggs.

"Come have some breakfast," she says, as though she had been there when we left earlier that morning.

Teresa hangs our coats in the closet. In front of the radiator we remove our sopping socks and flatten them on the radiator to dry. Teresa whispers, "I told you God would answer our prayers."

Mama doesn't explain her absence, nor do we inquire as to where she has been. We just pretend she never left, just as we pretend Joseph is coming back.

CHAPTER SEVENTEEN

In summer, when the only relief for city people is the hydrants, The fire department and police threaten to arrest anyone caught cranking them open, and we have no choice but to stay indoors, without exerting energy, lying in bed in the middle of the day with the shades drawn. If I could, I'd jump out of my skin to rally a breeze. Mama's permission to shave the hair on my scrawny legs, which is long enough to braid, is the only thing that keeps me sane.

Not even when the sun sets does Mama dare to turn on the stove. Instead, she dices onion and carrot and adds them to a can of tuna fish for supper. Just as we finish our sandwiches, Daddy barges through the door like a blast of chilled air.

"Antonette, girls, start packing. We're getting out of this hot box," he says, fanning himself with a stack of bills.

"Where did that come from?" she asks, her almond-shaped eyes widening.

Daddy chuckles, and the cleft in his chin deepens as he explains how the long shot named Shadow galloped to the finish line in first place, shocking the handicappers. His voice is throaty as he details how he won his fortune, and she listens as though he were some kind of superhero.

"I studied the program like I usually do, Antonette. I had my pick in my head before I got in line to make my bet, and then I recognized this old tauter I knew."

"Yeah, yeah, go on already," she interrupts him, anxious to hear the end.

"Well," I say, "tout man, who do you like in this race?" 'The long shot's going to take it home,' he says. So, I checked the program again."

"What's a 'tout man'?" Teresa asks, scooping up the bills Daddy tossed in the air; they've floated to the floor like snowflakes.

118

"Someone who studies horses," he says, patting her head like she's a good dog.

"And, what happened?" Mama's hands flail, motioning him to continue.

"The rest is history, baby." Daddy spins around on his heels, dancing the twist.

"How much is here?" Mama asks, counting the bills as Teresa places them in her palm one by one.

"Plenty," Daddy says, grabbing Mama's hands to twirl her around. The bills float to the floor again, and Teresa and I squat to gather them.

Mama tugs away from Daddy. She's giggling, and I think she's going to say okay, let's go; we ought to go on vacation. But instead she plucks the money from us and stashes it down her blouse.

"We're not going to waste money on a vacation. We got bills, and these kids need new sneakers for September...."

"We have plenty to do all of it," Daddy says, hushing her puckered lips with a finger and squeezing her breast with another. She slaps his hand, and he laughs.

"I'll wear my old sneakers; I don't need new ones," I say. I'm so excited I'm standing on the tips of my toes.

"Yeah, me too," Teresa says, reaching for my hand. Her cheeks are puckered as if she's about to explode.

"But, we have bills..." Mama says and then glances over at Teresa and me.

"Not another word about it," Daddy says, "We're going first thing in the morning."

———

The subway cars seem to be sweating men, women, and whining toddlers. Standing the entire ride, I occupy the time by visualizing the miles of sand and foamy waves at the shore. It's our first trip to the beach, but I've seen *Gidget* and *Where the Boys Are* at least ten times and can imagine what sand feels like squished between my toes.

The only time we've ever been swimming anywhere was when Adele had taken us to a lake. I remember there was a hefty entrance fee. Mama and Adele could afford for only four of us to go, and since there were five of us, Mama and Adele devised a plan while driving. They decided Joseph would hide in the trunk until they paid the attendant. I worried that he might suffocate and offered to go with him, but he refused to have me ruin the magical adventure he envisioned.

"He'll be fine, Rosie. Your mother and I did this all the time as kids. Didn't we, Antonette?"

"We sure did. Plenty of times."

"That's how she met your father. He was an attendant at the lake. He snagged us sneaking your mother out of the trunk one afternoon. Just her luck," she added under her breath.

At Penn Station we exit the subway car and board a bus destined for Asbury. In front of our parents Teresa and I sit quietly in high-backed cushioned chairs. She gazes out the window while I count in my head to one hundred and then start over again and again. Finally, the driver announces we have reached our destination.

Stepping off the bus and into a cool mist, I open my mouth and gulp the air. The unexpected taste of salt thrills me. Teresa's face shines with sweat, and ringlets pop up all over her head, just like Mama's. On the sidewalks mothers wheel strollers, toddlers skip in flip-flops, and cliques of teenage girls flaunt their bare skin in skimpy bikinis while boys lugging surfboards flirt with them.

Teresa and I marvel at the neon signs of dolphins and seagulls. At the end of a strip of hotels and motels we spot the only lit vacancy sign dangling on a single-story motel. Daddy disappears into the office to inquire about a room. Several minutes later he reappears clanking a key chain, gesturing us to join him.

A ceiling fan swirls above two full-sized beds, swooshing the damp, musty air.

"Wow, it's cool in here," Mama says, fussing with her damp ringlets in front of a dresser mirror.

"It'll be much cooler near the water," Daddy says, snapping his fingers.

Teresa rummages through the bag we stuffed with clothes for the trip.

"Let's change," she says.

The two of us squeeze into the square-tiled bathroom to wiggle out of our jeans and into cotton shorts.

The beach entrance is on the boardwalk. Teenage boys and girls, wearing wrinkled white shirts and grimy hats, grill sausages and hot dogs in kiosks overlooking the ocean. Several white-haired women crouch on benches, licking ice-cream cones and watching people zigzag in and out of trinket and memorabilia pavilions.

At the far end of the boardwalk a Ferris wheel, twice the size of the one hauled in every fall for the Feast of St. Gerard, towers over a roller coaster and a water slide.

"Mama, can we go on the Ferris wheel?" I say, pointing and slowing down for her to catch up with me.

"Maybe later."

I skip ahead to be first in line at the ticket booth manned by a teenaged boy brandishing braces that look as sharp as steak knives. A Yankee's cap hides his eyes and shadows his mottled skin.

"You a fan?" Daddy taps the rim of the boy's cap.

"Yeah," he says, "It's been a tough season, though." He smiles. Between his braces bits of his morning breakfast turn my stomach, and I look away.

"One of the worst we've ever had," Daddy says. "If Roy White can't get the job done, no one can."

"I hear ya."

"Do you go to many games?" Daddy asks.

When I tug his arm to hurry, he swats my hand like he's just been bitten by a mosquito.

"I used to go with my dad all the time." The boy chuckles. "Now I work all the time."

"That's too bad," Daddy says, scratching an ear. "I got a pair of tickets for tonight's game, back at the bungalow we rent for the summer over on Fourth Street. I'm looking for someone to take them off my hands."

"I'll go to the game with you, Daddy," Teresa butts in.

Ignoring her, Daddy whispers, "I only have two tickets; you can't take one without the other. You know what I mean," he adds, rolling his eyeballs.

The boy glances at Teresa and me and nods. "Gee, I'd die to go, but I can't afford them."

Daddy trips back as if he's been slapped. "I don't want your money, son. You can have the tickets."

"Wow, that's really nice of you, sir. I don't know what to say." Braces twinkle under the glare of the sun.

"Hey, you seem like a nice kid, and I'd hate for them to go to waste. What time do you get off duty today?"

"Four o'clock."

"Well, then, I'll meet you back here at three."

"Thanks, sir." The boy removes his cap and bows.

Digging into his pockets, my father says, "How much do I owe you for the four of us?"

"No charge, sir." The boy is waving his hand back and forth like Daddy's about to smack him with a hot iron.

"That's not necessary," Daddy says, holding a hand to his chest.

"No, really, it's on me."

"Thanks, pal."

The two shake hands, and the boy stamps our wrists with red ink.

Finally, Mama gives us the okay to head to the beach. Teresa and I race down the ramp, kicking our flip-flops on the sand.

"Hold on," Mama says. We stop in our tracks.

I'm out of breath, and the sun is beating on the top of my head. I place a hand over my eyes like an awning and spot Daddy swiping suntan oil off an unattended blanket and a pack of cigarettes off another.

"Let's settle here," Mama says, snapping open the matted wool blanket she took from the hotel closet. It's almost the same color as the sand.

Leaning on her palms, tilting her face toward the sun, she doesn't look thirty-five. She and Teresa could easily be mistaken for sisters, showing off their shapely legs in short shorts and muscular backs in halter tops. Like Teresa's, Mama's hair is pulled back into a pony tail; bangs hide furrows on her high forehead.

The beach bristles with group activities. A game of Frisbee occupies two preteen boys. Two girls construct a castle with pails, shovels, and sand. Frankie Valley and the Four Seasons blare from transistor radios, absorbing the incessant chatter.

Teresa oils her legs, arms, and chest and lies on her back beside Mama.

"Don't you want to swim?" I say, kicking up sand.

"Stop that," Mama says.

"I want a tan, maybe later," Teresa says, wiping her hands on the blanket.

"You're boring," I say as I fall to my knees. The sand is hot but smooth.

"You ready?" Daddy asks, tugging a T-shirt over his head. He tosses it on the blanket and rolls his heavy dungarees up to his knees.

"Yes," I say, racing ahead.

"Hold your horses; you can't go in alone."

"Daddy, I'm almost thirteen," I say, without looking back at him.

The ice-cold water takes my breath away as I wade into the crashing foam. Daddy suggests ducking my head under so as not to feel the cold. Once I do, the temperature rises. Imitating my six-foot-tall father maneuvering the waves, I swallow plenty of water, but it doesn't deter me from diving back into it. Daddy says I am a natural swimmer. He teaches me to dive into oncoming waves and to swim over them.

My nose tingles, and my fingers wrinkle like prunes, but I refuse to get out when Daddy tires.

"Come on; you can't stay in alone."

"Please, can I—I promise to swim by the lifeguard."

"Just for a little while," he says, trudging out of the thick wet sand and onto the shoreline.

Dodging the waves isn't as much fun alone, and after a while I'm bored. Glancing up at the blanket, Mama flails her arms above her head, motioning me to join them. To my surprise, a picnic of hot dogs, cheese fries, and Cokes awaits me. Teresa and Mama have been to the boardwalk.

"I want to go on the boardwalk, too," I whine, gobbling a French fry.

"You were having fun swimming. We didn't want to bother you," Teresa says, squeezing mustard out of packet onto a hot dog.

"Can we go again later?" I say, grabbing more fries.

"We'll see," Mama says, handing me a napkin and a straw for my Coke.

After our quick meal, Daddy sprawls on the blanket; his giant feet stretch way past Mama's toes. "I've had enough exercise for one day," he says.

"But I want to swim more," I say, kicking sand on purpose.

Daddy rolls onto his stomach, shading his head with his shirt. Mama douses her cigarette in the sand.

"Go for a walk or something," she says, massaging oil onto her chest and shoulders.

"I'll go with you," Teresa says, bouncing off the blanket.

Squishing our toes into the wet sand along the shoreline, we zigzag in and out of mussels and seaweed that have washed ashore and hop over jelly-fish we've been warned sting like a swarm of bees. A breeze whips around our heads. Teresa's long hair looks as though it's trying to fly away, and although I can't see mine, I'm certain it looks the same. The thought makes me laugh aloud—so hard I plop onto the sand. Teresa spins around. Now the breeze is on the back of her head, and her hair blows forward, concealing her face like a mask.

"What's so funny?" she asks, already beginning to laugh before she knows at what.

"You're hair looks like its flying away," I say, barely able to get the words out.

Teresa plops down next to me. Our fit of laughter lasts a few minutes. It feels good. When we finally calm down, we both stare out at the horizon. The water is so blue, it's hard to tell where it ends and the sky begins.

"This is really fun," I say, drawing a smiley face in the sand.

"Yeah. When Joseph comes home, we should come back. He'd love it," Teresa says, curling her knees under her chin.

"Maybe we can," I say, standing and stretching a hand to help Teresa. I don't say what I fear—that he's never coming back.

We stroll back to the blanket. Daddy stands and asks a neighboring worshipper the time.

"Ten of three," a woman more wrinkled than my father's shirt says.

"Come on, pack it up," Daddy says, rolling his pants legs down.

"I don't want to go," I complain.

"You're never satisfied." Daddy slips his shirt over his reddening chest.

Trotting past the entrance booth, waving to the pimply attendant, Daddy shouts, "I'll be back in about fifteen minutes with those tickets."

As he stamps the hands of an anxious huddle of girls, the boy responds, "I'll be waiting."

At the hotel Teresa showers and dresses first. When it's my turn, the hot water runs out, but I don't mind the cold. It soothes my singed skin and rinses the itching sand and salt clinging to my feet and ankles like ants. When I'm finished, I pull my sopping hair back into a ponytail and slip on a clean pair of denim shorts and a yellow tube top that accentuates my burn.

Mama and Daddy are sprawled on top of the floral bedspread, and Teresa is crunched in an armed chair by the window, flipping through a real estate magazine when I emerge from the bathroom.

"What are we going to do now?" I ask.

Daddy is stripped down to his boxer shorts. His shoulders are the color of tomatoes. Bouncing off the bed, he grabs a ten dollar bill from a wad of money lying on the lamp table. Fanning himself with it, he says, "You two go to the boardwalk, go on some rides, and get something to eat."

"Wow," Teresa says, clipping the bill.

"What are you going to do?" I say, slipping on flip-flops.

"We're too tired to walk around. I'm going to take a shower and relax," Mama says, getting up and disappearing into the bathroom.

"What about the tickets?" Teresa asks.

"The what?" Daddy says.

"The Yankees tickets you promised to the boy at the booth. Do you want us to drop them off to him?"

"Oh, thanks for reminding me," Daddy says, opening and closing the top drawer on the table. "I have them right here. You girls go ahead. I'll get him the tickets."

Teresa and I stroll onto the boardwalk. We stop at the first concession for a bite to relieve our gurgling stomachs. We splurge on a sausage and pepper sandwich, a slice of pizza, and lemonade with crushed ice. Sitting on a bench, relishing our freedom, we munch and eye the families lazily trotting by. When we're through, we toss the paper plates into a receptacle and continue down the boardwalk.

Drawn to the spinning wheels of fortune, we place nickels on Mom and Joe, hoping to win a case of electric rollers. After blowing five whole dollars, we decide to spend the rest of our money on ice cream for us and taffy for Mama. At ten o'clock we head back to our hotel.

Entering the dark room, I switch on the light, and the ceiling fan swirls. Daddy's white bare butt looks like a heap of snow on top of the fleshy blanket. Mama opens her eyes and quickly covers him. On the side of the bed her panties are rolled up in a ball. I switch off the light, and Teresa and I slip into bed in our clothes.

Glaring sunshine wakes us in the morning. Our parents share a cup of coffee while Teresa and I gulp pint cartons of cold milk and devour a box of jelly donuts. Peering out the window, I say, "It's another perfect beach day."

"Were not going swimming today," Daddy says, combing his hair back in front of the mirror.

"Why not?" Teresa asks, squirting jelly from a donut into her mouth.

"I'm all burnt. I can't sit in the sun today," Daddy says, bending to show us blistered shoulders. "We'll do something else fun today. Tomorrow we'll go back to the beach," he adds.

It's not our first visit to a horse track, but Monmouth is fancier than the others we've seen. Outdoors, rows of picnic tables, shaded with umbrellas, are packed with families enjoying picnics. Mama stands guard at a table of people finishing up. As soon as they clear their mess, we take the spot.

"Rosie, come with me," Daddy says, picking up a race program left by the previous family.

"Where are we going?" I say, practically parachuting off the bench.

"Daddy needs a good luck charm," he says, winking.

The betting arena is crushed mostly with men hiding behind newspapers. Ticket stubs, cigarette butts, and newspaper pages litter the floors. Cigar, pipe, and cigarette smoke clouds the air. Searching for a ticket window with the least amount of people in line, my father asks me a series of questions.

"What's your favorite color?"

"Green."

"What's your favorite number?"

"Three."

When it is our turn to place a bet, he speaks softly, as if fearing he'll be overheard.

"Fourth race; twenty on the three to win, ten dollar Trifecta, numbers three, six, and ten and a five dollar Exacta with numbers three and six."

"Hurry up, buddy. It's two minutes to post time; you're not the only one trying to get a bet in," an elderly man yells from the end of the line.

A cashier wearing a black visor counts the money and punches numbers into a machine. Within seconds a bunch of tickets sputter out. Daddy examines them before exiting the line.

"Keep your eye on the horse with the number three on it. You see it?" Daddy asks, tapping one of the many television monitors suspended from the ceiling.

A magnificent black horse, cloaked in emerald satin, with the number three imprinted on it, catches my eye.

"I see him. I see him," I say, bouncing on my toes.

"Okay, here's what you got to do, Rose Petal." Daddy's nose twitches, reminding me of Joseph. "I'm not going to watch 'cause it's bad luck. So it's up to you to keep an eye on that horse. When I ask his position, you tell me how many horses are in front of him. You got it?"

"Okay. I can do that."

"*They're* off," reverberates from speakers. The horses charge out of the holding area, their hoofs thrashing the dirt. My heart beats as loudly as their thunder. The crowd roars, shouting at the monitors, urging the horses to forge ahead, as though the huge beasts can hear them. The men riding the horses are petite like women, dressed in black-and-white striped uniforms. They whip the reigns and kick the horses' girths with their heels.

"Where's the three, Rosie Petal. How's she doing?" Daddy's back is turned away from the monitor.

The horses are meshed together, and I'm all mixed up. I don't want my father to blame me if he loses.

"Where is it?" Daddy asks again.

Refocusing, I spot number three. "He's second in line, but the number two is catching up to him," I say, as if his fate is mine.

The horses slow at a bend, and the gallant three suddenly takes the lead. Jumping up and down, I shout, "She won. She won. Our horse won."

Smiling, Daddy sheds years off his face; it is all because of me. The losers surrounding us curse, tearing their tickets and adding them to the pile of litter already on the floor. I feel small among these giant scavengers, chewing fingernails black from newspaper ink.

"Let's go study for the next race." Daddy loops my arm and drags me along with him.

Mama's still at the table, shaded by an umbrella. Teresa's peering over a barbed wired fence in awe of the parade of horses lining up for the next race.

"How'd you do?" Mama asks. She's not wearing makeup, and her face is bronzed and glowing. It looks like the sun is shining beneath the layers of her skin.

"We won," I say, running over to my mother. Hugging her shoulders, I add, "And it's all because of me."

Taking a seat on the bench, Daddy studies the program as if he is going to be tested. Two minutes before post time we hurry inside onto the same line where we placed the previous bet; it is bad luck to change tellers. Daddy examines the tickets before we stray from the line. It is also bad luck to switch posts, so we plant ourselves in front of the exact same monitor we watched earlier. Again, Daddy turns his back, relying on my eyes.

This time, I never take my eyes off the horse we bet on, and Daddy doesn't ask its position. The second race seems to be faster than the first. I hold my breath until the number two horse on which he bet whizzes past the finish line.

"You can look now, Daddy. We won. We won."

My father swings around, lifts me into the air, and twirls me around. It's been a long time since he has done this, and I'm embarrassed, feeling too big and gawky to be twirled around. I think he notices. He sets me down on my feet.

"You can have whatever you want, Rose Petal." His mood is as charged as the hectic atmosphere.

With his elbows on the counter at a food concession, Daddy orders a hot dog with the works and popcorn with extra butter for me. Nibbling on the jumbo dog, he reviews the program for the next race.

"It's two minutes to post, Rosie. Let's go," he says, swatting my butt with the program.

This time, at the window, Daddy empties his pockets of all the money he won on the previous races. He shoves it through the narrow opening.

"Shouldn't we save some for the next race?" I say, with my mouth full of popcorn.

"This is the last race," he says.

For the final time we take our places under the lucky monitor. Once again, Daddy turns away. He's gnawing the inside of his cheek and tapping his foot. He even covers his ears this time. Crossing my heart, my fingers, and my legs, I whisper good luck to the number five horse, but when the bell sounds, the five breaks coming out of the gate.

Unsure of what that means, I turn slowly to ask Daddy to explain; but when I see the sweat dripping off his forehead as he shreds the tickets into tiny pieces, cursing his dead mother and the father he never met, I understand it is not good news.

On the bus ride back to the hotel Mama rants, "You never know when to quit."

"You're a bunch of jinxes," he says, taking a seat in the back, away from us.

"Don't blame us for the mistakes you make," Mama says.

CHAPTER EIGHTEEN

On the third day of our trip Daddy's gone when we wake up. The room is sticky and dull. Without waking Mama for her permission, Teresa and I decide to take a walk. We mosey up and down the boardwalk, regretting having spent all our money. Too hungry and thirsty to hang around in the relentless heat, we return to the room to guzzle water from the bathroom tap. So we don't have to listen to the angry growls in our stomachs, we sleep.

Daddy barges in, just as the sun is beginning to set.

"What are you all doing in bed?" he says, clapping his hands. "Come on, get up; we're going out for supper."

Mama sits up. She looks around the room as though she has forgotten where she is.

"Antonette, there's a diner down the street."

"Yeah," I say. "Teresa, wake up; we're going to the diner."

Mama stretches and purrs like a cat. Sitting up, she clips the cigarette dangling from Daddy's lips and takes a long, deep drag.

"I got a headache. I'm going to stay here," she says, yawning.

"Please come," Teresa says. "You haven't eaten all day."

"Bring me back a cheeseburger," Mama says, stepping outside to breathe in some fresh air for the first time that day. She sits on a plastic chair and swings one leg over the other.

"Suit yourself," Daddy says, sweeping up pennies and nickels collecting dust on the dresser.

The restaurant is air conditioned. A blonde hostess with navy blue eyelids and red lipstick escorts us to a table in the far corner of the dining area. She tosses three menus on the table.

"Order whatever you want," Daddy says, skimming his.

Perusing the glossy menu, my stomach gurgles as if it can see and smell the quarter-pound of beef garnished with lettuce, tomato, and ridged fries.

"I'll have a hamburger with extra cheese, please. And a bowl of chicken soup with stars," Teresa says, when the waitress returns.

Unable to choose, I change my mind three times before deciding on a grilled cheese sandwich with bacon. Daddy requests a plain hamburger and black coffee.

Waiting for our meal to be served, I swing my legs under the table. Teresa flips through the mini-jukebox, reading off titles of songs. Scanning the dining room, observing the patrons, I eye a family in a circular booth. A girl and boy about the same age as Joseph and me sit regally with straight backs and hands folded in their laps. I assume the man is their father by the way he tweaks the tip of the girl's nose, triggering a squeaky giggle. Seeing that gesture, I reposition my chair to be closer to Daddy's and rest my head on his arm. But he doesn't respond. He continues to flip through the *Daily News* that someone's left behind.

Envying the family, I conjure up images of what I think they're lives are like. I imagine they're twins and that both have rooms of their own. Hers is painted pale pink, with a white dresser against the wall and a gold carousel of horses playing "Mary Had a Little Lamb." I visualize the boy's room to be like Joseph's at the Welles', and I wonder whether my brother still collects baseball cards and performs magic tricks.

"How long are we staying here, anyway?" Teresa asks, interrupting my thoughts.

"Don't know," Daddy says, tapping a fork on the table.

A waitress approaches, maneuvering three large platters onto the table. Large breasts bulge from her black-and-white uniform. Her fingernails are painted red and curve down. She plops the dishes onto the table.

"Would you like anything else?"

Glancing at Daddy, I ask, "Can I have a Tab?"

"Get whatever you want. Bring three of them," he says into the woman's cleavage.

She seems pleased with the attention he's showing her boobs. She winks at him.

"I'll be right back."

Biting into the sandwich, I singe my tongue on the melted cheddar. "Ouch."

"Stop acting like you never ate before," Daddy says.

I blow on the sandwich before I take another bite. Daddy gobbles his burger, and he and I finish our meals before Teresa is through salting and peppering hers.

Daddy picks his teeth with the edge of a matchstick and then lights a butt he picks out of the ashtray. When the waitress reappears with our Tabs, he asks, "Who wants ice cream?"

Although I'm suspicious of his generosity, a root beer float is tempting. Teresa chooses a strawberry hot fudge sundae and a hamburger to go for Mama.

Again, the waitress disappears and returns with our dessert and a burger wrapped in foil.

"Will that be all, doll?" she says, tearing our bill off a little book she keeps in an apron pocket.

"That's all," Daddy says.

Adding the bill, using her fingers, as I used to before I learned how to add in my head, she whispers, "The dessert's on me." She smacks the bill on the table in front of Daddy, leaning in a bit more than she needs to.

Daddy reaches into his left shirt pocket and then his right. He stands and skims his hands around his body.

"For heavens sake," he says, now towering over the petite woman. She has to tilt her head back to look up at him.

"What's wrong, doll?" she asks.

"I left my wallet in our room. I'll run back to get it. Do you mind?"

"Are you staying in our hotel?" she says, stepping closer to our father. I can see sweat prickles above her upper lip. I glance at Teresa, and she pretends to stick her finger down her throat. We giggle.

"We're in room 303. I'll be back in a second." He backs away from the aggressive woman. "Bring more Tabs for the girls," he adds, rushing toward the exit.

The woman stares at Daddy until he's out the door and then saunters over to another table requesting more coffee.

It's a while before the woman returns with our Tabs.

"Your Daddy come back yet?" she says, sponging the table.

"Not yet," I say, fiddling with a soiled napkin.

"You girls here alone with your Daddy?"

"No, our *mother's* here, too," I say, a little more rudely than I think she liked. She huffs away.

After a long while, Teresa says, "What's taking him so long? Mama's burger is soggy already."

Rising from the seat, I say, "I'll go see."

Outdoors, the humidity slaps me in the face like a sopping towel. I glance up and down the block, hoping to see my father's figure forging toward me, but deep in my burning chest I know he won't be coming back.

"Did you find him?" Teresa asks as I take the seat my father had occupied.

"He's not coming back," I say, wiping the perspiration off my forehead with the back of my sweaty hand.

"What do you mean?" Her eyes bulge with confusion.

"What don't you understand? He's not coming back." My tongue plows through my clenched teeth, and I sound like I'm lisping.

"What are we going to do?" Teresa makes the sign of the cross, and tears well up in her eyes. I regret warning her of my suspicion.

Behind her a round clock ticks above the cash register. Aware of people beginning to stare, I concentrate on the black handles clicking the minutes past. Finally, the manager approaches us.

"Can you please tell me your last name?"

"Scarpiella," I say.

He practically skips back to the counter for the black phone wedged between the register and a bowl of mints. He waves his hand like a conductor as he spits into the receiver. A voice screams in my head: "Get out of here." But my body doesn't get the message quickly enough, and before I can budge the manager is hovering over us again.

"I think there's been a mistake. No one by that name is registered in our hotel," he announces, loudly enough for the other diners to hear. "Is the man who left you here your father?" He directs his questioning at Teresa.

Teresa stands, opens her mouth to say something to the balding man, but rather than words, chunks of undigested meat, bananas, and strawberries explode out of her mouth, splattering the table, floor, and the man's starched white shirt.

"Please, mister, can we go?" I say, kicking back my chair to help Teresa. Every diner has stopped eating and is staring at us. Some gag from the rancid odor.

"Oh, dear, what a mess." The manager steps back and removes his jacket. He wipes his shirt with a towel a bus boy has come running over with. Another charges toward us with a mop, but Teresa is frozen in the puddle of vomit.

I wrap my arm around her waist to help her out of the mess. She's shaking and crying.

"You stop right there or I'll call the police," the manager shouts.

As I turn to explain I was only trying to get out of the way, another man shuffles toward us. His back is rounded as if a pillow is stuffed between his shoulder blades. His wife smiles at me from their table.

"Is that necessary?" the man says to the manager in a scolding tone.

"I have to call the police. I've been robbed." Thick blue veins protrude from his bald head.

"These kids shouldn't take the blame here. It's not their fault." The stranger places a warm and gentle hand on my shoulder.

"That's too bad. Who's going to pay their bill? This isn't a shelter for the poor," the manager says, rolling up his shirt sleeves.

Opening a leather wallet as worn as the flesh on his hands, the stranger says, "I'll pay their check plus give you an extra ten dollars. Just let them go; we both know what happened here."

"Well, that's very noble of you." The manager wipes his forehead with one hand and snatches the stranger's money with the other.

"Do you know where to find your parents?" The old man's eyes seem to be sinking into the loose dark skin around them.

"I think so," I say, clutching Teresa's trembling hand.

"You tell your father, if he ever steps a foot into this diner again…" the manager interrupts.

"Run along, then," the old man says.

Without saying thank you, Teresa and I scurry out of the diner like cockroaches. On the steaming pavement my feet thud in pace with my pulse. What if our parents have left us for good? What would we do? Bottled fear explodes into anger when I fling open the motel door. Mama is lying on the bed; Daddy is sitting on the edge, still picking his teeth with a matchstick.

"How could you?" I scream.

"What happened? Did he call the police?" he asks, standing.

"No, but he threatened to," I scream at my father but focus on Mama's reaction.

"What are you talking about?" Mama sits up.

"Daddy, how could you?" Teresa shivers as if she's trapped in a foot of snow rather than in a steaming hotel room in the middle of August.

"What else was I supposed to do? You were hungry, and now you're not." He shrugs.

"What did you do?" Mama says glowering at our father.

"What's the big deal?"

"You left them alone, you bastard?" She jumps up. Her shorts are wrinkled and baggy.

"Oh, come on, Rose Petal," he says, patting my head. "It wasn't that bad, was it?"

Swatting at his hand, I say, "Don't act like you weren't in on it, Mama. You knew what he was up to. That's why you didn't come with us."

"I didn't know," she says, fluffing a pillow. She lies on the bed with her shoulders leaning into the pillow.

"It's not Mama's fault," Teresa snivels.

"I'm out of here," Daddy says, tucking loose cigarettes in his front pocket before his second grand exit of the night.

From the inside out my body shudders as if my blood is boiling. Mama kneads her temples, staring into space like she always does when she can't lie quickly enough. I ache to smack her across the face, to see her lip bleed. Pounding both fists on the mattress, I grit, "How could you?"

Teresa blocks me, "It's not Mama's fault."

"I'm warning you, Rosie. Don't make me slap you."

Many times that tone frightened me, but it doesn't at the moment. I shove Teresa and rip the sheets off the bed. Yanking Mama's scaling feet, I drag her toward the edge. Twisting her torso, she manages to release a foot and jabs her toes into my chest.

Letting go, I scream, "I hate you. I hate you both."

Mama springs up like a jack-in-the-box, grabs a shoe, and flings it at me. The heel nicks my back. I dodge into the bathroom, escaping the second heel.

Leaning my back against the wall, I kick the door.

Mama's panting as if she just sprinted a mile.

"And I hate you, too, you little brat. If you know what's good for you, you won't come out of there."

"You let him leave us there. Just like you left Joseph."

In the middle of the night Teresa taps on the door. "Come to bed, Rosie."

My legs are cramped, and my back is stiff. But not as stiff as my heart. I open the door. Teresa is in bed. I slide in next to her. My back is toward her.

"You shouldn't have said those things to Mama," Teresa says, twirling strands of my hair.

"She deserves worse than that," I say.

The next morning a yellow-and-black station wagon motors into the motel's parking lot. The taxi driver estimates the fare to our destination to be twenty-five dollars.

"No problem," Daddy says.

The promise of home where I can find refuge in the familiarity of the tightly-spaced buildings and the grime of the city lightens my mood. When our journey began there was chatter and laughter, but on the ride home there is silence as thick as the humidity. In the backseat, my hair flaps in the hot breeze, slapping my face and tickling my nose. We drive past the Pine Barrens. It seems as though we're still and the trees are speeding by.

"I have to go to the bathroom," I announce half an hour into the ride.

"You'll have to wait until we get home," Daddy says over his shoulder.

"Stop the car," Mama says.

"Lady, the next rest stop is about three miles away," the driver says, his black bushy eyes blinking in the rearview mirror.

"She can't wait that long. Pull over."

"Jesus Christ," Daddy says. "That's the problem with these kids; they always get their way."

The driver careens to the shoulder of the road. I think for a second we are going to tip over.

"Come on," Mama says. She leans on the open door. "Both of you out now; we're not stopping again."

Scooting out of the wagon, I snub Mama and vanish into the tall weeds and thick brush. The air is cool within the denseness of the trees. The roar of the speeding traffic is muffled; the dank ground is soft beneath me. Mud squishes between my toes. The area is littered with beer cans and pine cones. There is evidence of a campfire, probably set by mischievous teenagers defying the "No Trespassing" signs. Teresa and I squat separately behind bushes. After peeing, I pick up a beer can and swig it; the hot liquid tastes like urine smells. I spit it out, ditching the can when Mama calls for us to hurry. As Teresa and I walk back to the cab, Mama stays behind to relieve her bladder.

The driver exits the highway and screeches up to a red light. Over his shoulder Daddy mouths words to Mama that are impossible for me to decipher, but apparently Mama can.

"Turn right at the next corner." Daddy dangles his arm from the opened window.

"That's it—the third house on the right. The white one with the red shutters," he adds.

The driver idles in front of a house with a southern-style wraparound porch, protected by a rusting chain-link fence. Teresa, Mama, and I scoot out.

"Oh, for Christ's sake, I forgot my wallet at the hotel." Daddy's tone is calm and even like it had been at the diner.

The taxi driver yells in an unfamiliar language.

"Hold your horses. I'll go inside and get your money. Just wait one minute; I'll be right back," Daddy says.

My feet twitch, anticipating our cue.

"Girls, the back door is open," Daddy says, shooing us away.

Stumbling through the gate, we startle a man in a straw hat, tending a tomato garden. Dashing across his yard, we bump into a teenage boy mowing a lawn in the next yard. We scuttle down an alleyway without stopping to visit with a stray cat nursing kittens in a rubber tire. Sweat pours out of my body, soaking my hair and clothes, but I don't stop until I glimpse the confectionery store. There, I finally collapse under the awning, kicking off my flip-flops. The skin on my big toe is torn and bleeding. Teresa plops down beside me, gasping for air. When we manage to catch our breaths, we don't speak; we just stare out onto the street, absorbed in our thoughts.

CHAPTER NINETEEN

It's rumored that Meredith Bailey, a twenty-five-year-old Irish Catholic widow, has purchased the duplex next door to the confectionery store with money awarded to her from a life insurance policy after her husband fell off a scaffold to his death. The young single mother occupies the second-floor unit with two toddler girls, Abbey and Ginny, and rents the first floor apartment to a single father and his sixteen-year-old son, Victor.

Mama and Meredith meet at the butcher's one afternoon and become fast friends, despite their age difference. They begin visiting each other, swapping recipes and parenting techniques. Meredith is spunky, and I am enamored of her boldness. Most mothers don't work, but Meredith is different. Not only is she the only woman on the block who owns a home, but she is also the assistant manager at the factory that manufactures snaps and buttons. She offers Mama a position on the assembly line on the day shift. At first Mama refuses, reluctant to give up the security of her monthly welfare check, but when Meredith explains how much more she'd make by working, Mama accepts. That's when I acquire the job of sitting for Meredith's girls every night.

When I first begin sitting for Meredith, Mama stops by to check on the girls and me before she retires to bed for the night. She snoops around in the cupboards, snatching what she assumes her young friend won't notice missing: cans of corn, packages of saltines, plum tomatoes. She doesn't stay long; Meredith doesn't allow cigarette smoking in her home, and Mama can't last more than fifteen minutes without one. Clutching her stolen treats, she says, "Rosie, lock the door behind me." One fall night, after the girls are asleep and Mama has come and gone, I go down to the rear yard to sneak a cigarette I clipped from her purse. The wind swishes around piles of leaves that Meredith had raked earlier. Victor, the boy who lives on the first floor, is on the stoop smoking. I'm in stocking feet, but he still hears me.

Tilting his head back, he says, "Hi."

I want to turn around and run back upstairs, but I'm more embarrassed to run away than I am to stay. He spots the cigarette squeezed between my fingers.

"Need a light?" he says, flicking a Bic.

My eardrums thump. I've been curious about the motherless boy. I've watched him come and go from the house, but I've never spoken to him. Victor's straight brown hair is centered, bobbing on his bony shoulders. Hazel eyes glint under the porch light, and when he smiles, his square jaw juts forward. Meredith told me he dropped out of high school and plays guitar during the hours when most people sleep. She complains that he and his band, The Pit Stops, hamper her sleep with their pounding drums and amplifiers, rocking the house from the basement up, and she threatens to evict them. But he lost his mother to cancer when he was only nine years old, and she feels sorry for him. Leaning into the blue flame, I inhale, tasting the butane.

"Are you the new sitter?" he says.

"Yeah."

"There's room here," he says, patting the stoop.

"No thanks."

Victor squeezes the lit head of the cigarette with his fingers and stands. In bare feet he's almost as tall as my father.

"Got to go anyway," he says. "See you around."

"See you around," I wave.

As soon as he disappears, I run upstairs, forgetting to put the cigarette out. I douse it in the sink and stash it deep into the garbage. Tossing around on the sofa, squeezing a pillow to my chest, I go over the encounter word by word in my head. I can hardly wait to tell Teresa I've finally met the boy next door. Stretching out on the sofa, rehearsing what interesting things I'll say to impress Victor the next time we meet, I doze.

On the way to school the following morning, I babble to Teresa about the encounter.

"Is he really a hippie?" she asks, balancing hardcover books under her arm.

"Just because he has long hair doesn't mean he's a hippie," I say, regretting telling her at all.

"Mama says he is."

"He's really cute," I say, trying not to sound too enthralled.

"He's too old for you."

"You're just jealous," I say, skipping ahead. But I know that isn't true. Teresa is going steady with a boy named Rocco Dibellis, whom she met at the ice-skating rink. Mama permits her to date him on Saturday nights with a nine o'clock curfew. Teresa is careful not to be late, even when our parents aren't home to know. Mama likes Rocco, noting that a smile says a lot about a person. But I can't get past his black eyes. To me, they're bottomless, a place to go if you want to vanish forever.

One Saturday morning while flipping the shade up, I spy Victor dashing through traffic across the avenue. Our paths haven't crossed since the night on the porch, but I'd like to learn more about him. I slip into sweatpants and a hooded shirt and hurry next door. Holding my breath, I turn the knob and exhale when it clicks open. I quickly slip inside. Above me I can hear the patter of Abbey and Ginny, like mice scrambling for food.

The apartment is similar to Meredith's but reversed in its layout. Entering one of the bedrooms, I stumble over a heap of dirty clothes. The shades are drawn, and only a sliver of light beams through a tear in the shade. When I open the closet, a light flicks on. The narrow space is crammed with dresses, skirts, blouses, and women's sandals and sling backs. I assume they belong to Victor's dead mother. On a vanity dust covers lipsticks, brushes, and eye shadows, as if they are expecting the woman's return. Before I have a chance to peek inside Victor's room, the strumming of a guitar jolts me, and I flee the apartment, sprinting up the stairs to Meredith's.

"What are you doing up so early on a Saturday morning," Meredith says, pouring oatmeal into bowls for Abbey and Ginny.

"Rosie, Rosie," the girls squeal at my feet, like hungry puppies. I lift Abbey, and Ginny begs for me to pick her up, too.

"Take your thumb out of your mouth, Ginny," Meredith commands.

Abbey giggles at her sister being scolded. I set her into a high chair, and Ginny climbs onto the chair next to me.

"Oatmeal?" Meredith says, scooping a full ladle into a third bowl.

"Thanks," I say, sniffing the cinnamon and butter.

"Hey, what are you doing tonight?" she asks, settling into a chair with a steaming cup of tea.

"Nothing."

"I have a date," she says. "Interested in earning extra cash?"

"Sure." I slurp the gooey oatmeal.

"Great."

Later that evening I center part my long, straight hair and brush on pink powdered rouge. I carefully iron Teresa's favorite paisley blouse and a pair of tied-dyed jeans I purchased at Haynes with the cash I earned from babysitting.

At Meredith's I bathe the girls and read them *Alice in Wonderland* three times before they fall asleep. From the living room window I strain to listen for Victor's footsteps on the back porch. It's late, and I'm about to surrender my post when I finally hear the thump of his bare feet.

I comb my hair and flatten it onto my cheeks, so just the tip of my nose and narrow eyes are exposed, just like Cher's. But when I'm done, I look more like Raggedy Ann than Cher, so I wipe the rouge off. I grab a cigarette from my denim jacket and bounce down the steps and onto the porch.

Victor sits on the stoop, pulling loose threads from the ragged edges of his faded Levis. It is damp and chilly the way fall is when winter is threatening to take control. I pull my sleeves down, and I hope Victor doesn't confuse my shivers with giddy nerves.

Waving a cigarette, I ask, "Can I get a light?"

Glancing up, he says, "Hey, Rosie." We have never been introduced. Accepting his butt to light my own, I wonder how he knows my name.

Joining him on the step, I inhale musk oil and burning incense. It tickles my nose, and I sneeze three times.

"Bless you, bless you, bless you," he says.

"Thanks," I say, hoping he can't see my moist nostrils.

"Are you sitting for Meredith's girls all night?" he asks, puffing a Marlboro.

"Yeah, they're asleep now."

"Why don't you stop down to the Pit and hang out for a while?"

"I don't know...the girls," I say, exhaling puffs of smoke into circles.

"They won't wake up," he says, pulling me up by an elbow. "We can use a real audience," he adds, smiling, revealing tobacco-stained teeth.

Victor flips the lit cigarette into a pile of curled-up leaves, and I crunch it under my sneaker before following him through the double doors leading to the cellar. My gut roils, warning me not to continue, but I ignore it.

The cinderblock walls are painted black. The only light source is a string of red Christmas bulbs dangling from the beams. Futons, ashtrays, and pipes are scattered across the cement floor. The burned rubber reeking in the windowless room blankets my hair and clothes.

The Pits consist of four members: an organist, a drummer, a lead vocalist, and Victor, the guitarist. The other boys appear to be a few years older than Victor, with long sideburns, mustaches, and cratered skin. Victor introduces us, and I wave, already forgetting their names. The young men pass around what I think is a cigarette. Inhaling it I find out otherwise. Launching into a hacking fit, I'm sure my cheeks are as red as the Christmas lights.

Victor chuckles. "It's a joint, not a cigarette."

"I know that," I say, too embarrassed to admit I learned about marijuana in health class but I never touched a joint before.

Holding the joint with the tips of his fingers, he inhales and seams his lips shut for a second before exhaling.

"That's how it's done." His eyes water immediately.

Taking the sizzling flat butt from him, I mimic Victor's actions, but again it singes the walls of my throat, and I cough and choke. Victor snaps open a can of Budweiser.

"Take a sip. You'll get used to the burn."

The ice-cold liquid soothes the lining of my esophagus, and just a few swigs relax me.

When the Pits begin to play again, I flop onto a futon as though I'm familiar with their routine. The music massages my tense muscles, and I smile effortlessly at Victor, banging his hips on his instrument, prancing on stage in bare feet. My tongue is dry and rough. Next to the futon on the floor is a six pack of beer. I help myself to another, snapping the can open like this is a regular habit of mine. I gulp it to quench my thirst.

The second beer relaxes me more, to the point where I don't think I'll ever be able to stand again. My ears buzz, and I worry I might be stuck on the futon forever. I try to focus on the music, but the cellar is black, and the room appears to be shrinking. Suddenly, I need to get out of there. Somehow I manage to pull myself off the futon. Waving goodbye, I stumble toward the double doors. In the dark I cling to the railing to climb the steps. My legs feel like bags of sand.

Upstairs, the light stings my eyes, and I switch off all the lamps. Just as I situate myself comfortably on the sofa, a car door slams in the driveway. The room is spinning, and I burp stale beer. Meredith fumbles with her keys, and the door clicks open. She flips the light on when she enters the living room.

"Are you asleep?" she whispers.

"You're home early." My words are slurred, and I hope she just thinks it's because she has woken me.

"Boring," she says, kicking off leather heels. "You can stay tonight, if you want."

"I think I'll go home. Teresa expects me to go to mass with her tomorrow." I rise slowly, as if a thousand-pound sack is on my shoulders.

Meredith rummages through her leather satchel and pulls out a ten. "Keep the change."

Avoiding her eyes, I swipe the bill and head toward the door, mumbling thanks, fearful she'll whiff the beer on my breath.

Relieved Mama is working the midnight shift and Teresa is still out on her date with Rocco, I scour my teeth and tongue and guzzle three glasses of water. Suddenly starving, I raid the nearly empty refrigerator, devouring slices of baloney hardening at the edges and half of a potato frittata stored under a plate.

Feeling refreshed, full, and not as high, I undress and flop into bed. I've taken to sleeping on the top bunk, which was supposed to be reserved for Joseph. Staring at the ceiling, I ponder whether or not I should confide in Teresa that I had been to the Pit; of course I won't tell her that I overindulged in marijuana and beer.

Below our window, which is cracked just a bit, I hear voices. I hop off the bunk and lift the window higher. I can clearly hear Rocco's accusing tone.

"I saw you looking at that guy in the diner."

"No. I wasn't."

"You're lying to me...." He mumbles something else, but I'm unable to make out the words.

"I love you," Teresa whimpers. And I imagine her full lips puckering.

"Swear on God," he says.

Teresa has managed to hold onto her Catholic faith over the years, and it shocks me to hear her use God's name in vain.

Rocco's footsteps float away. In a mousy voice Teresa shouts after them, "Don't go."

I want to scream out the window, "Don't beg him. Let him go." But I remain silent. I don't dare let on I've been eavesdropping. I shut the window and climb back into bed. Teresa comes in and doesn't turn on the light, but I can hear her sniveling.

"What's wrong?" I say in the dark.

"Nothing; I'm just tired," she says.

I hop off the bed to switch on the light. The rims of Teresa's eyes are pink and wet like the stray kittens that sleep out on the fire escape.

"Why are you crying, then?"

She turns away to undress behind the closet door. I wait for her to finish. She creeps out, tying a robe around her narrow waist. She sits on the edge of the bottom bunk.

"Rocco wants to get married after graduation."

I think I must have misunderstood and say, "What?"

"Rocco asked me to marry him." She twirls her hair and forces a smile.

I kneel at her feet. "You're not old enough to get married."

"I'll be seventeen. The same age Mama was when she married Daddy."

"Where will you live? Rocco doesn't even have a job." I'm on my feet again, pacing.

"Yes, he does, at the Hess station."

"Why do you want to marry someone who treats you mean?" My hands are on my hips, and I suddenly feel like Mama. The temperature seems to be rising. I crank the window up again, sticking my head over the sill. There is no moon, no stars, just blankness. I gulp the air and duck back inside, slamming the window down.

Teresa shivers. "He doesn't treat me mean. He loves me, and I love him," she says, untying her robe and slipping under the sheets.

"He makes you cry all the time, and he bosses you around like he owns you," I say, still pacing in front of her.

"You don't know what it's like to be in love." Teresa rolls away from me. Between her shoulder blades her nightgown hangs low, revealing a rainbow of bruises on her sallow flesh.

"What are those marks on your back?"

Ignoring my question, Teresa tugs the sheet up over her shoulders.

"I'm telling Mama," I say, snapping the sheet off her.

"Don't you dare." She pops up. Her eyes bulge, filmed with tears.

"What did he do?"

"It was my fault. Just forget it, Rosie." She lies back down. "It'll never happen again. If you tell Mama, I swear I'll never forgive you."

Suddenly, I'm exhausted and feel I've aged ten years in one night. Resting on the edge of Teresa's bed, I say, "Can I sleep with you tonight?"

She slides back to the wall and lifts the covers. I snuggle in next to her. I feel her breath on my neck. A chill rattles in my chest. I whisper, *Don't go. Don't you go away and leave me, too.*

CHAPTER TWENTY

Winter gloom hovers until early April like an unwanted guest. The power company has disconnected our service, the oil tank is dry, and the rent hasn't been paid for months. Daddy rigs the wires to get power from the landlord's service, but the landlord discovers what he's done and threatens to evict us. Over a cup of coffee Mama promises to work double shifts to catch up, and he agrees to let us stay.

Daddy doesn't even beg Mama's forgiveness when he loses his job at the port unloading cartons of produce. He is meaner too, hollering and criticizing us all the time.

One Saturday Mama is at midnight bingo with Adele, and Teresa is home early from her movie date with Rocco. In our room she's busy on the top bunk embroidering a vine of roses on her bellbottoms, and I'm snuggled beneath her, engrossed in the last chapter of *The Clue of the Broken Locket*.

Hanging her head over the bed, she asks, "Rosie, can you please get the scissors under the kitchen sink for me?"

Daddy and his buddies have been slumped over the table engaged in an intense poker game for the last twenty-four hours. At sixteen Teresa's breasts are full and her nipples pointed; she hates the way men gawk at her. At fourteen I pray for a sign that I'll grow breasts.

"I don't want to walk past those creeps either. Get them yourself."

Still looking at me upside down, she says, "If you don't, I'll tell Mama you've been hanging around with Victor."

"Go on and tell. I dare you. If you squeal on me, I'll squeal on you," I say.

"You're such a baby," Teresa says. Her head disappears. "I don't know when you're going to grow up," she adds.

This makes me mad. I crawl out of the bed and tug the bellbottoms out of her hands.

"Give them back," she says, hopping off the bunk.

Taunting her, I twirl them over my head. "Make me."

"Give them to me," she screeches, stomping her bare foot.

With that Daddy barges in without bothering to knock.

"What's the racket about in here?" His face is hard and uneven like a stone that has fallen and chipped. As if an invisible hand forces me forward, I lunge at Teresa, clawing at her skin. Tears huddle in the corners of her eyes as she scratches me back like a kitten pawing a mouse.

"Hey, guys, come in here and see this action." Daddy calls to his comrades. The men come scampering over to our room to see what the commotion is all about.

"Teresa, she's open on the right," Daddy says, circling us, as though he's a referee in a boxing ring. Our bodies twist, and Teresa's face looks as distorted as mine feels. But I refuse to be seen as the weak one.

"My money's riding on you, Teresa. Don't let me down, girl," Daddy says, fanning bills in our faces.

"I bet five bucks on the little one," someone wagers.

Bent forward, my head almost touches my knees, and I am unable to see the men who are rooting for and against us.

"I'll double your bet," Daddy counters. "The little one is going down. You got her now, Tre. Stay on your saddle, girl," Daddy adds.

But my sister releases the clump of my hair clutched in her fist; I lose my balance and fall hard on my knees.

"You were winning; what'd you go and quit for?" Daddy scoffs at Teresa.

Hugging her breasts, she slips past the gaping men.

"You kids don't know how to have any fun," Daddy says. And one by one the men return to their posts.

Glancing at my reflection, I can see scratches and trickles of blood, but it's the bruises swelling inside of me that hurt.

Wearing only a nightgown, I sneak out of our apartment in bare feet. Gravitating toward the music, I duck into the Pit, grateful for its painted black walls and colored lights camouflaging my mottled skin and red swollen eyes. I am relieved to find Victor alone, reclining on a bare stained mattress I had helped him haul from a neighbor's curb.

Beside him, his guitar is nestled like a sleeping dog. The heels of his feet are crusted; his chest is bare except for a blood red crucifix tattooed between his breasts. He sits up and hits on the joint smoldering in the ashtray.

"What's up?" I say, flopping on the edge of the mattress.

"Those losers didn't bother to show up for practice again. They just want to get high and get chicks." Passing the joint, he adds, "I want to be famous like Mick and the Stones."

"Yeah," I say, inhaling.

Leaning back into an uncovered stained pillow, he says, "Hey, why are you in your nightgown?"

Shrugging my shoulders, I say, "I just felt like a quick hit, so I didn't bother to dress."

"You're a funny girl, Ro," he says, massaging my arm. His raspy whisper of a voice caresses my hurt. He leans forward. "Hey, Ro, you ever kiss anyone before?"

"Sure, plenty of times." I lie effortlessly.

"I don't believe you," he says, maneuvering the guitar onto the floor.

"Have so." I take a hit. I am beginning to relax.

"Prove it," he says widening his smile.

His hair is silkier than mine, and I have an urge to stroke it, but I don't move a muscle. I had dreamed of kissing Victor, even practiced on my pillow. Before I take my next breath, his tongue is sliding in and out of my mouth. It's slimy and tastes like the scent of musk exuding from his body. I close my eyes and tilt my head back, like the actresses in the romance movies I stay up watching on the late show.

Victor releases my tongue, and I gulp a pocket of air.

"That wasn't bad, but there's room for improvement," he says, putting his arms around my waist, pulling me closer to him.

"Oh," I say. My chest burns, and my lips are drenched with his saliva. I want to quit, but I don't want to act immature.

"Don't be so stiff. Move your tongue around mine, like it's dancing," he says before plowing his tongue into my mouth.

Responding to his instruction, I swirl my tongue around his as he slowly begins massaging the tips of my undeveloped nipples. My tongue is the only muscle moving in my body. Bells sound in my ears and Mama's warning: *Only whores let boys touch them.* I curl my fists up and pounce gently on Victor's chest to make him stop.

"What's wrong?" he asks, slurring inside my mouth.

I shove him harder, and he falls back, panting.

"I have to go. I really do."

"That's too bad, man, I'm just getting warmed up," he says, reaching for my arm as I pop off the bed.

"See you around," I say, hurrying toward the steps.

Back home, our room is dark when I creep in. "Tre, are you awake?"

She doesn't answer. I climb into bed, wrapping a blanket around me. Shivering, I whisper, "Tre, I'm sorry."

On Saturdays Teresa and I scour the bathroom, change bed linens, and mop the floors. After our chores are complete, we trot to McDonalds for burgers and fries before Rocco fetches her in his Cougar. Peeking through the shade, I wait for the car to disappear down the road before sneaking off to the Pit where Victor and I make out until my lips swell and my crotch is drenched. I allow him to fondle my breasts, but when he attempts to caress other parts of my body, I always guide his hands back up to my breasts. Smoking pot, drinking beer, and cursing become habits of mine. I like how the swear words I learned from my parents roll off my tongue, especially the word "fuck."

One Monday afternoon the school nurse excuses me for a bout of bad cramps. I ache for my bed where I can crunch my knees to my chin and moan in private. But from the street I hear my parents shouting. I'm not in the mood to deal with their assaults on each other, so I head to the dank Pit. My eyes adjust to the darkness and focus on the outline of Victor's muscular frame as he lies on his back, his hands tucked under his head, gazing at the ceiling. His guitar is next to him.

"What's happening," I say.

"Hey, man, what'd you cut school today?" he says cracking his knuckles over his head.

"Yeah, I couldn't deal today." Perusing a pile of albums, I choose Carole King.

"Wait. Listen to this song I wrote first." Victor swings his legs off the bed. Strands of hair hide his eyes.

Cuddling the album to my chest, I flop on the mattress next to him.

Victor adjusts the strings on the guitar, which is more like a body organ to him than an instrument. I am close enough to smell the stench of his stale sleepy breath and oily scalp, but nothing about him repulses me. Victor strums the guitar and hums in a low raspy voice before the words begin to flow.

"It's nearly dawn and time to rise, And I don't want to wake you, To see the regret in your eyes, I need you to stay, Ro, You make me feel so good, I can't let you go, Taking pieces of my heart...."

He strums a few more bars and stops. "That's as far as I got."

"Wow. You used my name."

"You like it so far?"

I respond by parting his lips with my tongue. Gripping my right hand, he guides it slowly across his bare chest and down to his groin. I don't pull away when he maneuvers my hand inside his unzipped jeans. The sensation is frightening and thrilling. I grope his stiff penis. It's thin, soft-skinned, and damp like putty. Jabbing his tongue deep into my throat, he clasps his hand over mine and squeezes. A hot stickiness oozes all over like a volcano erupting in my fist. Gagging from a sudden bleach odor, I pull away, wiping the smelly slime onto my jeans. Victor's eyes flutter, and a wave of regret crashes in my stomach. Suddenly, he isn't this cute guy anymore. He's gross, and I'm gross.

Victor gasps for air as if he's just succeeded in a relay race.

"I have to go."

Too embarrassed to meet his eyes, I rush to the steps, climbing them two at a time. Tears stream down my cheeks, and I'm trembling all over. Staggering down the alley to the front of the house, I jaywalk across the small patch of brown grass and bump into my father.

"Where are you coming from?" His bushy brows join together when he scowls.

"Meredith's," I say, knotting my trembling fingers behind my back.

"Why aren't you in school?"

"I had cramps..."

"You're lying. You were down in the basement with that hippie." The whites of his eyes are spilling out of his bulging sockets like milk.

"No, I wasn't." Stepping back from his raised hand, I trip on a hose and fall.

My father lifts me up by my hair and drags me down the alley and into the basement. The Who blares from speakers wired to the stereo.

Victor is standing at the mirror; his dungarees are zipped but unsnapped. I can't look at him. My bowels pulse.

"What were you doing with my daughter; do you know how old she is?" Daddy releases the clump of my hair and flails a fist in Victor's face.

Victor tucks strands of hair behind both ears and rubs his nose. He doesn't look much older than I do at that moment.

"I was just jamming and asked Ro to listen to a new song." The tremor in his voice sounds like the rattle in my chest.

"You stay away from her, you hippie son of a bitch." Daddy inches closer.

Without wincing, Victor betrays me. "She came down on her own; I didn't invite her." The words sting more than the knot on my head.

"Just stay away from her," Daddy says, grabbing my elbow and dragging me out.

Back home, Daddy pushes me through the door. Mama is sweeping up fragments of a broken ashtray, remnants of their argument. I'm sobbing and more embarrassed than the time I was caught stealing licorice strings from the candy store.

"What's wrong?" she asks, dropping the broom.

"You see what you raised here?" Daddy screams like a man on fire.

Mama looks frightened, and her cheeks rise with blood. She brushes my forehead with her lips. "Are you okay? Why aren't you in school?"

"She was with that hippie." Daddy scrubs his hands under the sink as if he's just touched something filthy.

Mama shoves me away. I try to explain. "The nurse sent me home because I had cramps, and I heard you…"

"Jesus Christ, I told you to stay away from that boy." She picks up the broom, and as I think she's going to swat me with it, I raise my hand to block her; but she stashes the broom into the narrow space between the refrigerator and stove.

"What are you going to do about this, Antonette?" My father interrupts, toweling dry his clean hands.

"But we weren't doing anything; we were listening to music," I say, licking snot off my upper lip.

"This is your fault." Mama points to Daddy. "This wouldn't happen if you were home instead of out gambling to support your shylocks."

Daddy's hands flail above his head as if he's lifting a heavy object. Sweat beads on his forehead and chin.

"Figures you'd find a way to pin this on me. The last thing I need is another mouth to feed," he adds before slamming the door behind him.

Mama lights a cigarette. She isn't even looking at me when she says, "Get out of my sight."

Locking the bathroom door, I strip off corduroy jeans and a turtleneck and climb into the tub. I run the water and scrub Victor's sticky slime off my hands with scalding water and rinse my mouth with soap. Remembering Mama's constant warnings about whores who get pregnant before they're married, I swish my body around in the water to rid it of the shame.

CHAPTER TWENTY-ONE

After "the episode"—that's how my indiscretion is referred to—Mama requests a shift change at the factory so she can keep an eye on me. On weekends I'm not allowed to go anywhere without Teresa and am forbidden to sit for Meredith. I regret losing the forty dollars a week I've been saving to find Joseph, but I am in no position to negotiate my fate.

The only reprieve from Mama's repulsion is school, where I burrow into my studies, managing all As every marking period. I'm so much more advanced than the other sophomores that the principal requests to see me in his office.

"Congratulations," he says.

"Thank you." I know I'm squealing, but I don't care. I've worked hard, and Mama and Daddy don't even notice. He then informs me that in September I can skip junior year and jump right into senior year.

I'm so excited I sprint the entire route home, anxious to boast about the good news to Mama and Teresa. The apartment is dark when I enter, but I can hear the bathroom faucet running behind the closed door.

"Mama, is that you? Are you okay Mama?" I turn the knob. It's locked.

I knock again, and the door swings open. Teresa's skin tone resembles over-boiled Brussels sprouts. Her pouting lips are cracked and gray.

"Are you sick?"

"I think I have a stomach virus." She saunters out and flops on the sofa. *General Hospital* is just beginning.

Curling up next to Teresa, I am so excited. "Guess what?"

"What?" She barely responds, and I can tell by her faraway look she's not really interested in anything I have to say. But I don't care; I have to brag.

"The principal said I can skip eleventh grade and go straight to twelfth in September."

"That's great…." Unable to complete her sentence, she bolts up and dashes to the kitchen sink. Buckets of liquid pour from her mouth.

I rake Teresa's hair away from her face and hold it in a ball on the back of her head so she can finish her business.

"Teresa, I think you should see the doctor."

When there is nothing left inside of her, she collapses onto a kitchen chair. Her eyes are glassy, and she smells like a moldy pair of socks. She breathes deeply and exhales. "I missed my period."

"What's that mean? What are you saying?" I ask, knowing very well from health class that missing your period is not a good thing.

"I think I'm pregnant." She drops her head between her legs. Her hair sweeps the floor.

Talking to the back of her head, I say, "That would mean you had sex."

"What am I going to do? Mama's going to kill me." Her voice sounds thick like the word "pregnant" does to me.

I want to kill her, too. For yielding to Rocco. For being so stupid. For committing a mortal sin and cementing her fate in the hell she pretends to believe in. But she looks frail, like a broken-winged sparrow Joseph and I had found on the road years back. We couldn't walk away from it. We stayed and mended its wing with a Popsicle stick. I understand this crisis cannot be healed in such a simple manner, but I will not let my sister deal with it alone. Kneeling at her feet, I lift her head. It's heavy. Strands of hair stick to her sweaty cheeks. All I can think to say is, "Holy shit."

———

Meredith is folding a bushel of laundry heaped on the sofa. *The Price Is Right* blares on the console.

"What's wrong with you two?" she asks, as if the word "pregnant" is scrawled on our faces.

Teresa reclines in a painted blue wicker rocker. Succeeding in convincing her to confide the dilemma to Meredith was one step; getting her to actually spill the words is another. Understanding her shame, I blurt it out in one breath so she doesn't have to.

"Teresa might be pregnant…or she's pretty sure she is."

Meredith refolds a bath towel twice before she musters advice.

"Don't jump to conclusions. I missed my period many times. The outcome is not always pregnancy."

"But I'm never late," Teresa says, finally lifting her eyes to meet Meredith's. Meredith sighs and eases onto the sofa; the vinyl whistles like a teapot.

"How late are you?"

"Two months."

"Have you told Rocco?"

"No."

"Good. First thing to do is get you a checkup. A woman's body is not always predictable. Your cycle could be changing. You shouldn't worry until you have the proper exam."

"See, Tre. You could just be changing." I exhale and plop on the arm of the rocker and massage Teresa's trembling hands.

"Could all be a mistake," Meredith says, untangling a bunch of socks.

Teresa signs the cross three times.

"Yeah, it could all be a mistake," I say, getting up to assist Meredith with the folding.

Outside a clinic, in a distant town, Meredith wiggles her wedding band off her fleshy finger and slips it onto Teresa's. "You know what to say?" Meredith says, arching her eyebrows.

"I'm a newlywed and my husband was unable to take off work."

"That's it." Meredith squeezes Teresa's shoulder. "You'll be okay."

Teresa begs me to stay with her in the examining room. Behind a sheer cotton curtain her silhouette undresses and drapes the paper garment a nurse had slung on a metal chair. To respect her privacy, I look away and glance around the room. It's sterile in all its whiteness, without even certificates boasting the doctor's degrees on the walls.

Teresa reappears from behind the curtain and slumps on the examining table as if her spine is as mortified as she is. A doctor and nurse charge into the room. The doctor gets right to the point, inquiring about the history of Teresa's health, penciling her answers onto a form; the nurse checks her blood pressure and plunges a thermometer under her tongue as though Teresa were a mannequin and not human.

In a nonchalant tone, suggesting he has explained the procedure a thousand times before, the doctor instructs Teresa to lower herself onto the table and insert her feet into the stirrups.

Exposing her this way triggers a rash of hives on her goose neck. Pinching her knees together, she says, "Rosie, please don't look."

Obliging her, I turn away.

As the doctor proceeds with the exam, he assures Teresa it will only last a few minutes and that she should try to relax. She groans at the snap of his latex gloves, and I imagine him poking inside my sister with gleaming sterile instruments. He's humming "Candy Man," and, reflexively, I begin to hum it, too.

After only a few verses, he tears off the gloves. From the corner of my eye, I see him push away from the cot on the wheels of his stool. At a low desk he scribbles his findings. I can't tell whether he's written yes or no.

Holding my breath, I turn around. The nurse is lifting Teresa's feet from the metal stirrups and eases her forward to the edge of the cot. My sister looks as though she has lost twenty pounds in twenty minutes. Her cheeks are flushed, and beads of sweat ooze from the pores on her nose. The doctor stands in front her. She is unable to confront the eyes that have glimpsed her internal soul. Wiping his bifocals with the corner of his bleached jacket, he clears his throat with one harsh cough.

"Congratulations, you're approximately six week's pregnant, young lady. I suggest you make an appointment for your next visit at the front desk," he adds before exiting.

Except for the tune of "Candy Man" playing over and over in my head, the room is as quiet as its walls are stark.

"What am I going to do?" Teresa whispers, gaping at me.

"I don't know."

The next morning Teresa exposes the truth about her vomiting bouts; Daddy is perusing the paper, chewing a pencil eraser. The confrontations our parents have engaged in through the years have been vicious and shocking, but never can I recall an argument that lead to my father even coming close to striking Mama. This is why none of us expects him to flip the table, crashing cups and a pint of milk onto the floor. A cereal bowl rolls across the room, slams into the wall, and splits smoothly in half. Lunging toward Mama, Daddy raises his right hand. It's trembling like a kite losing its sail. She doesn't wince, daring him with her glowering black eyes. He drops his hand to his side, shrugs his shoulders, and shuts himself into his room.

Teresa appears relieved that the worst is over, but I know better. Mama reaches into the silverware drawer, grabs her choice of weapon, and chases Teresa around the sofa, swatting a soup ladle at the back of her legs like she's half mad.

"What have you done but ruined your life."

"I'm sorry, I'm sorry," Teresa says, hiding behind me.

"Stop it," I say, gripping the ladle in midair before Mama's able to whack me with it.

Mama's head swivels and her eyes bulge. It's difficult to distinguish where her pupils end and irises begin. Panting and sweating, she plops into a chair; the bent ladle crashes to the floor. Mama sobs in her hands, harder than the time Daddy told her he lost three thousand dollars. Teresa crouches on the floor and rests her head in Mama's lap.

She whispers, "I'm so scared."

In the days following the explosive confession Daddy stays in his room as though nursing the flu. No one dares to grumble a word about the pregnancy. It's like we believe if it's not talked about maybe it hasn't happened.

But one night Teresa and I are lying on opposite sides of the couch watching *I Love Lucy* reruns when Mama returns from work.

"Teresa, I want to talk to you," she yells from the kitchen, busy unloading groceries before she even unzips her jacket.

Dread is etched in the lines around Teresa's eyes. Together, we rise from the sofa and shuffle into the kitchen. A cigarette is already dangling from Mama's lips. Tapping the table with a ragged fingernail, she says, "Teresa you're going to give the baby up for adoption." Her tone is adamant as if it is her child to give away.

Teresa signs the cross. Mama's solution doesn't surprise me; she knows how to walk away from a child.

"How could you?" I say, clutching Teresa's thickening waist.

Ignoring me, Mama says that becoming a mother at seventeen will ruin Teresa's life like it had ruined hers.

"If I didn't have you kids so young, my life would have been different. Less of a struggle. Is that what you want? To struggle you're whole damn life."

"Rocco wants to marry me, and I want to marry him," Teresa says. Clinging to each other, we back away from Mama's rage.

Bulldozing her fingers through her stubbornly graying roots, Mama is trying hard not to shout. "You think getting married solves anything? What are you supposed to do for money? A baby needs food and clothes and a roof over its head."

"Rocco's got a job…" Teresa says.

"You're too young to get married; you'll do as I say."

"I could never give my baby up," Teresa says, covering the slight bulge as if to protect the baby swimming around inside of her from the harsh words.

"Well, then, you have one other choice," Mama says turning away from us. She's in front of the kitchen sink. Her head is bowed. "Adele knows a doctor who can abort it. She offered to pay for it."

"Mama, how could you? That's a mortal sin. I can't. I won't." Teresa stomps away, covering her mouth as if she's going to vomit up Mama's words. The front door slams, and her wedged heels thud down the steps.

Spinning around, Mama raises a fist toward my chin. I think I'm going to spit on her, but instead I start to cry.

"I hope you learned a lesson here," she says.

CHAPTER TWENTY-TWO

Mama doesn't consent with her heart, but after a second visit to the clinic, the doctor informs us that the baby is due on or before December 8th. Mama doesn't have a choice but to give her blessing.

The last Friday in June, as Teresa's classmates parade in caps and gowns to accept their high school diplomas, Teresa strains to sit still while Mama curls her hair with a hot iron. Ringlets dance over her smoky eyes, creating a veil.

"I didn't want this for you," Mama snivels as though Teresa were going to have an arm amputated or something.

"But I'm happy," Teresa says, blinking false eyelashes.

"You have no idea what it's like, Teresa. None." Mama rubs Teresa's lips with a clear gloss.

"We'll be fine," Teresa says, puckering.

Making up my own face in the mirror, I listen to them and suddenly feel limp like Gumby, as though the reality of Teresa leaving me has just revealed itself. Like Teresa, I've been excited and planning for the baby. It's all we talk about. Our conversations begin with, "When the baby comes" and end with, "Everything will be so much better."

All of a sudden I can't breathe, as though something has sucked all the air out of the room. I feel dizzy and hold onto the dresser. I take several deep breaths.

"What's wrong with you?" Mama says. "You look like you just swallowed a bee."

Teresa tilts her head and peeks at me through her veil of curls. Almost like she can read my thoughts, she says, "I'm not going far away."

Her words soothe me for a while, and I'm able to go into the bathroom to dress as the maid of honor.

There is no organist playing "Here Comes the Bride" or bouquets of white daisies arranged on an altar. The bride doesn't glide down an isle in a white satin and lace gown linked arm and arm with her father. Instead, Teresa settles for an ordinary cream knee-length slip dress and marches into the drab Municipal Hall, her arm linked with the groom's.

Overstuffed filing cabinets, a dusty conference table, and worn leather chairs crowd one corner. The guests include Mama, Adele and Roger, Meredith and the girls, and Rocco's grandmother, who spits phlegm into a handkerchief throughout the ceremony.

Even with a distended belly and wide hips, Teresa is a speck by comparison with her groom's broad frame. Tilting her head to gaze into her future husband's eyes, I witness their exchange of vows to love, honor, and obey each other until death do them part.

"I now pronounce you man and wife," the judge says. He slams the book he read from onto the desk and flicks the dandruff off his black cloak.

"Go on, you may kiss the bride."

Rocco obliges, and all in attendance applaud. Immediately after the couple's first kiss as husband and wife, we flee the stifling room for the outdoors where the breeze filtering through the dense trees is just enough to cool us down.

Back home, we feast on platters of baked ham, roasted turkey, and potato and macaroni salads that Meredith had prepared for the celebration. In the midst of all the chatter Rocco announces he has a toast. Squeezing Teresa into his side and raising a can of Budweiser, he says, "To Mrs. Rocco Dibellis, my wife and mother of my child." Teresa blushes while Rocco guzzles the beer and crushes the tin with one fist. Teresa winces and pulls away.

During the party I don't have much of an opportunity to speak with Teresa. Rocco holds onto her waist as though he's afraid she's going to disappear. Not until the guests have gone home do we have time alone. I assist Teresa with the task of packing her things in the large diaper bag Adele and Roger have given her as a wedding gift.

"I feel like I'm never going to see you again," I say, folding underwear and bras into the tote.

"I'm moving a mile away." Teresa collects her toothbrush, combs, and shampoos from the medicine cabinet.

"But I don't want you to go," I say, sniffing the bottle of Cachet that Adele had surprised her with.

"I'll stop by every day to see you, I promise. And besides, you can visit me whenever you want to," she says, zipping the bag closed.

In front of the confectionery store, at the curb, Rocco idles the car. Mama, Teresa, and I are in a tight hug. Cringing when Rocco honks, we loosen our grip on each other. Teresa staggers away to her new home, the basement apartment of Rocco's grandmother's house.

"Take care of my daughter," Mama croaks.

Rocco shouts out of the opened window before screeching away, "Promise I will."

———

Victor and his dad move out in the middle of the night, sticking Meredith for two months owed rent. I resume sitting for Ginny and Abbey. I even sleep there most nights, as going home to our apartment with Teresa gone stings like a stubbed toe. The smudged walls are duller than I've ever noticed, the frayed sofa pleads to be mended, and the unattended leak in the living room ceiling has finally blackened with mold. All of it looks as lonely as I feel.

One Saturday while Mama is working a double shift, I decide I need a change. It's not like me to spend a penny of Joseph's money, but with Meredith's help, we shop for paint, pillows, and a new lamp. Together, we roll cotton candy pink onto faded walls; it's the exact color I have always wanted for my room since I was a little girl.

Meredith searched her attic and found a white chenille bedspread dotted with pink rosebuds that belonged to her mother. We dismantle the bunk beds and set them side by side. We cover the two twins as a full-sized bed and hang a white wicker fan and a picture, which I found at a garage sale, of two little girls, sitting on a beach, their arms wrapped around each other. When we are through, Meredith and I sit cross-legged on the floor, the way Teresa and I used to do, admiring our work.

When Meredith leaves, I shower and change into a long-sleeved sweat suit, terry socks, and sneakers.

Switching on the television, I adjust the antennae and raise the volume. My eyes roam the dreary apartment. In the kitchen I search for a bite to eat, but the carton of milk in the fridge and the two ends of Wonder Bread on the shelf look pathetic. Slamming the door, I decide a cigarette will appease my stomach until I get to Meredith's, where I'm sure she'll be preparing a balanced meal before her date.

Like a fiend, I scour the medicine chest, cabinets, and silverware drawer for loose cigarettes. Mama switched from Pall Malls to filtered Kents after the surgeon general claimed they're less hazardous to your health. Tiptoeing into my parent's bedroom as if they are asleep in their bed, I creak open the nightstand drawer. Tubes of lipsticks, false eyelashes, and a deck of cards— but no cigarettes. The urge for a smoke intensifies, and I am more desperate to find one.

Caldor and Kmart shopping bags clutter the closet. The shock and shame of Teresa's pregnancy before marriage was absorbed by joy, and Mama started preparing for the baby's coming. Each payday she splurges for bibs, feetie pajamas, diapers, and bottles. She's even saving formula coupons from the A&P.

Fumbling over the packages, I grab a pair of Daddy's pants and Mama's factory smock and delve into the pockets. Zilch. Agitated, I rearrange the bags so Mama won't notice I've been snooping; then I glimpse a denim satchel dangling on a nail on the rear wall. I haven't seen Mama wear the purse in years and didn't even know she still possessed it. Unhooking it with trembling fingers, I feel warm and tingly all over, like when you stumble on something lost that you had forgotten you missed so much.

Sitting on the edge of the bed, I deposit the purse's contents onto the spread: rosary beads, a Saint Joseph's medal, the multicolored beaded wallet I gave to Mama one Christmas, and a stuffed envelope bundled with an elastic band. I reach for the medal first. After blowing stale tobacco flakes off it, I brush it against my cheek. It's cool and smells like a greasy nickel. I loop the strand of beads over my neck, pick up the envelope, and loosen the elastic.

Polaroid snapshots burst out as if they've been given oxygen to breathe. One photo is of a boy riding a bicycle, another of him brandishing braces under a glaring sun; in another he wears a blue-and-white striped baseball uniform and swings a bat. I line the photos on a pillow and, sitting cross-legged, rock back and forth over them. Something inside my head is clanking as the furnace pipes do when we turn the thermostat up. I burst into a wail, and snot trickles out of my nostrils and drips onto my brother's face. I wipe my tears off Joseph's cheeks, collect all the photos, and take them to the kitchen. I shuffle the photos of Joseph like a deck of cards and spread them on the table beneath the flickering fluorescent light.

Examining the details of each picture, I imagine my twin's thoughts when the camera clicked, capturing the awkward braces and the tailored navy suit that is too mature for someone his age. I chuckle at the thought of him pinching the lips of the first girl he kissed. In the snapshot of him diving off a board into a built in pool, the birthmark on his left shoulder is faintly visible. It is identical to the mark that taints my right shoulder.

By the time the canary springs from the clock, informing me it's midnight, the clanking in my head has stopped. It's just throbbing now, as it does when I've overindulged with marijuana. Minutes later heels thump up the steps. The door swings open. Tripping into the dim kitchen, Daddy yelps, "Shit, you scared me."

I had been rehearsing the verbal thrashing I'd give my parents when they came home, but when I look into my father's eyes, pink-rimmed and swollen from lack of sleep, the words are as lost as I am. Daddy scans the collage of photos, and I think he's going to deny having contact with Joseph—or that he'll pretend to be seeing the pictures for the first time. But he eases into a chair across from me, lights a cigarette, and exhales a breath of surrender.

"Your Mama thought it was the best thing for him," he says, chewing his inner cheek.

"What are you talking about?" I demand, gouging my knuckles into my eyes as if the gesture will help me to hear.

"They were good people. She did it for him. So he could have a chance at a good life."

He acts as though it is a normal occurrence to give one's own child to another.

The photos shimmy when I slam my fist on the table. "And she thought giving him to strangers was a chance at life?"

"They weren't supposed to take him away." He gazes at the pictures. The cigarette appears to be suffocating between his calloused fingers.

"And what about you; why didn't you do anything?"

Scratching the stubble darkening his jaw, he says. "He was one less we had to worry about. It was best for him."

"What are you saying?"

The door kicks open and Mama stumbles in, fussing with an armful of shopping bags.

"What the hell are you two arguing about?" She drops Caldor bags onto the floor and lights the pilot beneath the morning coffee before unzipping her jacket.

Bending, she rummages through the overstuffed shopping bag.

"Look what I found on sale." She yanks out a fuzzy yellow hooded blanket. "For the baby to wear home from the hospital," she says. "It'll be cold in December."

Coddling the soft blanket against her chest, she smiles. When we don't react, she drops the garment onto the table and, seeing the photos, lets out a slight gasp. Stroking the glossy pictures one by one, she says, "What were you doing in my things, Rosie?"

Scooping the photos away from her, I grind my teeth. "How could you? How could you give your son away?"

Shuddering, she presses her palms onto the table's edge. Her head bobs.

"What did you tell her?" she asks my father.

"The truth. That we thought it was the best thing for him. That those people could take care of him better than we could—that with them he had a chance. That's what I told her."

Mama flings her white-knuckled fists at Daddy. He blocks her with his arms.

"Why not tell her the whole truth?"

"That is the truth," he says, protecting his face.

"But the real truth is you gave your son up to save your own ass." Spit spatters from her mouth. A speck of tobacco sticks to her lip.

My eyes dart through tears from Mama to Daddy to the photos.

"What are you saying?"

"The Welleses paid us three thousand dollars for your brother. That's what your father needed to pay his shylock," she says, averting my eyes.

The scalding afternoon at the Welles' place flashes through my head—Joseph and me running into the kitchen, broken glass crunching under our feet, the adults shouting over each other's words. No one listening to anyone. Mama urging me to leave them alone to talk. Daddy crying and tucking something into his pocket when they stumbled out of the house. Mama guiding him down the steps. On the bus ride home she caressed his back, easing his sobs, as if he had suffered a sudden loss rather than one he had brought upon us.

"Where is my brother now?" My fists are clenched like my teeth.

"The pictures stopped coming a few years ago," Mama says. "The postmarks on the envelopes were from New York."

Kicking my chair back, it topples over. "I hate you both. I wish you were dead."

In my room I cradle the photos of Joseph in the crook of my arm, whispering to him, "Everything is going to be all right. I'll find you."

———

When the sun peeks into my window, I crawl out of bed. I empty my dresser drawers of socks, pajamas, underwear, Levis, and my favorite paisley blouse into a large black plastic trash bag. I clear a shelf of the series of Nancy Drew books I have collected over the years, stacking them in the bag along with the milk cartons, which harbor Joseph's cash fund. The cartons are bulky and heavy, and I make a mental note to open a bank account as Meredith suggested I should when I began sitting for her.

Before I leave the apartment I pause at my parent's bedroom. Daddy's snores whistle as though he doesn't have an ounce of guilt, and Mama's breath doesn't skip a beat. Kicking the door with the heel of my shoe, I hear them stir, and then I storm out.

It's early, and few motorists are on the road. There's a rush of customers at the confectionery store for newspapers. Jaywalking across the avenue, I gaze up at the fire escape where Teresa and I had blown our wishes out to the blinking stars. I wave to the empty wrought-iron terrace as if she's standing there waving back.

En route to Teresa's apartment to confess what I know about Joseph and to show her the photos of the brother we both love and miss so much, I'm drawn to the church Teresa had often convinced me to attend with her. Stepping into the dimly lit cool dome reminds me of the Pit, but rather than Led Zeppelin posters nailed to the walls there is a series of vibrant stained glass, depicting Jesus Christ being lowered from a cross and his Mother swaddling him in white cloth.

Haggard women draped in black raincoats and kerchiefs, clutching Bibles, rosary beads, and tissues mourn in pews. Yearning to unload the garbled truth swimming around in my head, I slide into an empty pew and wait my turn for the confessional. When I am the only person left in the church, I creep into the booth and kneel.

"Bless me Father, for I have sinned. It's been two years since my last confession."

In the midst of the potent incense burning, peppermint swirls off the priest's lips.

"Go on."

Except for the rattle in the priest's chest, the box is still and quiet. Although my shoulders shudder from the chill, sweat trickles under my windbreaker. Without uttering a word into the silence, I stand and exit the booth.

I drag my sack down the marble steps and turn right. My arms are numb from the weight of the measly treasures I haul over my shoulder. At the crosswalk, as I wait for the light to turn green, I glance in the windows of the Laundromat. The windows are so clean I can see my reflection. As I step off the curb, someone shouts, "Rosie, is that you?"

I stop and turn. It's Scraps.

"Oh, hi," I say. I haven't seen him since the day he returned my doll.

Scraps dangles keys in one hand and grips a brown bag in the other. I'm almost as tall as he is short. "You look like you can use a ride."

"No, I'm fine." I feel silly dragging the bulky sack.

Scraps must notice. He takes the bag. "Come on. My car is right here." He points to a Cadillac the color of a red plum and tosses the bag inside.

"Wow, that's heavy."

He opens the passenger door, and I climb in. The leather seat is polished and slippery. A gold horn bobs on the rearview mirror.

"How are you doing?" He views a side mirror before he lurches out onto the street.

"I'm good."

"Where to?" he asks.

I blurt out Teresa's address, and Scraps screeches left.

"How's your mother?" He lowers the volume of the blaring radio.

"She's fine," I say, looking straight ahead.

He bobs his head back and forth. "I was emptying the change machine in the Laundromat while you were waiting for the light. And I said, 'That's got to be Antoinette's daughter, Rosie.'"

"Yeah. It's been a while since you drove me to the hospital. Thanks again," I say.

"No big deal. You look just like your mother," he adds.

I appreciate his kind compliment, but my skin is cratered from picking pimples, not bronzed and smooth like Mama's. My hair is fine and straggly, not thick and curled, and my legs are stumpy like Uncle Carmen's, not long and slender like my mother's.

"I'm sixteen now," I say.

"Wow, time flies. Do you have your permit yet?"

"Not yet."

Scraps parks and turns the ignition off in front of Teresa's place. He swings the car door open and retrieves my bag from the backseat. I hop out of the car and slam the door.

"Can I help with anything else? Do you need money?"

"No, thank you." I can feel my cheeks blushing. "I'm good."

He stands there for a while grinning at me. His teeth are grayer than I remember, but his skin is still smooth and taut like the skin of an apple. I could stay there all day looking into his bright blue eyes. I feel safe like I did the night he took me to the hospital when my father wouldn't. He taps his cap and grins.

"You'll be all right then," he says.

"Yeah. My sister lives here. I'm going to visit."

"I see," he says, pinching my nose as if I'm still a little girl. It makes me want to cry, but I hold back.

Whistling, he trots back to the car. As he yanks the door open, he yells out, "If you ever need anything, I'm at the tavern most days."

I wait for him to drive away before I turn to scuttle through the alleyway to the basement entrance. My cheek is still warm when I knock. No one answers. Dropping the sack next to the door, I turn the knob and let myself in. The single room is barely lit by a busted lamp flickering on a shag remnant. Picking up the lamp and setting it on the table, I glance around the room. The lace curtains I recently helped Teresa wash and starch hang off an unhinged rod. Shattered glass splattered with blood glistens on the linoleum.

"Teresa, Teresa," I shout, running into the only other room. My heart is racing. I kneel down beside where my sister sprawls on the bathroom floor. Her hair is sopping in blood, and I can't tell where it's coming from.

"Oh, my God, Teresa what happened?" I lift her head onto my lap.

Slurring as if she's swallowed a pint of gin, she says, "Rocco said my fat stomach is ugly and that he can't stand the sight of me."

"Shh. You're safe now. I'm here." Gently, I caress strands of hair from a gash at the edge of her left eye.

As she speaks, I can hear her heart beating out of her opened mouth. "He stuck my head in the toilet. He says that's where I belong, with all the rest of the shit."

She's sobbing so hard her belly is bouncing like a ball.

"Can you stand up?" I maneuver her shoulders off the tile. She looks dazed and confused, but she understands. With what little energy she has, clutching my strong, steady arm, she hauls her lopsided body onto her bare feet. I close the toilet lid, and she squats down.

Soaking a washcloth in the sink, I say, "Teresa we have to call the police."

"No."

"Then I will." I dab the gobs of blood.

"No, he's my husband; I can't." She winces as I press the slit at the corner of her eye to get the bleeding to stop.

"That doesn't give him the right to whack you in the head whenever he feels like it."

Swatting my hand, she croaks, "He didn't mean it. He's under a lot of pressure with work and the baby coming."

I'm so angry I'll try anything to get through to her. Swiping a sheath of broken mirror off the floor, I hold it in front of her bruised, toothless face. An imprint of a fist is plastered on her jaw.

"You see how he didn't mean it. He'll hurt the baby, too."

She drops her head into my chest. Her entire body shudders. I fold my broken sister into my arms like a soft pillow and rock her. The odor of clotted blood on her matted scalp takes my breath away.

"I don't want to lose you," I say.

Teresa refuses to see a doctor but agrees to come with me to Adele's. Hauling my bag over my shoulder, I grip Teresa's elbow and guide her out of the basement and through the alleyway.

"What's in the bag?"

"My stuff."

"What stuff?"

"I'll explain later." Looking up and down the street, expecting Rocco to show up any second, I hail a cab at the curb.

The driver hops out of his vehicle, helps Teresa into the backseat, and relieves me of my heavy sack, tossing it into the front seat.

"You go to hospital?" he says, latching his seatbelt.

"No, no," I say.

He looks at us through the rearview mirror.

"You sure?" He looks confused.

Understanding that he thinks Teresa is about to give birth in his cab, I chuckle and say, "She's not ready yet."

I give the man Adele's address, and he speeds off. She lives only five blocks away. Before we can catch our breath, the cab driver's idling in front of her house. Again he hops out to assist Teresa from the backseat. I delve into one of the milk cartons in my bag for cash to pay the man. I think I've given him more than he asked for because he tries to give it back, but I'm already nudging Teresa up the stairs.

"Thank you for your help," I say.

Adele answers the bell with a cheerful grin that quickly disappears at the sight of Teresa's bruises.

"Oh, my, what happened?" she says gesturing for us to come in.

"I'll explain later," I say, guiding Teresa through the door.

In Adele's guest room Teresa sheds her bloodied smock; it puddles at her ankles. Normally, being exposed in such away would humiliate my sister, but she doesn't seem to care. Adele wraps her in a robe, and she climbs onto the bed. She's asleep in an instant.

In the kitchen Adele fumbles in the cabinet for the pack of cigarettes she keeps hidden from Roger behind a Christmas bowl. She strikes a match, inhales, and exhales.

"Tell me what happened."

Skipping my discovery of Joseph's photos and the argument with my parents, I tell the story of finding Teresa lying beaten on the bathroom floor. Adele listens to the details without interrupting. When I'm finished, she goes to the counter and scoops coffee grains into a percolator. Locking the lid in place, she says, "We have to tell your mother."

"Why? So she can say she was right and talk Teresa into giving the baby away?" I swat fruit flies away from a bowl of ripened bananas.

Spinning around, Adele leans against the counter. "She's not going to do that, Rosie. She can't wait to spoil that baby."

"You don't know her like I do. You don't know what she's capable of." I stand to retrieve milk from the refrigerator and sugar from the pantry.

"But what I do know is that she's been the best mother she could be to you girls."

"What about her son? Doesn't he count?" I say, slamming the milk carton on the table.

Ignoring my questions, Adele takes the smoldering cigarette from the ashtray. She drags on it as if it will be her last. Glimpsing sorrow in tears she blinks away, I ask, "Do you know anything about Joseph?"

She exhales the smoke through her nostrils. Her voice quivers like my insides.

"Your mother will know what's best for Teresa."

————

In front of the medicine cabinet Teresa's bulge rests on the edge of the porcelain sink as she dabs her bruises with Cover Girl. She has lost weight in the past week, and from the back she doesn't appear pregnant at all. I sit on the toilet lid. She grins and covers her mouth to hide a missing tooth.

"Teresa, are you sure you want to do this?"

"It's the right thing; I have to."

"I'm scared. I don't want you to go."

"Don't worry. Once the baby is here, Rocco will be calmer."

Breathing on her neck, I wrap my arms around my sister's waist, clasping my fingers over her hard, tight belly. We sway, holding on to each other, weeping bubbles of pain clotted up in our insides. Our eyes lock in the mirror, and the reflection of our sad selves sends us into hysterical laughter. Facing each other, we clutch our bellies. Tears are rolling down our cheeks, but they tickle rather than burn.

It's a while before the bout of giddiness subsides and Teresa becomes very serious. Sitting on the tub's rim, spreading her legs so that the ball of her stomach dips between her thighs, she intertwines her fingers with mine. "Rosie, do you still think about Joseph?"

Even with the rainbow of bruises around them, her eyes still shine. I had planned to confess everything I know about Joseph's disappearance the morning I found her beaten. But at this moment I refuse to burden her with anything more. Not now. Maybe not ever.

"All the time," I say.

"Why do you think he didn't want to come home?" She releases my fingers to twirl her straggly hair.

"I don't know. But I have a plan to get him to come home."

"How? What kind of plan?"

"I don't want to tell you yet, but I promise I will soon." I grab for a brush on the window sill.

Before Teresa attempts to prod the secret from me, the bell chimes. I brush her hair and then mine, and together we go to the living room. Adele is unlocking the door. Mama strides in with a woman I don't recognize.

"Jesus, what did he do to you?" Mama launches toward Teresa.

Embracing, they both weep. "I'm okay, Mama; they'll heal."

"What about the baby?" Mama cups both palms on Teresa's roundness.

"We have to talk. Come, sit down," she says, brushing past me as if I'm a shadow on the wall.

"This is Martha."

"Nice to meet you," Teresa says, looking at me and shrugging her shoulders.

Martha resembles a man, rigid and starched in a gray wool pantsuit and white shirt.

Teresa sits in Roger's favorite recliner, and I perch on its wide arm.

Eyeing Teresa's swollen lips and bruises, the woman speaks. "I'm a volunteer at the shelter for abused families. I'm here to help."

Teresa shifts her gaze from Mama to Adele to me as though she's lost and trying to find a familiar face.

"Just listen to what she has to say," Mama says, clutching her pocketbook in her lap.

"I don't need help. Everything's going to be okay."

A single tear streams down the woman's reddened cheeks as the tale flows from her mouth. She and her husband were quarrelling, and he swung a telephone; it missed her but struck their three-year-old son in the head, crippling him for life. She warns Teresa that the same horrific incident could happen to her.

"That's not going to happen to me or my baby," Teresa says. "Why are you telling me this?"

"Something horrible is bound to happen, if you don't do something about it," Martha says.

"No. I just have to be a better wife to him. That's all. It is my fault."

Martha raises a hand. "It's not your fault. It's his problem, not yours. You don't have the power to make him stop."

"Mama, what is she saying?" Teresa stares straight into Mama's wet eyes.

"You can give the child up for adoption," Martha continues, pulling a thread off her slacks.

Teresa leaps up so fast she loses her balance and falls back onto the chair.

"I'm not going to give my baby away."

"You're a young girl. You have plenty of time for a family," Martha says as though she has the right.

"Rocco would never hurt our baby."

"He hurts you; you can't be sure he won't hurt a child," the woman insists.

Teresa melts into the cushions. She glances at Mama; a child's fear shrouds her eyes.

Glowering at Mama, I say, "Why did you do this?"

Biting down on her lower lip, she says, "Because I'm her mother."

CHAPTER TWENTY-THREE

Adele offers me the guest room, just as she offered it to Mama and me years ago. It's supposed to be temporary, until Mama and I can work out our issues. But I have no intention of ever going home.

Adele and Roger appear to enjoy my company. Adele launders and irons my clothes and prepares eggs and pancakes for breakfast. Roger seems genuinely happy to drop me at the high school, wishing me a good day as I wave goodbye. They've even installed a teen line in my room, but it's not a habit of mine to mingle with anyone, so I rarely use it.

When I return from school, warm cookies are heaped on a plate beside a glass of milk. After supper, Adele prepares lunch for the following day for Roger and me, scrawling flowers around my name on the outside of the brown bag. She doesn't seem to notice or maybe doesn't care that I'm sixteen and too old and weary to be fussed over.

One night, after a shower, I'm sulking in my room, missing my old life. Adele knocks on the door before entering. The scent of Jean Naté talcum follows her in and tickles my nose. She carries a basket of creased jeans, folded turtlenecks, and ironed underwear. She balances the basket on the foot of the bed and begins to replenish my empty drawers. I jump up. I do not want her to find the photos of Joseph that line the bottom of the dresser.

"I'll do it," I say.

"I don't mind. I like having someone to take care of."

"You've already done enough for me." I take the pile of clothing.

Adele shrugs and sits on a fringed ottoman while I complete the task she began. She sighs. "I saw your mother today."

"Oh."

"She really misses you."

Snapping the drawers shut, I spin around.

171

"I bet."

"Don't be sarcastic, young lady."

"I'm sorry, Adele. But that's how I feel."

"You're a tough cookie. Just like your mother."

"I'm nothing like my mother," I say, more high-pitched than I intended.

Ignoring the snide comment, she continues, "Have I ever told you about the time your mother and I were forced into identical pixies?"

I've heard the story one thousand and one times, but I say, "No."

Adele kicks off her heels and tucks her feet under her skirt.

"Your Mama was a real tomboy. If I didn't agree to do everything she wanted to do, she'd throw me on the ground and straddle me until I had no choice but to agree to whatever mischief she was eager to get into."

I listen to Adele paint a picture of a strong young girl filled with confidence and desires and roll my eyes.

"Your Mama had volunteered to restack the library shelves. Of course, gum was not allowed on school grounds. Well, she hid a wad under her tongue and absentmindedly popped a bubble that almost popped off the librarian's glasses."

Adele laughs and dabs the corners of her eyes with the tip of her painted nail.

"'Spit it out right this minute,'" the librarian demanded, running over to Antoinette with her palm opened to catch it. So your mother spit the gum into the tyrant's hand, and she stuck it on Antoinette's nose. Everyone giggled. Not just me. But your mother was so mad her face turned the colors of the Italian flag."

Adele laughs again, swats her leg, and continues. "Well, all of sudden she charged at me, pulled the gum off her nose, and squished it into my ponytail. My mother had no choice but to cut it out."

"How did you ever forgive her?"

"I got even. The next day our classmates made fun of my short pixie, and your mother, of all people, came to my rescue. 'I think it looks pretty,' she said. 'You think so,' I said. And then, just as she inched closer, I squished a pack of chewed gum hidden in my hand into her curls. And the next day we trotted to school, hand in hand, in identical pixies."

"You and Mama are so different to be friends."

"Not really. We have the same heart."

"Why didn't you have any kids?"

"It's not what God intended for me," she says, slipping back into her heels.

"Adele, I know you don't want to get involved, but do you know anything about where Joseph might be?"

"Rosie, when you become a mother, you'll understand." She smoothes her skirt before she gently closes the door.

CHAPTER TWENTY-FOUR

I don't know whether it came to me in a dream or the answer was right there in front of me the whole time and I just didn't see it. One night, I wrote a list of all the people in my life I could trust to help me find Joseph and checked the names off one by one. Nona was too old, Uncle Carmen too mean. Adele would never do anything without telling Mama, and my father was worthless. But one name danced in my head, and when I wrote it down on the white-lined paper, I knew I was going to find Joseph.

Entering the pub is like backpedaling into my past life. The bar is more ragged than I remember it to be. The pine floors are scuffed and faded from the steady rays of sunlight that manage to peek through slivered blinds. Patrons are slumped over a mahogany counter, their skin sagging like the worn leather chairs that comfort them. I wonder whether they're the same men who drank the days away years earlier.

"Is Scraps around?" I ask the bartender. The lines around his mouth point to his toes like arrows.

"Who wants to know?"

"Rosie Scarpiella," I say, loudly and firmly.

The bartender pokes his head through the checkered curtain and grumbles my name.

"He'll be right with you," he says, holding a spotted glass to the light.

The curtain is drawn aside, and I'm greeted with a hug. I'm awkward in Scraps' unexpected embrace.

"Don't you look beautiful today—just like your mother?" His eyes brighten the dull restaurant.

"Thanks."

"Let's go sit. Are you hungry?"

I follow him into the familiar dining area. Scraps deposits coins into the dusty jukebox and makes a selection. Bobby Sherman's voice fills the room.

"I think this is who you kids are listening to these days."

"I like Bobby Sherman," I say.

"How about a pizza pie?" Scraps asks, removing his cap. His white hair has thinned, and the top of his head is completely bald. But his face still glows like I once believed God's did.

"Sounds great." I fold my hands on the red-and-white checkered vinyl tablecloth. Scraps waves to the waitress, and she rushes over with menus.

"Just a pie," he says, shooing the list of specials for the day.

"Any toppings?"

"Pepperoni," he says.

I diddle with a straw; my raw nerves feel exposed.

"And how is your mother these days?" he says, stretching back into his chair.

"She's good, thanks."

"Your mother is a great lady," he says, with sincerity that causes my eyes to fill.

It's the first time I wonder about his family. Sitting there, staring into his eyes, it occurs to me that he might have a wife, kids, and grandchildren of his own. I'm ashamed of my selfishness, embarrassed I haven't shown the same concern for his family that he has for mine in the past.

"How many grandchildren do you have?"

"The last time I counted, I had twelve."

"Wow."

Scraps smiles and crosses his legs. He fusses with the crease in his tweed trousers.

"So what is it you want to talk to me about?"

Staring boldly into his eyes, I say, "I'd like to hire you to help me find someone."

Scraps squeezes a lemon rind on the rim of a Coke.

"Who?"

"My brother. His name is Joseph."

Scraps leans on his elbows and inhales the Coke through a straw like a kid would.

"He was living with a family for a while. It was supposed to be temporary. But then they moved away and took Joseph with them." Fumbling in my handbag for the crisp bills I had withdrawn at the bank that morning, I add, "We didn't expect never to see him again."

Scraps' blue eyes cloud like steam. Raising a hand, he says, "I don't want your money."

"But I saved it up…"

"Did your parents call the police when they took him away?"

I'm struggling to hold back the tears and swallow them before my voice cracks into a million tiny pieces. Scraps pats my hand.

"Never mind about all that. Do you have any information about him at all?"

Putting the envelope stuffed with Joseph's photos on the table, I say, "Harold and Doris Welles are their names. They're not a young couple. These photos are all I have. They were mailed from New York."

The waitress interrupts, clattering a metal pizza tray onto a rack.

"Need anything else?"

"Two more Cokes." Scraps selects a slice of pizza and blows on the melting cheese. Before he takes a bite he says, "Does your mother know you came to see me about this?"

"Yes." I avoid his eyes as I soak the excess oil off a slice with a paper napkin.

"Well, let me see what I can come up with," he says, dabbing sauce dripping down from the corners of his mouth with his knuckle.

Under the table my legs are dancing, and they collide with Scraps' shins.

Grinning, he says, "Calm down; I can't promise anything." His lips are shiny from the oily pizza.

When we're through devouring the whole pie, I jot down my telephone number for Scraps.

He walks me through the bar to the front entrance. "I'll touch base with you in a few weeks."

"Do you really think you can help?"

"It's a long shot. But I'll see what I can find out."

"Thank you. I just know you're going to find him for us."

Swinging open the door, I have to squint to keep the glaring sun out of my eyes.

"Say hello to your mother for me."

"Will do." I wave goodbye, giddy as if I drank pints of beer for lunch rather than Cokes.

————

On Thanksgiving, the first holiday I am to celebrate without Mama, I join Teresa at her church. Since Rocco has agreed to counseling to manage his anger, she attends mass every day to thank God and to pray for Rocco to stay strong.

After communion we stroll to the corner diner for our traditional post-mass breakfast: coffee and fried eggs. Massaging her pointed belly, she prods me to join her and Rocco for dinner at Mama's. Teresa has forgiven her husband, but my vision of her lying in her own blood hasn't begun to blur. And there's no way I'm about to breathe the same air as my parents, let alone eat with them.

"Are you ever going to tell me why you're not talking to Mama and Daddy?" she asks, gulping orange juice to wash down her vitamins.

Teresa has begged me one hundred times to divulge what it is that separates me from my family. But I have vowed to myself not to tell her until after she has the baby.

"Drop it," I say, buttering a slice of toast.

"Okay, okay. Now don't be grouchy. I have something important I want to ask you." Teresa rests her palms on her belly, which brushes the table.

"What?" I ask, scraping the yolk off the plate with rye toast.

"Will you be the godmother?"

A crust of bread lodges in my throat.

"What's wrong? Don't you want to be the godmother?"

I swig iced water to force down the bread. Leaning over, I reach for her hand. We pinky lock. "I'll be honored to be the godmother."

Shivering outside the diner, Teresa wraps a scarf around her head and knots it around her neck. We hug goodbye with a promise to meet at Kmart the following afternoon to take advantage of Black Friday sales.

"Are you sure you don't want to come to Mama's?"

"Positive," I say, waving goodbye as I head in the opposite direction to Adele's.

After sharing a quiet turkey dinner with Adele and Roger, I decline pumpkin pie and retire to my room. I'm totally engrossed in *The Thorn Birds* when the telephone rings. I roll across the bed and lift the receiver before the second ring.

"Hello."

"It's time," Rocco says. "We'll meet you at the hospital."

"Oh, my God." I hang up, without inquiring about how many minutes apart the contractions are or whether my sister is panicked.

I bang on Adele's door. "The baby's coming, the baby's coming."

We throw coats on over our pajamas and hurry to the car. The night is black and cold; it takes a while before the hot air gushes out of the car's vents. Adele races through the green, yellow, and red traffic lights. It's a bone-chilling night, yet my throat is dry like dirt after a summer drought.

"We should have telephoned your mother before we left the house. We'll have to call her as soon as we get to the hospital."

"Don't do me any favors." I massage my hands in front of the hot air blowing out of the vents.

Skidding into the hospital parking lot, Adele says, "Your mother is not the enemy, Rosie Scarpiella."

The emergency area is crowded with patients moaning on gurneys and dozing in wheelchairs; doctors and nurses scramble to aid them. In the waiting room, we spot Rocco, crouched in a chair, resting his elbows on his knees. We take a seat across from him.

"Any word yet?" Adele asks.

"No, not yet." Rocco leans back into his chair. "Thanks for coming."

A woman sits across from us, clutching a black leather purse as crinkly as her hands. At her feet a little boy writhes on his belly, lining up green toy soldiers, begging his unresponsive father to join him in combat.

As the hours pass, the room seems to expand to accommodate all the people. Adele and I cringe and tighten our intertwined fingers each time the door creaks open, as if to keep from falling off a cliff. After a while Adele gets up and disappears into the corridor. Standing, I stretch my arms over my head and pace back and forth several times before resituating myself on the chrome-and-vinyl chair.

I'm searching in my purse for loose change to purchase a Coke from the machine when a doctor half the size of Rocco glides into the room. His skin is sallow underneath the white jacket; his bloodshot eyes sink into dark spongy circles. Adele is behind him. When he speaks, the lines in his forehead deepen, reflecting the burden of a messenger of grief.

"Mr. Dibellis, you're the father to a fine, healthy boy," he says, extending a hand to Rocco.

Rocco bolts off the chair. Saliva sputters off his lips.

"How's my wife?"

"We had to do an emergency cesarean. But she'll be up and about in no time."

"Oh, my God—they're both okay," Adele breathes, and we embrace each other for a long time.

"A baby boy," I say. The blood begins to circulate in my toes again and flows through my veins. I'm warm and bubbly. "I'm an aunt," I gush to the people waiting to hear their family members are okay, too.

The room applauds just as my parents step in. Adele leaps toward her friend with a huge grin.

"Congratulations, Grandma. You have a grandson."

The two of them embrace, and Daddy opens his arms toward me. A single tear rolls down his cheek.

"Rose Petal."

I turn my back on him and walk away.

CHAPTER TWENTY-FIVE

After graduation Adele secures a job for me at the Hair & Now Beauty Salon, where she's been working since I've known her. The duties I'm responsible for absorb my thoughts like a sponge: stacking the operator's stations with curlers, brushes, bobby pins, and cans of hair sprays. I also launder loads of towels stained with dyes and sweep cut hairs from the linoleum. When the day is over, I stop at the diner to swig down a bowl of soup before I head to night school to complete the hours necessary for a beautician's license.

One Saturday, the busiest day at the shop, I arrive early to double check that the inventory is in order for the stylists. I'm in the back room, where the hairdressers gobble their lunch in between appointments, when the telephone rings.

"Good morning, Hair & Now Beauty Salon."

"Just the girl I wanted to talk to."

Like the touch of a hand, the tone of his voice gently pushes me into a chair.

"Scraps?"

"I don't want you to get your hopes up, but I have an address in Queens and a telephone number. But keep in mind he could have moved by now."

"Queens. That's so close."

Scraps says, "It appears the Welleses passed away a few years ago, and Joseph moved to Queens with one of their daughters."

"Thank you, thank you, thank you," is all I can say.

Scraps laughs, and I swear I can see his eyes glistening through the wire.

There is no paper around, so I jot the number on the wall next to the telephone.

"Let me know how you make out," Scraps says.

I hang up and tug at the cord to get it to reach into the stockroom.
Inhaling, I dial the numbers, praying the operator won't inform me the number I'm attempting to reach has been disconnected. On the fourth ring a man answers.

"You just called hell; if you're looking for heaven, deposit another five cents."

There's an unfamiliar sarcasm in the voice, but I recognize the curled *r*'s.
I'm unable to catch my breath to speak. Joseph, assuming the caller has misdialed, hangs up. With my eyes shut, I count to ten before redialing. The phone is answered on the first ring.

"Hello."

"Joseph?"

"Who is this?"

Sliding down the wall onto the floor, I curl my knees to my chin; my voice crackles.

"It's Rosie."

Clearing his throat, my twin says, "You have the wrong number."

I hang onto the receiver until I can't stand the screeching tone.

———

Joseph has no idea that in less than two hours his other half will shadow his doorstep. I've called him many times, and he continues with his charade—that I've dialed the wrong number. But because he never warns me not to call again, I think he needs to hear my voice as much as I need to hear his. I don't stop.

Since I've never been out of New Jersey, I research public transportation from Jersey to Queens. It's not an easy trip. I hop on a bus to Penn Station, board a train to Manhattan, and then take a subway to Queens. Glancing out the window, I watch the drizzles of rain create puddles on the outskirts of the rails.

I wonder whether Joseph is as tall as Daddy and is going steady with a pretty girl. There are so many questions swirling around in my head they make me dizzy. I almost miss my stop.

The platform stinks like urine, so I clasp a hand over my mouth as I dash up the steps. On the street I exhale and breathe in clean air. I button up my raincoat and snap open my umbrella. Following the directions I've written down, I saunter by red brick buildings attached to one another. They're trimmed with wrought-iron railings, and bars shield cellar windows. In front of one building, on a patch of overgrown weeds, the Blessed Virgin Mary is tilted forward as if she's searching for something she's lost.

I squint up at the foot of a narrow flight of brick steps nestled between two sculpted lions. One's tail is chipped off, and the other's nose is split down the center. Above them on wood trim, etched in brass, is the address I'm looking for.

Closing the umbrella, I climb the flight and scan the mailboxes at the top of the landing. The name Welles swims in thick blood red magic marker next to the letter E. I thumb the bell and am buzzed in without an inquiry as to who's there. Traipsing up the steps, I begin to sweat. The corridor is poorly lit, but I spot the door branded with the letter *E*. I tap, and it swings open. I'm not sure whether it's anger or surprise that flushes his cheeks. A copper-haired girl with matching freckles sprinkled all over her face, chest, and arms stands behind him. Her belly is round and taut.

"This is a surprise," Joseph says.

The copper-haired girl is scowling, but before she can ask, Joseph says, "Brenda, don't be going and getting all worked up. It's my sister."

"Come in. I didn't know you had a sister," she adds, as she kicks the door closed.

I step into a room cluttered with piles of unfolded laundry, an unmade sofa bed, and a cradle crushed between the refrigerator and a café table. Joseph is in front of a mirror, splashing on cologne. He is tall but not as broad as Daddy. His curls are cut short to his scalp, kinking around his earlobes. The skin under his eyes is as dark as his brows, and a mustache hides his thin lips. He appears older than his years, older than I.

"Don't mind the mess," Brenda says, clearing the floor littered with newspapers and racetrack programs with one swoop. In the far corner of the room ashtrays, overflowing with cigarette butts, are strewn on a card table.

"When are you due?" I ask.

"In three months," Brenda says, poking her protruding belly button. "Just in time for summer."

I feel like an intruder standing there in the center of my brother's home. I'm still clutching the directions in one hand while my umbrella is soaking the carpet.

"Teresa has a baby, too," I blurt out, staring at the back of Joseph's head. "She named him after you."

Spinning around, Joseph pulls on a hooded Jets sweatshirt and a denim jacket over that. "I'm on my way out. I got this tip in the second race at Belmont, and I don't want to miss it. But you stay and have a visit with Brenda."

"Your sister just got here, Joe," Brenda says, darting a not-so-pleased look at him.

Ignoring her, he trots to the door. I hope he can't hear my heart ticking louder than the clock hanging crooked on the single bare wall in the room. His hand is on the knob, and he pauses and turns around.

"Hey, you want to bet a couple of bucks on a sure winner?"

I walk toward my brother and stop so close to him I can taste tobacco on his breath.

"Joseph, I'm not interested in horses. I've come a long way to see you."

"Yeah, well I didn't ask you to."

Without shutting the door he disappears down the dark corridor. My cheeks are stinging as if he's just smacked me.

Behind me Brenda sighs. "You don't know your brother very well."

"That's what you think," I say, chasing after him.

The rain slants toward me, but I don't bother to pop open the umbrella as I make my way through pedestrians also caught in the downpour. Joseph ducks into a coffee shop, and I follow him. When I plop down on the stool next to him, his dimples deepen in the way they always did when he was agitated. Joseph unfolds a newspaper and orders coffee. More annoyed than him, I poke him on the shoulder. He doesn't look at me.

"Joseph, I want to talk to you."

"Don't have time to chat. Just stopped in for a quick cup of coffee," he says, nosing the paper.

"Why are you angry with me?" I hate how my voice sounds so pleading.

"I'm not angry." He folds the paper and adds cream and sugar to his mug.

I tug at his elbow, and he pulls away. "We haven't seen each other in years. Give me a few minutes." My words are stronger now, more in charge.

"That's not my fault," he says, slamming the mug on the counter. The black liquid swishes over the rim but doesn't spill.

"It's not my fault either."

"Then whom should we blame? Mama…Daddy…who? You tell me," he says, staring into the black gunk.

"Joseph, I never stopped thinking about you after those people took you away."

His head swivels like the stools we're sitting on. Gritting his teeth, he sounds just like Daddy. "Those *people* were all I had."

"I wanted you to come home. Truly, I did." I'm trying to whisper, but the words topple out loud, and people start to stare.

"Yeah, well then, what happened?" Joseph slings back the coffee like it's a shot of whiskey. He tosses quarters on the counter. I tug his sleeve. He jerks away, and I trail behind him to the outdoors.

"Please don't blame me." I'm thrashing through puddles; my shoes squeak.

Joseph halts and spins around. Shouting over screeching cars and honking horns, veins bulge out of his neck.

"Why me?"

"I don't know…." His cheeks are soaked. I can't distinguish the raindrops from the tears.

"Why was I the one they gave away? Why didn't they want me?"

"It's not because they didn't want you. They wanted you to have a better life."

"Our parents gave me away like I was a sack of dirty laundry. Not you, not Teresa. Me." He pokes his chest with two fingers.

I yearn to throw my arms around his neck and bury my head on his shoulder, but I'm certain he'll shove me away.

"It just happened to be you." The pellets hurt, crashing down on my head, so I finally open the umbrella.

"Get underneath," I say, gesturing for Joseph to get closer.

But he turns on his heels. I watch his familiar slouched shoulders as he hustles down the block with his fists tucked inside his jacket pockets.

CHAPTER TWENTY-SIX

In a square, windowless room I kneel over the empty human shell of my Nona. The fragrance of the daffodils and lilies surrounding the coffin causes my head to throb. Braided between her gnarled fingers is a rosary of roses, the color of dried blood. A white satin ribbon draped across them reads "Your beloved daughter." To the left side of the coffin is a heart designed with white carnations; a row of red roses cascades through the middle, splitting it into halves. The ribbon reads "Your devoted son."

"Rosie, its time to say goodbye," Teresa says, nudging me.

For the final time we kneel together to pray. On wobbly legs we stand. Then we rub Nona's ice-cold hand and whisper goodbye.

It is tradition to drive past the residence of the deceased before the actual burial, and we do so before heading to the cemetery to bury Nona beside the grandfather I've never met. The black leather seats in Roger's sedan are stiff and cold, and not even the smoke from his cigar overpowers the scent of their newness. My head is buzzing, so I roll down the window and stretch my head out as far as I can to breathe fresh air. But I inhale black smoke from leaves burning in a distance. I cough and draw my head inside.

At the cemetery Teresa and I huddle in a patch of sun glaring on the stones and brown earth. Remnants of curled-up mums and dead bouquets of carnations wilt under an early frost. In the front row of mourners Daddy grips Mama under one arm. Uncle Carmen stands in front of them all, alone, as if his pain requires more space than the rest of ours.

Numbly, I listen to the priest's final prayer and watch Mama's shoulders shudder under the black sweater cloaking her. When the deep hole swallows Nona's coffin, Mama moans and pleads with the pallbearers to stop, as if they are shoveling the heavy dry dirt onto her. Teresa fumbles in her purse and hands me a tissue.

Grieving friends and family drop a carnation on the grave before they head back to their cars. Teresa joins our parents in a huddle. She'll be going home with them—to rehash Nona's life over cake and coffee with other friends and relatives.

Walking back toward Roger's Cadillac, I stop under a tree to block the breeze from blowing out a match. Someone taps me on the shoulder.

"Aren't you too young to be smoking?"

Spinning around, I exhale the smoke above my mother's head.

"Too young to smoke and too old to be lied to," I say, stepping away.

"Rosie, how long are you going to keep up with this?" Mama tugs on my elbow. I stop and turn around to meet her eyes. They're swollen. Gray roots tug at her scalp.

"I found your son," I say before sucking more nicotine into my lungs.

"What are you talking about?" Mama asks, blowing her nose into a tissue.

"Just what I said. He lives in Queens, and he's probably had his baby by now."

Mama scowls at me. "What baby? How did you find him? Where is he?"

Holding my two hands up to prevent her from coming nearer, I say in a sarcastic tone, "Whoa, one question at a time." I drag on the cigarette before throwing it on the dirt. I stub it out with the tip of my shoe.

"I asked your old friend Scraps to help me find him. And he did."

The wind is picking up. I pull my collar up to block it.

"Scraps. What possessed you to ask for his help?" Mama says, leaning on a nameless tombstone.

"Why not?"

Mama's face is all bunched up and crinkly like a head of wilted lettuce. As she squeezes my forearm, I feel her fingernails gouging my skin.

"Why? Because he's the one your father owed the money to. That's why."

I wiggle out of her grip. I'm shocked and confused. And yet it all makes sense to me.

I push her out of my way, and she trips on a stone.

"You're pathetic," I say, trotting away.

She yells after me. "Rosie, tell me how to reach your brother."

Without turning around, I yell back, "Find him yourself."

———

Adele's house is dim and quiet when I stagger in after the funeral. She and Roger have dropped me off and head to my parents to eat, drink, and recall fond memories of Nona. I stretch out on top of the pink chenille spread. No matter how much anger clenches my heart, I still miss Mama. Sometimes I imagine her sitting in a cloud of smoke, clanking her spoon on the rim of a coffee cup or at the stove frying chicken cutlets with her free hand on her hip. Despite my anger, I smile.

Bouncing off the bed, I smooth my black knit skirt. I pick up the telephone and dial. "Hi. Is Joseph around?"

"Hello, Rosie, how are you?" Brenda asks.

"Great. I need to speak to my brother."

She cover's the mouthpiece. "Joseph, your sister's calling."

Joseph mumbles, and Brenda returns. "He just went out for a paper."

A baby gurgles in the background.

"What did you have?" I ask.

"A boy. We named him Sammy."

"Sammy?" I practically shout into the phone.

"Yeah, after your father," she says, as if I don't know my own father's name.

"Congratulations. I can't wait to meet him."

Brenda doesn't respond to my comment with an offer to visit or anything at all. I remain on the line a bit longer, hoping Joseph will change his mind and decide to speak to me. But Brenda interrupts my thoughts.

"It's time to feed the baby. I really have to go."

"Well, I only called to let him know that our Nona passed away. A heart attack. I thought he'd want to know."

"Oh, my. I'm sorry. Joe's told me lots about her. I'll let him know you called."

"Thanks."

And without a goodbye she hangs up.

CHAPTER TWENTY-SEVEN

It's baby Joey's first birthday. After work I rush to Teresa's with bundles of packages. There's a bib that says "I Love My Aunt," boots and a snowsuit for the dead of winter, and blocks and LEGOs for him and me to play with.

Teresa is decorating Rocco's grandmother's house with pinups of Big Bird and Cookie Monster. Rocco blows up blue-and-white balloons while Joey fusses in his highchair, Cheerios squished between his fingers.

"He won't take a nap. He's going to be cranky for his first party," Teresa says, wiping his mouth with a sponge.

"Hey, Joey. Let's open some presents," I say, placing a box on the highchair tray.

He swats the box, which crashes to the floor. He starts wailing, and I lift him out of the chair. He's kicking and screaming. When I stick a bottle in his mouth, he calms down.

"He's teething, too. What am I going to do? Everyone will be here in an hour," Teresa says.

I was planning on a short visit and then darting out of there before my parents showed up. But Teresa seems so distressed, and I want to help.

"How about if I put him in the car and take him for a ride," I say. "That'll put him to sleep. He'll be refreshed in an hour."

"Oh, could you, Ro? That'd be great."

While I bundle my nephew up in a thick, bulky coat and tug a wool hat over his blonde curls, he clutches a bottle with one hand and rubs my cheek with his other. His lids are already drawing like a shade.

"He'll be asleep before we get around the corner," I say.

"Thanks, Ro," Rocco says, opening the door for us.

"I'll be back in an hour."

Latching Joey into the car seat, I kiss his head then tighten the strap on his hat. As I turn the key, I glance into the rearview mirror. He's already fast asleep. I drive around the block several times and then turn right onto the avenue. I pass the confectionary store and turn into the park.

Although it's November, the sun is bright like May, and it's warm in the car. I turn off the ignition and crack the window a bit. The breeze carries with it the aroma of chocolate that our landlord is no doubt churning into fudge in the back of his store. Licking my lips, I can taste warm, gooey liquid oozing into my mouth.

There are two young boys on a seesaw that wasn't there when Teresa and I used to play in the park. They're giggling with joy, which reminds me of when my parents had taken us to a park for our very first picnic. Joseph and I were about five years old and Teresa seven. Mama sprawled on a blanket, picking blades of grass and watchful of Joseph. Daddy stood at the edge of a pond, feeding ducks stale bread. Teresa sang "Itsy Bitsy Spider" as she pushed me on a swing, from where I could see Mama blowing bubbles with Spearmint Gum. I jumped off, skinning my knees on the patch of macadam. Without so much as a flinch I ran over to Mama. Kneeling in front of her, I said, "More bubbles, more bubbles."

Mama raked her fingers through my tangles, wiped a smidgen of dirt off my cheek with her saliva, and tightened Teresa's pigtails.

"Blow more bubbles, please," I said, clapping my dimpled hands.

Mama snapped and blew as many bubbles as she could before the gum flattened. Daddy and Joseph trotted over to us, giggling. On the grass, in a family circle, we shared peanut butter sandwiches and sliced apples.

Joey stirs and groans. I lean over the seat to shove the bottle back into his mouth.

"Just fifteen more minutes will do you good, pal," I whisper.

Starting the ignition, I roll up the window and drive off. I circle the park several more times and then drive toward Teresa's.

The baby is so peaceful in his seat I hate to disturb him, but his guests will be here any minute, and I've got to go before they arrive. I lug him out of the seat and over my shoulders. Climbing the front steps of Rocco's grandmother's house, I hear laughter seeping through the closed door. Maneuvering Joey, I turn the knob and kick the door open with my foot.

Teresa rushes toward me, flapping her arms like a seagull preparing for landing. A smile stretches across her face.

"Rosie, you're not going to believe this. It's a miracle." She takes Joey from my arms.

I follow her through the kitchen and into Joey's room. Mama is cross-legged on the plank floor, bouncing an infant in the crook of her leg. Joseph is sitting on a chair bent over them. My twin has shaved his mustache off, revealing a yellowing smile.

"Hey, what do you say," he whispers, locking eyes with mine.

Gaping at him, I manage to ask, "Why are you here?"

Joseph lifts the infant from Mama's lap and positions him between two pillows set up on the floor.

"I got your message about Nona last month. And I just figured I should look you guys up."

Teresa situates sleeping Joey on the opposite side of the pillows. Gripping Mama's hand, Joseph boosts her up. Looping one arm through Joseph's and one through mine, Teresa coos at the infants.

"Don't they look like twins?"

"Yeah. Like Rosie and Joseph," Mama agrees, rubbing Joseph's back.

Joey is sucking on his thumb, and the infant Sammy curls his toes to his chest. Mama slings an arm around my waist, and I stiffen.

"I better be going." I turn from the precious boys. My lunch is threatening to surface. I think I'll never be able to eat tuna fish again.

Joseph grabs my wrist. His hand is calloused. "Don't go; stay."

"Who's hungry?" Mama asks.

"I'm starved," Joseph says, rubbing his flat stomach.

"Come on, let's eat," Teresa says as she switches on a Donald Duck night-light.

Joseph brushes his hand across my back, and he and Mama scoot out.

Taking one last peek at the boys, Teresa whispers, "Now do you believe in God's miracles?"

I don't know what to say because I can't describe how I feel. The babies look so peaceful; I don't want to ruin the moment. I tilt my head and rest it on Teresa's.

"They do look like Joseph and me, don't they?" I say.

THE END

ABOUT THE AUTHOR

Photographer John Bonnet

Donna C. Ebert was a real estate broker and founder of Ebert Home Inspection Company. She was awarded Realtor of the Year in 1996 in recognition of outstanding contributions to the community and the real estate industry. She has attended writing classes at Gotham's Writers Workshop in New York City and was a semi-finalist in the 2004 William Faulkner Creative Writing Competition. A native of New Jersey, she resides in North Caldwell with her husband Paul. Her interests include reading, walking, and travel.

Give the Gift of

PENNIES FOR JOSEPH

to Your Friends and Colleagues

CHECK YOUR LEADING BOOKSTORE OR ORDER HERE

❑ **YES**, I want _____ copies of *Pennies for Joseph* at $14.95 each, plus $4.95 shipping per book (New Jersey residents please add $1.05 sales tax per book). Canadian orders must be accompanied by a postal money order in U.S. funds. Allow 15 days for delivery.

My check or money order for $_____ is enclosed.

Please charge my: ❑ Visa ❑ MasterCard
❑ Discover ❑ American Express

Name _____

Organization _____

Address _____

City/State/Zip _____

Phone_____ Email _____

Card # _____

Exp. Date_____ Signature _____

Please make your check payable and return to:

Pen-it Publishing
878 Pompton Ave., Ste B2
Cedar Grove, New Jersey 07009

Call your credit card order to: 888-845-4708
Fax: 973-226-4563

www.PenniesforJoseph.com